THE STRINGS OF HARMONY

Written by Jacob Cole Turner

Edited by Andrew Littrell

TABLE OF CONTENTS

PROLOGUE

Before the world, there was nothing. Only silence, darkness, and chaos were found in the empty void. Among the endless void of space was the one known as the Conductor. With an existence that could flow out of deep passion and the power of music, the world of Symphonia was born. Many who exist in this world pondered at the mystery of its creation. The stories tell that the Conductor used a harp with seven strings to form Symphonia and all its wonders.

The first String of this Harp was one that played the music of love, which was the source that inspired creation to come about. Deeply moved, the Conductor's desire to create led him to embed the world with his love. Thus, the String of Ahaba was used and its music ranged across the universe. Soon, those who would inherit the world, whom the conductor shared his providence with, will be woven with this power.

The Second String was the string that played the music of the sky, the String of Sahaq. The Conductor used this to create an infinite blue. From the blue came the clouds and from them poured the ocean. The ocean would then give back to the clouds, reforming them, making the dance of the heavens and the sea.

The Third String was the string that played the music of the Earth, the String of Eres. Like a sheet of music, it stretched beneath the boundary of the sky. It rested next to the vast sea and stood as a firm foundation for what is yet to come.

The fourth string was the string that played the music of Life, the String of Nepes. When the sound of this music ran across the newly ordered world, life sprouted from all places. The seas contained marine creatures and the Earth below gave birth to all the land-dwelling creatures, as well as mankind. The sky served as a place for all the winged creatures to come and go.

The Fifth String was the one that played the music of trust, the String of Aman. With the world now teaming with life, it was crucial to all that everyone coexists with one another just as the world would coexist with its creator. Now, the life of creation relied not only on themselves but each other to thrive.

The sixth String was the one that played the music of balance, the String of Mozane. In many aspects, balance is woven throughout creation. It took the form of moderation, justice, and tamed the infinite complexities of the created world and all its wonder.

The seventh String was the one that played the music of Truth, the String of Emet. The values of the creator are woven into the entire world. This music let those truths be self-evident and further intertwined to all the sounds of the world. This music stood for the truths

After the Conductor played his Song of Creation, he scattered the Strings that played his very song across the created world to maintain its harmony. Mankind, with the guidance of the divine Concertmasters, ruled over the lands and spread across its vastness. This was the great song of Creation.

CHAPTER 1 LIFE

In a distant peaceful village, in the green fields of the not so far north, was a boy. This boy's name was Lutcas, and he lived a happy life after being born into this beautiful world of Symphonia. Lutcas learned the ways of music from the Concertmaster that resided near his home village. He and the others would grow harvests with the power of the music taught to them. The village was always fed, the animals always tended to, and the harvest festivals were always joyful.

Often, he would take walks in the forest with his dog, which he loved to do. His dog's name was Note, and oh how he loved Note, the most loyal dog any boy could ask for! Note would never leave Lutcas's side even as a puppy. Note was about as big as a typical dog, with a clean white fur coat and floppy ears that hang from the side of his head.

As Lutcas strolled through the dirt path of the forest, he would skip flat stones across the running waters of the creek. Lutcas would occasionally look in the creek to see the small fish, along with his reflection. Looking back at him from the water was the reflection of a young adolescent boy with white skin and blonde hair wearing a simple tunic. He wasn't very muscular, like some of his friends, nor was he very tall. However, Lutcas was skilled with his Lute and loved to play it. It brought him and his dog great joy to play it. His favorite spot to sit and play was at the Theater of Nepes, which was where he was heading now.

The Theater of Nepes was a place that rested in the woods near his village. This theater held one of the Seven Strings of Harmony, this one being the String of Nepes. Despite being only one string, music would emit from it and could be heard throughout the forest and all the way in Lutcas's village. Sometimes, when it is time for harvest, the String of Nepes would be heard loudly from the village and everyone would dance to its music. The music that normally came from the string was calming, steady, and yet invigorating. Some people in his village described it as rhythm; as that of breath leaving and entering something.

When Lutcas got closer to the theater, the music became louder, and the birds and bugs were in harmony with it. Finally, Lutcas made it to the Theater of Nepes. The theater was mostly constructed of trees that had grown into shapes of seats that made almost a giant bowl shape. In the middle of the theater was a small tree, mimicking a podium, that stood below The String of Nepes. From this small tree-like altar, flowed water that ran in many directions. Some of the water ran into the nearby creek, some into the ground, and some into unknown places. The String itself hovered over this podium as it emitted its relaxing music.

When Lutcas arrived, he sat at the front of the theater, leaning his back on the wood that constructed it, and began to play his Lute. Lutcas loved to play alongside the music produced by the String of Nepes. The melody he was playing didn't hold any power to it, but it was like a melody of contentment and thankfulness for this life.

After relaxing at the theater for a while, Lutcas was approached by his friend Bendzo. Bendzo was bigger, burlier, and a little older than Lutcas. He was gentle despite being so large and was close to Lutcas almost like a brother. From time-to-time, Bendzo would meet Lutcas out here to play.

Bendzo sat down with Lutcas and asked him, "So Lutcas, are you ready for the festival tonight?"

Lutcas stopped playing and turned to him surprised, "Wait! That is tonight?"

Bendzo laughed out loud and said, "No! I was just messing with you! I think you are worrying about it too much. You shouldn't be afraid to ask her you know."

Lutcas rubbed the back of his head a little embarrassed and said, "Right, that is tomorrow, isn't it? That's when I said I would do it. I don't know why I am so anxious about asking Sonare to marry me. "

Bendzo replied, "I don't know why you are so worked up about it either. The worst she can say is no. Besides, I'm certain there is one lovely girl who would love to live with someone as good with music as you are."

Lutcas smiled and was thankful for Bendzo's encouragement, "Your right. I shouldn't worry so much about it."

Bendzo's stomach rumbled loudly, "Speaking of being good with music, perhaps you could assist me in finding something to eat?"

Lutcas smiled knowing well the compliment may have been intended to invoke his assistance, "You know you have that banjo that could be used to do this too."

Bendzo shrugged his shoulders, "Sorry, I haven't been too fast at learning how to deal with plants yet. Really, I'm just good at moving around dirt and stuff for things to be planted."

Lutcas reached into his small bag that he carried with him and pulled out a seed and asked, "Well do me a favor and give me a spot to plant this then."

Bendzo took his banjo and played a minor tune of moving earth, which created a little hole in the ground for Lutcas to plant the seed. Lutcas then put the seed in the hole and played a minor tune of growth after covering it over with dirt. From the ground, sprouted a small plant producing cherry tomatoes. Bendzo began to pluck the fruits from the plant, which grew back as soon as he broke the stem from the root.

"This is why Sonare would want to be with you, Lutcas. It is because you can do this!" Bendzo exclaimed holding up the fruit like a prize.

Lutcas said while laughing, "Well hopefully my wife won't eat as much as you do you, oaf. I would be forced to play till my fingers fall off."

"What can I say? I am a growing boy and I need to eat."

After a while, the sun began to descend on the horizon, illuminating the forest in an orange aura. Lutcas and Bendzo decided to go back towards the village. So, they grabbed more Tomatoes on the way back while Note followed closely behind them.

On the way back, Bendzo began speaking again, "You know Lutcas. I think one day I would like to travel around Symphonia."

Lutcas responded, "Travel? You want to travel? It is so beautiful here, why not settle down?"

"I know it is nice here. But think about how beautiful it is elsewhere in Symphonia. It is all the artwork of the Great Conductor, so why not see the rest of his masterpiece?"

Lutcas hesitated to answer for a moment, "Maybe you are right. Tell you what? If we don't settle down here, why don't we go and travel? We could see other villages and maybe find people to settle with there?"

His friend smiled and answered, "Ya! One place I would like to see is the Great Kingdom of Podiem. I have heard so much about the greatness of that place from travelers that pass through from time to time. How great it would be to see the Conductor and his great podium."

Lutcas replied, "I have heard the stories too. Now that you bring it up, I think I would like to go there as well one day."

After getting out of the forest, they finally made it to the outskirts of the village. They were welcomed with big rolling fields of green. Some of which was now populated with the numerous crops that were brought up in melodies and tunes by the villagers. As they got closer to the village, more and more cottages appeared until finally they found themselves in the village of Zoi. The village consisted of cottages, dirt paths leading in different directions, a water well, and a Silo where they stored the crops.

Shortly after they got to the village, a group of strangers arrived. They were riding on the backs of horses while wearing armor and capes, creating quite the display for fashion. The armor was black and the people on the horses had large noses compared to those who lived in the village, along with darker toned skin. This was the look of someone from the middle lands of Symphonia. These are people that lived near the Great Kingdom of Podiem. The village greeted this group of people that numbered about twenty with two distinct leaders in front. The capes on the back were black just like the armor they were wearing, which had a red symbol of a man standing on a podium.

One of the leaders spoke, who sounded young, but was a little older than Lutcas, "Greetings! We are from the new kingdom of Orchestrasus. We have come to observe the wondrous String of Nepes."

Kindly, the villagers gave the directions for the Theater of Nepes. A crowd began to emerge from the village, observing the knights that had appeared in their home. Since no one had heard of such a kingdom before, nor have they seen such clothing, they stared in awe. Lutcas and Bendzo were stuck near the back of the crowd. Between two of the cottages, Lutcas saw someone peek out and move in the shadows of the buildings that were close together. Lutcas tried to tell Bendzo what he saw, but Bendzo's attention was solely on the awesome Knights entering the town. Curious, Lutcas went to investigate what he saw. When he turned the corner, he saw a hooded figure in the shadows who pulled him in and pressed his hand against his mouth, preventing him from making noise.

The figure whispered to Lutcas, "Be calm and be quiet. You must hear what I have to say to you." Lutcas, confused, nodded his head in compliance with the figure's demands.

The figure spoke, "Listen to me. My name is Guil. I have come to warn your people, but I have arrived too late."

Lutcas, whose voice was muffled from the hand, asked, "Warn. What are you talking about?"

Guil, who still understood him, answered him, "I am too late. Even now these Knights are influencing your people. I came to protect the

String, but I will not be able to. Perhaps I can at least save one of you. Will you hear me out?"

Lutcas, still confused, answered, "Sure? I still don't understand. Why would the String or my fellow villagers need protection? These Knights are simply on a pilgrimage to see the String of Nepes."

They turned after hearing the Knights move out, "Listen. Please come with me and I will show you what is at stake."

Lutcas agreed and followed. Naturally, Note followed him as well. Lutcas wanted to bring Bendzo along, but he was conversing with one of the knights that stayed behind. Guil and Lutcas were observing the company of Knights from a distance. After moving into the light, he noticed that Guil looked much like the Knights who arrived. Lutcas knew the path towards the Theater of Nepes, so it was easy to navigate unseen. Eventually, they arrived at the theater. The Knights got off their steeds and walked into the tree-like structure. One of the leading knights went into the theater and brandished a lyre. This lyre was a deep purple that emitted a chaotic aura. The knight grabbed the string and ripped it out of its tranquil floating state.

As soon as the string was removed, its music fell silent. The birds and animals that were at this theater now fled in haste. The nearby trees began to wilt, including the trees that formed the theater. The grass below everyone lost its lush green color and became dried up. Additionally, a few of the Knights around him fell limp to the ground and were silent. Witnessing this caused great fear to erupt.

The Knight arose from the ruined theater and said, "I, Prince Lyle of Orchestrasus, has now claimed the String of Nepes! Now we, as the people of Orchestrasus, are one step closer to becoming conductors ourselves! The men who have just fallen will not be forgotten, since they were a part of the first steps of exaltation and salvation. Thanks to them we need not fear their same fate." The knight then put the String onto his Lyre, in addition to the one string already on it which glowed purple like the Lyre did.

Lutcas was confused and afraid of what he just witnessed. "Guil... What is this madness?"

He answered him, "My brothers have turned against their creator under the command of my parents, the new emperor and empress of Orchestrasus. They are now on a pilgrimage to take the Seven Strings of Harmony for themselves."

Lutcas felt the new silence of the forest around him, and it made him afraid and angry at what happened "Why would anyone do such a thing?" he asked.

Guil looked down in sorrow, "They have been deceived. They are now blind. A single deception has led to this madness that you see before you."

"What do we do now?"

"I have no instrument to play. My brother Lyle shattered it. Even though you seem like you can play, you are no match for any of them, especially my brother. Tell me, does your village commune with a concertmaster?"

Lutcas answered, "Yes, but Selaphiel said he wouldn't be back for a while. He had to do something, but he didn't speak about it."

Guil's face grew sad, "Perhaps a Concertmaster could detain my brothers? However, that place is not here."

Note began whimpering after the string was pulled. Eventually, this became frantic barking and howling. Guil and Lutcas looked ahead to see that the Knights had noticed them. Some of the Knights readied their instruments and approached the hiding spot that the two were at. Immediately, Guil and Lutcas took off into the woods away from the Knights. Lutcas stopped and tried to play a tune of growth to make more obstacles grow between them and their pursuers. However, something was wrong, and the tune was weak and not very effective. Which forced Lutcas to use his knowledge of the area to lose them. Eventually, the three lost their pursuers after heading deeper into the forest.

As they were regaining their breath, Lutcas asked, "Guil, what about the villagers? What will this do to them and my family?"

Guil answered, "If what happened the first time happens again, it is too late. They will convince your village to go with them to Orchastrasus. There, they will fall into this deception, if they have not already."

Lutcas, feeling scared said, "We need to go back to my village. I need to warn them!"

Guil felt sorrow for Lutcas and warned him, "We are a great deal away from the path. They will reach the village before we will."

Lutcas, full of fear, began to head towards the village, ignoring Guil's advice. Lutcas was not entirely sure where to go since he ran off from the part of the woods that he was used to seeing. Eventually, he was back on the right path, and then made it to the village. Guil, who followed Lutcas as he and Note ran, insisted they stayed out of sight. Lutcas obeyed and stayed behind a cottage near the edge of town. The Knights were already there, and Lyle was standing on a box while playing a tune with his ominous Lyre, speaking to the people of the village.

Lutcas noticed Sonare in the crowd, with her long blonde hair flowing behind her. Lutcas began to worry even more since she was about to fall into their deception. Lutcas begged Guil to let him go in, but Guil refused.

Lyle said to the villagers, "Dear people of the village; as you can see, I now possess two of the Seven Strings of Harmony. You all may be confused, but I tell you this is the sign of a new era that is for each one of you. This is now a time where we can be conductors ourselves and break away from the song that was forced upon us since creation!"

The other leader knight took off his helmet and approached him, grabbing his arm and pleading, "Elder brother, please stop this! I don't want to be a part of this anymore! We have defied our good creator and we have done horrible things. Please let us stop this!"

Lyle was shocked as he looked at the people and looked at Zamir, the one who spoke to him. The people began to stir after hearing these words from Zamir. Guil's face sprung with hope as he saw one of his brothers stand up against what was happening, hoping maybe there would be sense.

Lyle's face then grew angry, and he said, "If you want no part of our exaltation and glory, then do not tarnish it with your poison brother!"

Lyle swung his arm, throwing Zamir to the ground. When Zamir fell, his head smashed into the edge of the stone well. After his head hit with a great smack, he remained motionless and silent. The people fell silent because they have never seen anything like this before. Lutcas and Guil were speechless and couldn't move. They weren't sure what happened, but they felt something horrible just occurred. Fear swept over the people, Lyle knew this and took it to his advantage.

Lyle turned back to the people and spoke to them while playing his tune, "My dear people; this is where the path to your precious creator leads you to. If you come with me and my brotherhood, then we can work together to prevent this. Come with me and you will all be like conductors, so powerful that you will not need to fear!"

Guil began to tear up and he shouted from the depth of his heart, unable to hold back his elegy, "Zamir no!"

Lyle and his men were alerted to Guil's voice. "It's my traitor brother! Let him share the same fate! For he wants to take our exaltation away so that we will be silent and motionless."

The men began to pursue them once more. This time, Lutcas played a melody of mud, which molded the dirt behind them into slippery mud. The Knights slipped on the mud as they began pursuit. One of the knights with a flute began playing a melody of dry ground to counter it. However, this bought Guil and Lutcas enough time to escape back into the dark forest and out of sight. It was now nightfall, and the forest hid them well. The knights were once again unsuccessful in their pursuit.

When the sun came up over the horizon, Guil and Lutcas returned to the village. They found the village abandoned. Zamir was still where he rested and most of the villagers were scattered across the streets motionless and silent.

Lutcas saw their motionless state and asked, "What happened to them? Why are they not moving?"

Guil began to tear up as he looked at his older brother Zamir, "My teacher was told by a concertmaster what would happen if the Strings of Harmony were disrupted. It was a long time ago for me. If I can recall, I believe this is something called death."

Lutcas looked at everyone who lay motionless and began to weep in the deafening silence that lay over the empty town. Even though the concept was new to him, he understood that life no longer flowed in his fellow villagers. This was the moment when death began to plague the world.

CHAPTER 2 LOVE

Lutcas walked through the lifeless and silent streets that used to be his village. Now, this once busy town was reduced to a husk full of bodies. Lutcas looked at the silent corpses that littered the dirt roads. He recognized each of them, but he did not find his parents or close friends among them. This broke Lutcas's heart to see his fellow villagers now dead. However, he noticed that most of them aren't here. He realized that most of them had to have gone with the Knights. Many thoughts raced into Lutcas's mind, asking himself if any of the villagers turned on each other or if he could have done anything to stop it.

Guil was mourning his brother and after a while, he stood up and said, "I must apologize. I haven't asked what your name was."

He slowly looked up at Guil with his eyes watering up, "My name is Lutcas."

Guil approached him, "Lutcas, you have seen the devastation my elder brother has cast on you and your village. I apologize on behalf of him and my family. But I need help to stop him, please join me in finding the other strings."

Lutcas was a bit scared at first when presented with this task. He looked at the bodies of the villagers, the wilted crops in the distance, and his dog who was whimpering while sniffing the corpses of the village. Lutcas knew that there had to be a reason that he was spared from this influence and death. Besides, there was nothing left for him here if he refused.

Lutcas shook his head and said, “Yes. I must. When do we need to leave?”

Guil answered, “We need to leave as soon as we can. Now if we can.”

Lutcas was shocked, “Now? So soon?”

“Yes, we need to go now. My brother is taking your villagers back to the kingdom. It will take them a while to get there, so it will buy us some time to get to the next String.”

Lutcas understood, but looked at the dead villagers and said, “Can we at least give them the respect of not being laid about? Let me return their bodies to the earth where they came from.”

Guil hesitated and then looked at his brother and agreed, “Fine. But we need to be quick. After you're done, gather all the things you need, and we will depart from here.”

Lutcas took his Lute and played a major tune of moving earth. The ground underneath the bodies of his fellow villagers shook and opened to let them sink in. After this, Lutcas played a tune of shifting rocks, which took rocks from the well and moved them to serve as markers for the bodies now beneath the ground.

After Lutcas buried the bodies, he went to his house to find the things he wanted to take with him. Like the other houses, Lutcas’s was a cottage built by his father. When Lutcas entered his house, he found most of the belongings in the house gone. He went into his room and found a handful of things still there, not that he had much to begin with. He had a waterskin that he used to collect water, spare strings for his lute, spare clothes, and a backpack. Lutcas gathered all these things and prepared for his journey.

Lutcas went outside and met Guil there, “I have gotten all I need. Where do we need to go?”

Guil answered, “We used to have a map of where the Strings were. It was written in a vision from my master. In an act of defying my brothers, I destroyed it and fled after memorizing all the general locations. So, we need to head east from here to find the Theater of Ahaba."

Immediately, Guil and Lutcas began their pilgrimage to find the remaining Strings of Harmony. When they headed east, they followed the dirt road, with the forest on the north side of the road and the open fields to the south side. Lutcas noticed that many of the crops appeared wilted. Lutcas decided to grab some corn for the road by picking it off the nearby stocks. However, when Lutcas removed the corn, it did not grow back.

Lutcas looked at it shocked and said, "What is happening? The Corn doesn't grow back anymore."

Guil observed the stock of corn and said, "It is just like what my master said. It will be much more difficult to get food now. Life doesn't actively flow like it used to without the Strings in their rightful places."

They continued down the road when Lutcas asked, "So you have brought up this master of yours. Who is he?"

Guil answered him, "My master was a kind, old man. He was a seer and was blessed with dreams. He foresaw what was going to happen to the kingdom and the strings, but by the time he acted, it was too late. The people of my kingdom smashed his instruments and forced him into exile."

Feeling guilt for asking, he replied, "I'm sorry about what happened to him. But if he ran off, how did you get this information?"

"Before he was exiled, he warned me of what would happen and told me where his notes were kept in secret. I read his notes, and out of fear that they would be misused, I got rid of them. Not long after, my family knew of what occurred and they exiled me. He was a great teacher to me, and I intend to fulfill his wishes of protecting the strings." he answered

"Well, I wish to help him too. What the kingdom has done to my village was evil and frightening. I cannot imagine if the world fell into this sort of horror and chaos."

Not long after they left, the fields of crops became fields of tall grass moving to the flow of the wind like a dance. The forest began to spread more and more across the fields and the hills. At this point, plant life didn't seem to be physically affected by the String of Nepes's absence yet. Eventually, the dirt path was besieged by the forest. The forest trees were a bit different from the ones near Lutcas's village. There were tall narrow pine trees that littered the forest floor with their pine needles.

Once it became dark, the two stopped and made camp. Lutcas and Guil gathered wood and started a fire. Lutcas didn't know any tunes or melody of fire, so they had to start the fire by hand. While Lutcas was hungry, he planted a cherry tomato seed. He then played a tune of minor growth to grow the seed. However, the process was slow and Lutcas had to put more effort into playing his lute. After a minute, the plant finally grew and spurred forth a single cherry tomato.

He looked at Guil embarrassed, "Usually this takes a lot less time and effort to do."

Guil replied, "Interesting. It seems that the absence of the string has made it more difficult to play tunes and melodies involving life. See what happens when you take the tomato?" Lutcas reached for the tomato and when he plucked it off the stem it did not grow back as it usually does. "This is very interesting. It appears that this is affecting everywhere, not just near where the theater used to be."

Lutcas thought that now might be a good time to get to know Guil, since they will be traveling together. "You sound smart Guil. What did you do before you got wrapped up in this mess?"

Lutcas, at first, was afraid he might strike his feelings after the words left his mouth. But instead, this put a smile on Guil's face as he remembered better times.

Guil answered him, "I loved to study. I loved observing the beautiful masterpiece of the Great Conductor. Everything is flowing with such magnificence and beauty that I felt the need to study it and observe. So, I wanted to become a scholar like my master."

Lutcas was happy to hear the positive side of Guil's life and answered, "I love looking at creation too. It brings me joy to play music in its melodies. I would have a hard time reading and writing about it though. I can't say I'm much of a scholar."

Guil smiled and asked, "What did you do back in your village?"

A smile was also cast on Lutcas's face as he answered, "I used to help my family and my village grow crops. I loved to play music and watch the plants spring to life from the ground like people once did."

Note began sniffing Guil, which made him reach out to pet him. "I see you had a little bit of help too."

Lutcas chuckled a little, "Sure do. He is my trusty little companion. I grew up with him. He loves to play around and roll in the grass whenever I play my songs."

Guil asked, "If you don't mind, would you play me a tune? It has been so long since I have heard good music."

Lutcas took his Lute and played the tune that he played when sitting at the theater before the knights came. The tune was like the music coming from the String of Nepes. Note began wagging his tail happily when he heard it. When Lutcas played it, he began to remember the life he had and realized he would never have again. But the music also helped him stay thankful for what he did have. Lutcas stopped playing the tune after tearing up a bit and wiping away the tears.

Guil commented on his music, "That was a nice tune. It did not have any power behind it. But it was pleasant to my ears."

Lutcas replied, "Thank you. It is a song that I would often play, with Note by my side, whenever I would be out and happy. I suppose it is my tune of thankfulness."

Guil added, "You know; in a way, you sort of remind me of Lyle. Well, before he was deceived. Like you, he liked making life grow with music. He would go into the fields of the kingdom and make many crops, flowers, and trees grow. He could do much more with his music too, but he gave it all away for some false ideal. But I look at you and see a bit of my brother that I miss seeing."

Shortly after talking, they went to sleep and then headed out at sunrise. Guil and Lutcas continued exchanging stories of their homes with each other. Lutcas had never met anyone as studious and smart as Guil.

Note got to like Guil as well, and Guil would occasionally throw a stick for Note to retrieve and fetch.

Later in the morning, they came to a crossroad in the tall pine forest they were walking in. Leaning on the tree near the crossroad, was a girl. Lutcas saw her and saw that she was beautiful. She had long, red hair, with freckles populating her pale white skin. She appeared older than Lutcas, maybe closer to Guil's age. While leaning against the tree, she played the violin that was in tune with the birds who were singing in the nearby trees. Guil and Lutcas looked at each other after looking at the girl and decided to proceed, minding their own business.

When they were about to pass the girl, she looked up, stopped playing her violin, and drew her attention to the two, "Excuse me. Can I ask you a question?"

Lutcas froze at the sound of her voice. Her voice matched her physical beauty so much that he became nervous and awkward. Guil, on the other hand, seemed to be handling the situation with a much cooler head than Lutcas was.

Guil turned to answer her and asked, "Sure. What do you need?"

The girl approached the two and observed the two closely. Guil stood there confused but levelheaded as the girl walked in circles around them. Lutcas's heartbeat raced whenever she would look at him. Note approached her and was wagging his tail, being the happy little dog, he was.

The girl crossed her arms and said, "You both seem to fit the vision, but that means little to you. Who are you guys?"

Guil, not knowing what she meant by vision, went first, and spoke bluntly, "I am prince Guil of the middle lands of Symphonia, from the kingdom of Podiem."

Lutcas was staring at her, so Guil nudged him prompting him to speak, "Oh I um. I am Lutcas, a farming musician."

The girl happily said, "Great! Just like what the village seer said! A farmer and a prince on the road to obtain the Strings of Harmony."

Lutcas was surprised by how much she knew just by looking at them and he asked, "That's right! How did you know?"

The girl put her hands on her hips and said, "Did you not just hear what I said? A seer told me."

Guil narrowed his eyes skeptical and asked, "How can we know that you are not here to do us harm?"

The girl added, "Fear not! I assure you both that I mean no harm. By the looks of things, it seems that you both are here with good intentions as well. So, our trust must be mutual since I am taking you to my home. If you don't mind, I need you both to come along. Our village elder needs to see you first."

Guil called Lutcas in a huddle with Note walking over in curiosity.

Lutcas asked Guil in a whisper, "What do you think of this?"

"I think she is beautiful," Guil said jokingly, being aware of Lutcas's awkward behavior.

Lutcas was mildly annoyed with Guitheth's tease and said, "No not that! Do we trust her?"

Guil answered, "I don't think she appears to be under the influence of my brother. I think we can trust her."

Guil broke the huddle and said, "Alright we will go with you. Where is your village?"

The girl pointed in the direction and said, "My village, Phileo, is north of here. It isn't terribly far. We should be there around noon."

The three-headed towards the village. The girl led the way while Lutcas, Guil, and Note followed her. The girl was not only beautiful from her appearance, but when she spoke or moved, it radiated a joyous energy. Guil would occasionally pick up nearby branches and throw them for Note to fetch. Lutcas tried to look at the nature around him, but he kept finding his eyes dart towards the girl.

Guil noticed this and began to whisper to Lutcas to pick at him, "You still looking at her?"

Lutcas whispered back honestly but embarrassed, "If I am honest, she is one of the most beautiful women I have ever seen."

Guil teased him, "Then go speak to her."

Lutcas answered, "We can't do that. What if she is in union with someone already? Besides, she is probably not interested in someone younger than her anyway. Not to mention, I planned on asking another girl to be with me anyway."

Guil replied, "Well, you will not find out any of those things if you do not speak to her. Though it's sad to think about, that girl back at home may be gone. It would be healthy for you to explore options my friend, since I don't know what the outcome of this fixing will be. Let me show you. It is key to speak with confidence!" Guil turned forward and walked by the girl and said to her, "You know I couldn't help but notice we never got your name."

The girl answered, "My apologies, prince. My name is Violina."

Guil continued, "Violina. That is a nice name. What do you do?"

Violina answered, "I am under training to be a musician. I seek to learn about all sorts of music that flows in the wisdom of the world and master its many wonders"

Guil replied, "Interesting. So, are you pursuing this by yourself or are you in union with someone?"

Lutcas widened his eyes at how straight forward Guil was with his question. Lutcas knew that he struggled to speak with girls and would never take such a straightforward route to ask a question like that. Nevertheless, Lutcas wanted to know the answer to Guil's question.

Violina answered, "Oh I am in union with my lovely husband. He just departed on a journey earlier. He is one of the fastest riders in our town, which was why he was sent."

Lutcas jumped in, "What was he sent for?"

"Same reason I was. But I cannot explain the specifics until we speak with my village elder," she answered.

They continued down the road a little while longer and Guil asked, "Hey Lutcas. Why don't you play that song that you played for us earlier?"

Lutcas took out the lute and began to play his tune of thankfulness. He was a little nervous to do it in front of their new friend, but he wanted too anyway. As he played, Note began to bark happily and run-in circles around the group.

After he was finished Violina asked, "That was a nice music piece. Did you come up with it yourself?"

Lutcas blushed at her comment and answered, "Thank you, and not exactly. I got inspiration from the String of Nepes. I play it whenever I think about my friends, family, and Note." After saying this, his face became shallow, and he felt saddened by the thought of his family and friends.

Violina looked at Lutcas concerned, "What are the people of your village like or the String of Nepes."

Lutcas, still feeling sad, answered in a strange burst of non-aggressive frustration he never experienced, "What are they like? Well, they are all gone now."

Violina's face showed concern and confusion. She felt compassion for Lutcas and felt bad for asking about it. She didn't know what he was talking about, but she didn't want to press Lutcas about it any further.

Around noon, they arrived at the village that Violina was leading them to. The village was different from Lutcas's. The surrounding area was mostly the towering evergreens that they encountered along the way here. They couldn't see it but, in the distance, there was the sound of rushing water. In the not so far distance, there was a small mountain that stood a bit taller than the surrounding hills, which all contained various holes that ran through them. The wind would blow through these holes making a strange musical sound. These were the famed Embouchure Hills.

Not long after spotting these hills, they arrived in the Village of Phileo. The cottages of the village were made of pale stone with thatch roofs. The road, once it reached into the village, was made of various pieces of flat stones. Like Lutcas's village, there was also a well in the center of town. The people of the village looked a lot like Violina. They were pale, red-headed, and covered in freckles.

As Lutcas, Note, and Guil were walking through the village, the villagers studied them, pausing their daily activities. The looks were not that of hostility, but of curiosity. Violina was leading them to what appeared like a chapel-like building. When they finally arrived at the building, Violina led them in.

Violina shouted to an old man at the other end of the room, "Elder! I have brought the ones that you have sent me to find!"

The old man at the end of the room turned to reveal a long, bushy red beard, and small size. "Ah I have been expecting you all. I am glad to see you have made it here even with such strange occurrences."

Lutcas, feeling confused, asked, "There have been strange occurrences? Like what?"

The elder answered, "Some of our villagers have been harmed doing certain tasks and activities. One of our littler ones fell into the nearby river and his head collided with a large rock making his body still and silent."

Guil rubbed his chin in thought, "I was afraid something like this would happen."

The old man continued, "Before I go on. I am the village elder and seer. I have received dreams after the departure of our Concertmaster. The visions I have received have been disturbing. I need you two to tell me who you are and why you are on the road."

Lutcas and Guil explained everything while Note sat patiently on the floor. Guil explained who he was and why he was on the journey. Lutcas explained what happened at the village and how his village was now empty and that the String of Nepes is gone. As the two explained this, the elder's face grew with concern.

The elder answered, "It seems my visions were right. Violina, your husband didn't leave for nothing. The dreams were true. However, if I realized we needed to take the strings, I would have told him to do more than simply warn the other settlements." The elder turned to Lutcas, "My boy, I have had a recent dream about the tragedy of your village and about the new horror that now looms in our beautiful world. I am so sorry for what happened to your people."

Lutcas's sorrow resurfaced at the mention of his village, and he answered, "There was nothing you could do about it. It hurts to see what happened to my people."

The elder continued, "Guil, you said that your brother and his men headed back home. This will buy us some time to leave. I will instruct the village to use this time wisely, for I fear that the same thing will happen here, like it did your home Lutcas. If you two are trying to protect the strings, then Violina will lead you to the Theater of Ahaba. It is not far from here, and you can probably hear its tune further in the forest. Once you get it, leave here and find the next string. The raw power that those Strings possess should not be wielded by this new order of Knights."

The three left immediately to retrieve the string. They understood that this was all a task in which time was of the essence. They moved as quickly as they could north, to the small mountain they were instructed to go to. They rushed down the road that led through the evergreen forest and over the rushing river, leading into the Embouchure Hills. Eventually, they made it to the mountain. When the party found themselves at the base of the mountain, they were presented with a large cave mouth, leading into its surface. Pouring out of the sides of the cave's mouth was a stream of water that formed a creek that flowed into the nearby river. Upon getting closer, they heard the melody of the nearby string. The melody was warm and welcoming, almost embracing all who heard it as if it were a hug.

Lutcas turned to Violina and asked, "So, I'm guessing this is the theater?"

Guil responded with Sarcasm, "No, it is in the other really majestic mountain standing above the rest of the village."

Violina chuckled and replied, “Yes. When we go in, there will be a series of tunnels that lead all over the mountain. They enter and exit the cave at all different points and places. The one we need to take is the one that leads straight past the mouth of the cave.”

Lutcas felt hope and said, “You know, I am glad that we are getting at least one of the Strings of Harmony. Where is the next one after this?”

Guil answered, “If I can recall correctly, it is further east. That would be the String of Eres.”

The party then proceeded to enter the cave. The cave’s massive mouth began to narrow and split into various tunnels. They listened to Violina’s instructions and followed the path that led directly forward. After taking this path, they found themselves in a great opening in the cave. The cave’s ceiling shot straight up into a cylinder, allowing the light from the sky to shine through. The floor of the cave went from stone to grassy terrain with flowers and other various plants inhabiting it. Birds had nests around its walls, bees jumping from flower to flower, and furry cave dwelling creatures piled up around each other resting. Around the center of the room was a formation of rocks that appeared like seats facing a podium. Surrounding that was a network of small streams making their way around the Podium, which rested in the center of the room. Above the podium, were the String of Ahaba that floated and emitted a warm red aura. This was the Theater of Ahaba. The warm music that they heard from outside radiated in the dome-like room, filling everyone with joy and energy.

The three approached it and Guil said, “At last, a string that is not removed from its home. We can at least save one.”

Lutcas remembered seeing what happened when the String was taken by Prince Lyle back at the Theater of Nepes. He remembered the flowing water ceasing its flow from the podium. He remembered life leaving all the things around it and the music falling silent. Lutcas was afraid that would happen once again.

“Wait!” Lutcas shouted, which gained the other’s attention, “What if something terrible happens like it did in my village?”

Guil studied the String, "Well Lutcas, we don't have much of a choice. It's either we take it, or my brothers take it. If something bad happens, we will have to find a solution until we can stop my family."

Guil reached out and grabbed the pink glowing string. Lutcas braced for the worst while Violina watched with great curiosity. Note was not paying attention and was proceeding to roll around in the soft terrain. Once Guil grabbed the String and pulled it out of its place, there was a moment of silence. Lutcas had his eyes shut in a brace of the worst but opened to find that nothing happened. Violina studied the string and the room to see if anything changed. Suddenly, the silence was replaced by a low humming sound from the string. The string began playing its music, but at a lower volume than usual. It was as if the string was whispering its melody.

Lutcas smiled and said, "We got a String? We got a String!" he turned to his dog, "We did it boy! We got a String!"

Lutcas's joyful voice excited Note and he ran around in circles barking and wagging his tale playfully. Note then darted between Lutcas's legs causing him to fall over on the soft ground. Lutcas laughed and continued to play with his dog.

Guil held the String of Ahaba in the air and studied it, "What a magnificent object! I should figure out how my brother managed to place this on his instrument. Though I suppose it can't be that difficult right?

Violina added, "I don't know if I would fiddle with right now. It may be safe to take it back to my elder. He may know how to put it on an instrument or if it is even safe to do it. Here let's return to my home."

As they were about to depart the cave, Note's ears raised high, and his teeth began to show. Lutcas had never seen this before and became worried. Upon listening carefully, they could hear movement down the way they came. Not knowing what this was, the party hid in some thick greenery near the cave wall, suspecting the worst. They barely found cover in time when a small group of black clothed knights entered the room. There were about five of them, all wearing black, steel armor; completed with helmets and cloth marked with the man and podium symbol. Among them, there was one knight that stood out. He wore no helm and was large compared to the others. He was extremely muscular, with no hair on the top of the head, and a large brown handlebar mustache. Wrapped around him, was a large Sousaphone Tuba, complimenting his size. Despite being muscular in the arms, he was fat, as implied by the shape of his body armor. The large man, with thundering footsteps, marched towards the podium with a displeased look.

The man stroked his unusual mustache and complained, "Curses! Only I would be this unlucky to come all the way here to get the String of Ahaba and it be missing! Now I will fail to retrieve this String and fail my superiors! To add to my problems, we also don't know where the other Strings are! That darn old hag had to escape interrogation before we squeeze out the locations of the other theaters" In anger, he turned to his men and said, "Men! Our power to become conductors is slipping from our very grasp! I need each of you to turn this mountain upside down! Once we find it, we will catch up to our brothers and those villagers heading back to Orchestrasus."

Lutcas tried to keep Note calm and in place while whispering to the other two, "What do we do? They will find us."

Violina whispered back, "There is something I can do. I can play a melody of mist. I can make the water around us into a cloud of mist to limit their vision. But we won't be able to see either and my song will be heard across the room for it to have full effect."

Guil looked at Lutcas and said, "I don't have anything to play. Lutcas, is there any way you can help?"

Lutcas wasn't sure how to help. "Well, I don't know what I can do. All the music I can play is related to farming. I can do stuff with the plants and the dirt."

Guil rested his chin on his fist in thought and came up with an idea, "Lutcas and Violina, I think we can get out of here. Lutcas, if you can play some music to stir up the plants and distract them, then that will be helpful. Preferably anything to hinder their movement. Violina, you play your melody of mist and cloud their vision. Once they can't see, we will run for it."

Violina added, "Remember we won't be able to see either."

Guil replied, "It wouldn't be the first time I've taken risks. Just remember that we are on the other side of the room from the entrance. Run straight there! And if you touch anyone, push them over."

Lutcas asked, "What if there are others waiting outside?"

Guil added, "Well then, we can't leave out that way. We will have to work our way through the tunnels. Try to meet on the east side of the mountain."

The party agreed while the knights were continuing to search for the string. Lutcas readied his Lute and Violina rested her chin on her violin. Lutcas quickly played a tune of major growth. It was more difficult to get the tune correct, but he managed to pull it off correctly. The flowers and plants beneath the feet of the knights began to grow quickly in large size. The Knights panicked, trying to move their feet around the rising growth. Violina then took her bow and played a melody of mist, which created a fog that enveloped the room. They knew it was the time to make a run for it. Lutcas dashed towards the entrance, no longer able to see Violina or Guil. Note was running right with Lutcas to ensure he was safe. Lutcas could make out the entrance to the dome-like room that was right in front of him. Before he could reach it, he heard a massive sound come from the center of the room. From this sound, came a powerful gust that blew Lutcas and Violina right off their feet.

When Lutcas turned to see what happened, he saw that the fog was gone, and the knights were blown against the edges of the wall. In the center of the room was the large knight wielding the tuba. In the hands of the knight was the wrist of Guil, who was holding the String of Ahaba. He must have grabbed a hold of Guil before playing that tune. Lutcas turned to see Violina by his side looking at the scene in horror.

The large knight laughed and said, "haha! I Tubiat, the first in command under Prince Lyle, Emperor Anthropo, and Empress Theyls, have claimed the String of Ahaba!"

Violina's face was painted with a look of fear and frustration. Violina readied her bow to play a song against this great foe. Lutcas saw her and readied his Lute. He wasn't sure what to do against such a powerful being. He had never seen an instrument like this, nor one used with such power. He realized he must have played some sort of wind song that did all this.

Guil tried to struggle free, and he shouted, "Run, get out of here! You can't let him catch you too!"

Tubiat looked at Lutcas and Violina while effortlessly holding Guil in the air, "Go on and try... Fight me! My men will be on their feet and ready to take you on! But I am in a good mood, so I'll let you two scrams since I got what I need. Consider it an act of love. Hahaha."

Violina looked at the knights getting back up after being thrown across the room. Violina understood that they were outmatched and outnumbered. Violina didn't want to leave and neither did Lutcas. He was overwhelmed with fear and sorrow while watching his friend helplessly struggle. Note snarled and barked at Tubiat, ready to engage. Lutcas took a step forward and Violina stopped him.

"Lutcas please, we need to go. We can't beat them. We need to go now." Violina said urgently.

Lutcas protested, "But he has Guil and the String of Ahaba! We can't!"

Violina asked again, "Lutcas please, we need to go!"

Even though they didn't want to, Lutcas, Violina, and Note fled through the tunnels of the mountain. Like they had originally planned, they worked their way towards the east side of the mountain. They waited there patiently in some small chance that Guil would have escaped. As time passed, the reality became clear that he was gone.

When the sun came up over the horizon, the three headed back to the village. When they got there, they found it empty. It was clear that the knights had been through here already. The buildings were looted. There were bloodstains that were splattered around, but strangely there were no bodies this time. For Violina, this was an all-new nightmare; but for Lutcas, this was an encore of a nightmare. When Lutcas saw this, he developed a feeling that didn't exist in him before. It was a sort of animosity that consisted of strong negative emotions and burning desire to win this fight.

Lutcas began to hate the knights that did all this and grow a passion in his heart that could change his life forever.

CHAPTER 3 ELECTED

Lutcas and Violina didn't stay in town for too long, there was no reason to. All that was there for them was sorrow and a reminder of their failure. They looked through the houses of the village to find anything they would need to continue their journey. The two remembered that Guil said something about moving further east to the String of Eres. They also remembered Tubiat implying that they didn't know where the other Strings were, but they could use Guil to find out. Lutcas understood that Guil didn't know precisely where the strings were, so they would still have to search for it themselves.

Once the two had all they needed and searched all the buildings of the town, they departed on the road. The further the party went east, the more mountainous it became. The road they took was through a valley, between mountains that's tops couldn't be seen because of the present fogs. The forest, at one point, dispersed and scattered. Later down the road, it appeared like more open fields. The sight was beautiful, as if the land appeared to meet the sky like a kiss.

After a period of silence, Violina spoke. "This is breathtaking, isn't it? I have only been able to see this a few times. But it never fails to impress me. It makes me want to play music."

Lutcas, still a bit nervous speaking to her, said, "I don't mind if you want to play a song. When Guil and I were on the road, there was a certain tune I played that he enjoyed a lot."

Violina took out her violin and her Bow. Her skill showed since she was able to do all this while walking, as if it were as natural as breathing. Violina rested her chin against the violin and moved the bow over the strings. Her music was full of grace, passion, and elegance. Lutcas had heard of violins but never saw one in action before. He couldn't take his eyes off the instrument and Violina's beautiful face as she cast a smile while creating such marvelous music. The music, like the tune he would often play, didn't wield power but was pleasant to the ear. Lutcas was so entranced by this music that he tripped over a rock and fell to the ground. Violina was startled by his fall that she played a note wrong and stopped in her tracks.

Violina leaned down and asked, "Oh Lutcas! Are you okay?"

Lutcas was really embarrassed by his clumsiness, "Oh sorry about that. You were so wonderful that I wasn't paying attention."

Lutcas's leg stung a bit and he saw that he had received a scrape from his tumble. It scared Lutcas for a moment because he had not received physical pain like this before. But it was merely a minor wound and nothing to fret about. Lutcas noticed that some blood came out of the wound as well. Note whimpered and licked the wound to help Lutcas.

Lutcas said, "This is annoying. I never had this happen before. I wonder if this is because of the absence of the String of Nepes."

"Things like this started occurring in my town not too far from you and Guil's arrival. I wonder what the effect of the missing String of Ahaba will be." She said as her face became downcast at the mention of the String and her old town.

Lutcas noticed this and wanted to see her radiant happy face again. "I know it must be sad to think about your home. When Guil and I traveled, we told each other about our homes. It makes me sad to think about it sometimes, but it also makes me feel better in a strange way."

Violina's face brightened up a bit as she asked Lutcas, "Well then, I would like to know more about Guil. I knew him briefly, but I would like to know more. He seemed intelligent, like a teacher of mine."

"Well, Guil explained himself to your village elder plainly. He was royalty of the middle kingdom. He said he did a lot of music studying. He even talks like he is smart sometimes."

Violina thought the remark was funny and asked, "If he was such a student of music, why did he not carry an instrument?"

Lutcas answered, "Well he told me his family smashed it after he defied their actions. His brothers embarked on a journey to claim the strings while he tried to get the strings first. But one of his other brothers stood against his family like Seth did but died because of it. So, we traveled in hopes of attaining the other strings. He was a kind friend and I hope we can complete his mission now." Lutcas noticed he was feeling downcast, and he asked Violina, "Maybe you could tell me about your beloved? The man you are in union with?"

Violina began to twirl her hair in the thought of her partner, "Oh well, Tekoa is his name. He is the fastest horse rider in the town. Maybe even the world."

Lutcas noticed her desire to be with her husband and felt lonely. He wanted to know why Violina loved this man so he may give Sonare a reason to love him, "So did you love him because he was the fastest rider?

Violina answered, "No I wouldn't fall for someone just because they knew how to tame a horse. I just found him so alluring. He was warm, kind, and would listen to me. To be honest, he was awkward sometimes but even that was cute. He treated everyone with love and wouldn't hesitate to help anyone in the village."

Lutcas thought this guy must have certainly been something, "Wow it seems like you fell for the right guy. I can't wait to meet him sometime. Is that what you made that bit of music for?"

"Yes actually" Violina said almost teasingly, "So tell me Lutcas, where is the special woman in your life?"

Lutcas thought about Sonare and said, "Well, there was this girl that lived in my village. Her name was Sonare, and she was beautiful. But now she is gone, wherever the Knights took her."

Violina didn't want the conversation to grow gloomy or provoke sadness in Lutcas, so she asked, "tell me more about her. Did she play an instrument? Was she a farmer like you and your other villagers?"

Lutcas continued, “Sonare was good at playing the Mandolin. But she wasn’t a farmer, she was more of a gardener. Sonare and her family had this garden where they would grow beautiful flowers. Sometimes she would weave some of them into her long-braided hair. I was always so anxious to talk to her but sadly it seems I won’t get that chance again. After all, I am not as great as Tekoa.”

After Lutcas said this, a feeling began to fester inside him. He thought about the people he knew in his life and compared them to himself. Thoughts of despair and self-doubt filled his mind. He thought to himself that he couldn't even save his own village and friends. Maybe if he was better, he could have prevented this.

Violina felt compassion for Lutcas and said, “Nonsense. Once we get the strings, I'm sure you will see her again. If she isn’t the one for you, then I’m certain you will find another girl in the land of Symphonia who will love you for who you are. Besides, she may not need a Tekoa in her life. She might need a Lutcas?”

Lutcas understood that Violina was trying to be kind and encouraging to him. He even remembered having a similar conversation like this with Bendzo. Making this connection, Lutcas was glad to have a friend that was encouraging like his old beloved friend. But the feelings of pitty for himself couldn’t be shaken.

Later down the road, Lutcas and Violina found a village. The village rested at the foot of a mountain. It had no villagers except the ones that were dead. The streets were littered with the lifeless bodies of men. The once wooden lodges were now piles of ash, with only a small amount of evidence to what they were before. Note sniffed the bodies and whined loudly, nudging them to see if they moved. This was the same silence that rang through Lutcas’s town.

After Violina saw the ruin, she exclaimed, “I can’t believe that they could do such a thing. Those knights wreaked havoc and destroyed these people's lives. Yet they still proclaim exaltation and salvation.”

Lutcas agreed and noticed something. “Wait a minute. Something is off. When they came to my town, they took almost everyone. At your village, they left with no one, not even a few. But here seems like this could have been all the men in the entire village. There isn't a single woman or child's corpse here."

"This is strange. I feel terrible for not being able to do much about this. But who would do this apart from the Knights of Orchestrasus?"

"I don't know. I hate for them to be exposed like this. Let us give them a burial before we continue. That way, they can return to the earth where they came from."

"Right. We also may need to rest. We haven't gotten too far but we are traveling on foot, and it will get only more difficult. Especially with these mountains" Violina suggested.

Lutcas looked at all the destruction around him and was a bit nervous about staying here any longer, "I don't know. This place makes me uneasy. What if they come back and do the same to us?"

Violina folded her arms and began to think, "Well, I couldn't imagine why they would come back here. They left nothing. Not even any of the buildings are suitable for good shelter."

Lutcas, still uneasy about the whole place, agreed to stay. He played a tune of moving earth, allowing the bodies to sink into the ground and out of sight. Soon after, a snowflake fell from the sky and a cold breeze came in from over the mountain. They knew they needed to stay warm; so, they found that some of the village still had remnants of wood and a building with a wall still standing. They began to build a fire at the ruined structure that could protect them from the cold wind. While they were doing this, Note was chasing the snowflakes that were ever so slowly falling from the sky. After setting up camp, Violina played a tune of minor flame, kindling the wood they gathered into a proper campfire. At this point, the sun was down, and the snow kept falling.

While sitting by the fire, Lutcas was curious about the music Violina could play, "Violina, I know you mentioned that you study a lot of different kinds of music. What kinds of music can you play?"

Violina answered, "Oh, well I know tunes of fire, water, air, and some earth tunes. I know melodies that can change the properties of water into ice or mist and such. I can make hot or cold air. But I can't play all of those highly efficiently yet. Those are the ones I can think of off the top of my head."

Lutcas was impressed, "Wow, you sure know a lot of different music. Could you teach me some of the songs?"

"Unfortunately, I know the songs only by the way of the violin. I cannot teach you. If anyone could, it would be the one who taught me." she replied.

Lutcas was curious as to who taught her all of this. "That's incredible that you had a single teacher that was able to teach all of this to you. Who was your teacher?"

Violina looked up into the snowy sky remembering, "He was a kind man with many years on him, from the middle kingdom. He would travel from the middle kingdom to see the other villages when he wasn't teaching his students. He found interest in me and two of my friends and decided to teach us. He knew how to play multiple instruments and claimed that concert masters would teach him in his dreams. He offered to take me and my friends back to the capitol, but I refused since I wanted to live in my village with Tekoa. So, he went back home and took two of my friends with him."

Lutcas couldn't help but think of Guil and said, "You know Guil's master was from the middle kingdom as well. It wouldn't surprise me if they knew each..." Lutcas was interrupted by a fireball flying past their heads.

Startled, Note began to bark in the direction where the flame came. Lutcas got out his Lute while Violin readied her violin. They were in silence for a moment, waiting for the slightest sign of movement in the dark snow-filled void. They were so distracted that they didn't hear the direction the music came from. Suddenly, there was rustling in a nearby bush. Quickly, Violina played a melody of melting then with a tune of moving water, turning some of the falling snowflakes into the water and launching them at the bush. Before the water contacted the bush, a boy jumped out from the bush who was holding a pan flute. The boy, after dodging the splash, played a tune of roaring flame, combusting the campfire. Violina and Lutcas moved away from the raging fire and scattered. Lutcas took cover behind the wall and played a tune of moving rock, throwing nearby stones at the stranger. However, the stones flew past him. While he was dodging the stones, Note rushed him and knocked him on his back, making him drop his instrument. Violina quickly went to recover the instrument while Lutcas went to help wrestle the boy to the ground. After a brief struggle, Lutcas and note pinned the boy down.

After the boy was pinned down, he shouted, "Chornelious now! This is the emergency signal!"

Another boy emerged from another nearby shrub wielding a strange instrument, "Randomness goes!" he shouted while winding the instrument and pressing the keys on it.

Water, earth, and the air moved around him at random intervals in an unorganized and wild way. At first, Lutcas and Violina were frightened, but then quickly realized he didn't know what he was doing. After all the craziness, a big puff of snow engulfed him and once the snow settled, it revealed him trapped in a block of ice with his head sticking out. He said nothing and grunted as he struggled to move. Lutcas and Violina looked at the frozen boy and then turned to the one who was pinned.

The pinned boy with an embarrassed and inconvenienced look said, "We surrender."

After getting a close look at the boys, they realized they were not wearing kingdom uniforms; they looked like regular villagers. To be safe, Violina played a tune of moving earth to warp the dirt and rock around the pinned boy's arms. When Lutcas saw the boy, he reminded him of Bendzo. He was tall like Bendzo, but not quite as defined as he was. Maybe he was a little younger than him as well? He had brown hair that was brushed over to the left. His clothes were made of fur, keeping him warm. The other frozen boy was shorter than Lutcas but looked to be around his age. The boy's eyes were narrow, his hair was straight and black, and his body appeared to be thin. Violina played a melody of melting to remove the ice around him. After the boy slumped to the ground, Lutcas played a tune of moving earth to pin him to the ground as well. Now that Lutcas and Violina had pinned them both down, they weren't sure what to do.

"What now?" Lutcas asked Violina.

Violina replied, "I'm not sure we can leave them. But if they work for the kingdom then letting them go is a bad idea."

The taller boy somewhat sarcastically suggested, "Why don't you start by interrogating us? Since you don't know what to do."

Lutcas yielded to the suggestion, "Alright then who are you?"

"I am Pan and my very cold friend over there is Chornelious." the boy answered.

The three looked over to see Chornelious on the ground shivering and chattering his teeth. Note went over to smell him and then began licking his hands and fingers. Once Lutcas saw this, he knew that they must not be that dangerous since Note was comfortable around them.

Violina, still confused, asked, "Alright we know your names, but we don't know who you are and why you shot a fireball at us!"

Pan looked away a bit embarrassed but keeping his composure, "That was my mistake. I had thought you may have been the people that laid waste here."

Lutcas asked, "People? You mean this village was attacked by the Knights?"

Pan answered, "That is what my fellow villagers were expecting, an attack from the knights. A rider wielding a trumpet came through town and warned us of the Knights."

Violina knew that had to have been Tekoa, "It's him! I know who that was! That is my husband."

Pan continued, "Well we listened to your husband and prepared to go into hiding. Not long after, we saw a group of men approach town. We thought that they were friendly, maybe giving the same warning we did, but then they attacked us. They killed all the men with music and metal tools like scythes and axes. Out of all the horrible things they did, taking the women and children was the worst. I, along with a handful of people, managed to escape."

Lutcas answered, "This is strange. I wouldn't imagine why anyone other than the knights would try and kill. Well, I'm glad you both managed to escape. I'm sorry that you both lost your village."

Pan corrected Lutcas, "Well actually, Chornelious isn't from here. He is from a different village not terribly far from here. I know him since our peoples usually trade. This is a mining town, while Chornelius's town is an exceptional smithing village. I even went to his village to learn how to forge. When I returned here, the town was being attacked. So, we fled through the tunnels and found help. I came back to see if any bandits were around and if there were any signs of survivors."

Violina felt sympathy for them and said, "I am sorry that happened to you. Lutcas and I have lost our villages as well. We are looking for the Strings of Harmony, so this doesn't continue to happen."

Pan curious asked, "You are searching for the Strings of Harmony? Maybe that old coot wasn't as crazy as I thought he was."

While shivering, Chornelious called out, "Hey! Could we move this conversation towards the fire?"

Lutcas moved the earth with his tune to free them both. Chornelious, still shivering, rushed towards the fire to warm himself up. Pan didn't waste much time getting to the fire either. Note, now in a playful mood, ran with them while his tongue hangs out of his mouth.

After sitting down, Lutcas examined Chornelious's instrument and said, "So uh, Chornelious. What is that instrument you have right there?"

Chornelious picked it up and said, "This is my master's beloved creation. He calls it the Hurdy Gurdy. You won't find another one of these."

Violina leaned forward and studied it, "Interesting. how does it work?"

Chornelious answered, "Unfortunately, I do not understand the instrument as my master did. I originally had a Pipa. But the attack here resulted in it being destroyed. I was able to save my master's instrument which is why I have this. He told me that this instrument has the power to play two tunes or melodies at the same time! I don't know how it works so it gets a bit wild sometimes. I wish to see him after his travels so he can show me more of how it works."

Lutcas kept studying the Hurdy Gurdy while Violina asked Pan more questions, "So, you said you found help? Where?"

Pan answered, "If we go through the mine, we will end up on the other side of the mountain. Not far from there we will find the sanctuary where we received help from the old man. He said that he was expecting a student of his to head this way. That is according to a dream he had."

Lutcas looked at Violina and said, "Hey, could that be your teacher Violina?"

Violina wasn't sure yet the thought of seeing her old teacher gave her excitement. "We must go! Can you take us there please?"

Pan didn't seem to care and said, "Fine by me. But we can't leave yet. I am assuming you're here to rest awhile. So, while you two rest, I am going to go find clues to who attacked and why. The women and children are in their clutches, and I need to find them."

Lutcas and Violina went to sleep while Pan and Chornelious searched the ruins of the town. Morning came and the four departed to their next destination. The ground was now covered in a thin layer of white snow. Note rolled around and played in the snow while they moved forward. Not too far from where they were was the mine. The mine's entrance was somewhat hidden by the forest. If someone passed by there without knowing beforehand where it was, they wouldn't have noticed it. It seemed that whoever passed through there last made sure they weren't followed either, since the entrance was covered with rocks. Pan took out his flute and played a tune of moving rocks, clearing the way into the mine. After the rocks were moved, they were presented with a dark tunnel that looked a bit ominous. To fix the darkness issue, Pan, with one hand, played a tune of minor flame. A little ball of fire flew from the flute and floated next to Pan. The group walked a bit further into the cave with Pan, maintaining the flame with his song. They found an unlit wall torch that Pan grabbed and moved the fire onto. As they continued, they found more torches and lit them with the fire from the first torch.

Lutcas was rather uneasy about moving into the cave. Some passages that branched off from the one they were on appeared like shadows until they were right next to them. Lutcas could only imagine who could jump out at them in surprise.

In order to distract himself from the rattling suspense, Lutcas decided to go and talk to Pan. At first, Pan didn't seem very approachable. Really, Pan looked dead serious, and a frown seemed to be his favorite facial expression.

Building up the courage to talk to him, Lutcas said, "So you said your village was attacked by a group of men. Do you know who those men are?"

Pan continued to look ahead while he answered, "No. I don't know what their deal was exactly. They had no reason to be provoked and we had no reason to think random travelers would do such a thing. As far as I'm concerned, they are just evil filth that plagues this world." Pan looked at Lutcas and asked him, "What about your town. You said your village was attacked by knights?"

Lutcas answered, "destroyed more like. Basically, they came into town and stole the String of Nepes. After that, they convinced the town to join them and killed those who didn't."

Pan looked back at Violina with his empty glare, "So the same thing happened to her town?"

"Yes. except we couldn't find any dead." He replied, "But thinking about it makes me sad and angry... I hate them."

"Well, my hatred goes for those who have done such a thing as well. In fact, once I see those people again, I will wipe them off the face of our beautiful world. Then I will do the same to the knights who did this to you and Violina."

After continuing down the dark tunnels, they finally found the exit point. The light from the exit was harsh on the eyes, but they were glad to be in it again. Upon their exit, they were presented with a slope leading down into a valley that had a river between the mighty mountains that laid siege to it. In the distance, they could make out a civilization by the river. Pan and Chornelious led them down to the riverside.

The town was right next to the riverbank. Sticking out from some of the wood buildings were docks for their boats. Fishing nets were dangling from signs and beams protruding from the buildings. Lutcas also took notice of many people that were sitting on the streets. He could tell that they were above capacity here. In the middle of town, Pan and Chornelious led them to a large stone building that resembled a chapel. Upon entering, they were greeted with an old man who was absorbed completely into whatever he was reading.

Chornelious went up to him and tapped him on the shoulder, "Harper, we have brought travelers. I think one of them may know you."

The old man Harper turned around and studied Lutcas and Violina before speaking, "It has been a while, hasn't it young lady?"

The man was completely unkempt. His beard was long and gray along with his hair. He was thin, almost malnourished looking. His clothes seemed to resemble something that was once fine, but now has succumbed to dirt and tears. But even with all of this, Violina recognized who this was.

Violina ran up to the old man and said to him, "Teacher, it is really you! What happened to you?"

The man stood up and said, "Oh my dear Violina, it is a long and tragic story. The kingdom I once called home has fallen to a great deception and is now in a state of rebellion against our creator the Conductor. But it brings a spark of joy to see at least one of my beloved students alive. It was foretold that one of my students would arrive here, but at first, I believed it to be Guil."

Lutcas burst out in astonishment, "You were Guil's teacher?"

Harper's eyes widened, "You know Guil? How is he?"

Lutcas face became downcast as he now had to explain what happened, "Guil had tried to save my town from the knights. He was too late, and he let me come with him to retrieve the Strings of Harmony. Upon finding the String of Ahaba, he was captured along with the String."

Harper's eyes watered with sadness and his voice began to choke up, "My dear Guil. Oh, I knew how dangerous this would be for you. He barely escaped his family and now he falls back into their clutches. They will do horrible things to him to get information on where the remaining strings are; as they did me. Oh, how the world will wilt at the hands of the very beings that exist in it." Harper looked back at Lutcas, "Is your journey leading you to the Strings of Harmony still?"

Lutcas answered, "Yes. We are trying to find the String of Eres right now."

Pan, a bit shocked by what he was hearing, asked, "Wait, what happens if they are all taken by Orchestrasus?"

Harper went on, "I will share what happens with the corruption of the Strings. The String of Emet, the first one taken, maintains the integrity of the inherent truth of all creation. Upon its absence, those inherited and self-evident truths can become twisted and manipulated. The String of Nepes, that which grants bountiful life to all things, will bring death and mortality into the world. The String of Ahaba, that which upholds the passion of creation and the interactions between creations, will stir hatred. Love will be replaced with power and the desire to love will be replaced with the desire to dominate and rule. Those are the effects of those corrupted strings."

Lutcas now understanding the effects of the String of Ahaba, understood why Pan's village may have been attacked. Lutcas, for a while, understood the effects of losing the String of Nepes. But he wanted to know more about the other strings.

Violina beat Lutcas in asking the question, "What of the remaining Strings?"

Harper continued, "I don't know entirely. But there are the String of Eres and The String of Sahaq. These both keep the harmony of the earth beneath and the sky above. To allow these to be taken will throw both into discord and chaos. I could only imagine the effects. After that, the String of Aman. This String is what helps maintain coexistence between beings in creation as well as their relationship with their creator. However, I imagine this String is only doing so much at this point. For it is very similar to the String of Ahaba. The final string of the seven is The String of Mozane. This string maintains the stability of existence; to lose this string is to risk many becoming unstable creatures of chaos."

Violina, afraid, asked, "But what do we do now? The army of Orchestrasus is searching for these Strings. What are we to do against them?"

The old man was silent for a moment, and then walked toward the back of the chapel, signaling the group to follow him. The old man led them to a room in the back that smelled of incense.

Harper said, "Fortissimael! I request a word with you."

Nothing happened for a moment, but then a brilliant light appeared in the middle of the room. Among this light glowed the silhouette of what appeared to be a man. Lutcas was not afraid of what he was seeing. He knew that this was a concertmaster. Concertmasters were celestial beings that had many forms. But it wasn't uncommon to see them in towns and villages, like the one that used to live at Lutcas's village. Fortissmael's features could not be made out, only a silhouette of light could be perceived.

The Concertmaster Fortissimael spoke, and his voice echoed, "Fear not, I am Fortissimael. I am the humble messenger of the Creator King, The Conductor. I have come to provide wisdom from the creator king."

Harper asked the entity, "Oh Fortissimael, I have in my company those who seek the Strings of Harmony. We request guidance."

Fortissimael took a moment before answering, "Indeed the Strings need protecting. The Conductor has elected these four to retrieve the remaining strings."

Chornelious, feeling confused, almost protested, "Four. Including me and Pan?"

"Precisely." Fortissimael answered, "Even though you four are already infected with the effects of this discord in your world. You will receive guidance and blessing on your quest."

Lutcas was also confused, and he said, "The Conductor chose us? Why did he do that? There are surely better musicians than us to perform this task."

Fortissimael answered, "The will of the creator is not for me to question or know. I am merely a celestial messenger. But he has elected you four to undergo this task. However, it is up to you to take on this journey and stay on this path. Now, will you hand me your instruments so that it may receive the blessing from the Conductor? Upon accepting this blessing, you are agreeing to take up the quest presented to you."

Lutcas didn't want to see any more damage and wished to complete the quest, so he vowed to fulfill the journey. Violina agreed so no more would need to suffer and she could be reunited with Tekoa. Pan wanted the chaos to stop and to see the end of the evil, so he accepted. Chornelious never had been called to such a task before and wanted to honor his friends and creator, so he accepted.

The four-handed over the instruments and they were enveloped in the light. Shortly after being consumed by the light, the instruments were given back. The string of the instruments now had a faint glow to them. Other than that, the instruments didn't appear to be changed.

Fortissimael then informed them, "Your instruments now can play the music of Purity. These will be tunes that will help protect you from the main foes you now face. Your instruments will not easily break and those with the stringed instruments can place a String of Harmony on the instrument. This is a powerful blessing that will not be bestowed freely, for you four face a great and terrible journey. I will now teach you the music of purity.

Suddenly, as Lutcas was standing there, his mind was flooded with information. It stopped as if he didn't just learn the information but had known it all along. Lutcas and the others were astonished at what had just happened, now they learned the music of Light.

Fortissimael then directed his voice to Harper, "Harper, I must go to the domain of the creator. I will not be here to give you more guidance. I must tell you what has happened in your homeland. Ever since the String of Ahaba was claimed, the kingdom has fallen under a great civil war. Emperor Anthropo and the Empress now wage war on each other for the throne. Due to this, their forces are thinned out in search of the Strings. They wander in this region searching for the Theater of Eres. Let them rest and send them out." Fortissimael moved his attention to the group, "You four, once you obtain the strings, go to the far west lands of Symphonia where you will receive further instruction. I wish you all blessings on your journey and stay on the path of the creator's wisdom."

The light that the being emitted vanished. Harper's mind was now a hurricane of thoughts. He now wandered and worried about his homeland that was now in the civil war. In this thought, he requested to be left alone for a while and he dismissed the four and requested to see them before they departed the next day.

For the rest of the day, they were given a place to rest, though it was crowded. It was a once large and empty building that were now used to house many refugees who had no place to go. Lutcas asked many who were with them what happened to them, and they were all either attacked by bandits or by the Knights. To hear these stories allowed Lutcas to see even more clearly how The String of Ahaba's absence plagued the world.

CHAPTER 4 EARTH

After the four rested, they began their preparations to go to the Theater of Eres. Before departing, they went by the Chapel to see Harper again. Harper appeared to have stayed up most of the night either taking notes, reading, or just thinking. They asked him for guidance in getting to the other Strings of Harmony. Harper gave them a map of the known world of Symphonia. Lutcas gazed upon the map in fascination looking at places he didn't know existed. There was a great lake to the north, a sea to the west, sky-high mountains, deep valleys, swamps, everything. Harper's only request was that this not fall into the hands of the enemy. The four agreed of course and they took the map and headed to their next destination.

The village was kind enough to lend them a boat that would carry them downstream. If they continued to go downstream, they would eventually be at the village of Siderous. There they will get to the Theater of Eres. So, they all set out and went down the river to begin their journey together.

Lutcas wanted to get to know Chornelious and Pan a bit more, so he waited for a good moment to speak to them. There wasn't much to time this with since they were just on a quiet boat ride. Pan would spend most of his time staring off at the mountains or rowing if needed. Chornelious spent most of his time studying his Hurdy Gurdy. Violina now was playing with Note who was either getting belly rubs or sticking his nose in the water. It occurred to Lutcas how Chornelious and Pan had gotten thrown into this whole mess, which made him feel a little guilty.

Lutcas with a bit of guilt said to the two, "Guys I am sorry that we wrapped you up in this whole wild chase. I know this was all so sudden."

Chornelious answered while still studying his Hurdy Gurdy, "It is alright. It wasn't like I was doing anything better. Besides, we are heading to my hometown right now. So, I get to see if it is okay."

Violina confusedly asked, "Wait, your village is near the Theater of Eres?"

Chornelious paused what he was doing and answered, "Yes. Though I never did go to the theater much. It will take us a bit to get there so we will still need that map to navigate. I don't know the way from my village."

Pan looked over his shoulder at Lutcas and said to him, "I don't mind. I have got nothing left to go back to anyway. Besides, I am a little bit glad that you are letting me tag along. This feels like I am helping fight what was brought upon my hometown."

Lutcas was astonished to hear Pan emit any sort of positive feeling, "Wait you are?"

He nodded, "Yes, I am. Because of you and Violina, I can now wipe out these people that have caused all this ruin to come into our world. I have been equipped with tunes of purity to stop this evil from spreading. Plus, I can try and find where those men took my fellow villagers and my family."

He agreed with him completely, "Well I'm glad we don't just have two people trying to do it anymore. Now have the help of two more people."

Violina cleared her throat sarcastically, "Ahem! You are forgetting our other little helper." She then began to scratch Note's chin, which Note wagged his tail in bliss.

Lutcas was happy that they have had some support given to them, "Why don't I play us some music for the boat ride."

She answered, "Yes, I like the tune that you play. Please play it again."

He took his lute and began playing his tune. Note knew exactly what tune that was about to play. So, he sat while wagging his tail ready to hear its music. Lutcas played the tune that he always liked to play, his tune of gratefulness. After Lutcas played the tune, he found something he didn't think he wouldn't see. He saw Pan with a bit of a smile.

Pan turned to Lutcas after the tune was played, "I do like that tune. It reminds me of the tunes my little brother would play."

Violina asked Pan, "Did your little brother play the Lute like Lutcas does?"

Pan answered her, "Yes, actually very similar to it. He even has a tune he likes to play when he is happy. He had such an innocent heart. " Pan's fist tightened and his face went from that smile to a look of hate, "Now he is gone."

There was a moment of silence before Chornelious spoke, "You know I could try to play music for ya'll with this thing."

Worried that the Hurdy Gurdy may go haywire again they all at once yelled, "No!" which followed with some laughter from the group.

On the rest of the way on the water, the group practiced the tunes of purity they had just learned. To everyone's relief, Chornelious was able to play these tunes properly since he was given the knowledge of how to do so. However, he still didn't know how to play normal tunes with his odd instrument.

Finally, Chornelious told everyone to dock at the upcoming shore, where village Siderous was. Just by looking at the town, it was extremely different from the ones they had been to. Mostly this was due to their architecture of the village. The roofs were not flat and triangular, but rather curved and with the edges of the roofs pointing up. Smoke came out of some of the buildings that had furnaces in them from smelting and burning. Siderous also had a stone gate that surrounded it while it sat on the foot of a nearby mountain.

When they approached the village, a few people poured out from the gate to greet Chornelious. This consisted of his family, friends, and town leadership. They all had very similar features to Chornelious. They all had black hair and narrow eyes. The most distinct between all of these was the town leader with his thin and long beard and mustache. But they varied in different sizes and body types. Lutcas observed this and wished he could go back to his village and see his people pour out of it with welcome arms.

One of the town leaders asked Chornelious, “Young man. Who are these people that you bring with you?”

Chornelious answered, “Tenor, we have been sent on a quest with my new companions here to retrieve the String of Eres.”

Tenor, the town leader, was surprised at this claim and said, “You all follow me.”

Tenor led them to the town hall and back into a room with a chest, “Chornelious I trust you. But there are some things I need to know.” Tenor opened the chest revealing some armor and a strange tool.

Just by glancing at the armor, they could tell this was from the knights. It had the same color and design to match them. Along with this, there was a strange tool with it. It was a bladed tool that had a handle. It was like that of a large knife but with both sides of the metal being sharp. They didn’t know it, but this was one of the first swords of many that will be made.

Tenor continued, “We were warned by a trumpet wielding rider that there would be people coming to try and take the Strings of Harmony. We found a couple of knights searching around this region. They asked and after some of our villagers questioned them, an escalation occurred. We killed one of their knights and they took a couple of our peoples. I need to know what your friend’s intentions are for the String of Eres.”

The group was quiet till Violina spoke up, "Right now all we can do is keep the String away from the Knights of Orchestrasus. If they don't take these strings, we can prevent damage being done."

Tenor looked at the group critically, "I see. Even though Chornelious and Pan seem to trust you, I require something more to give my trust."

Pan and Chornelious looked at each other and then looked at Violina and Lutcas. Meanwhile, Note was rolling around on his back. Lutcas and Violina weren't sure of definite proof they could offer.

Lutcas forced himself to bravely speak up, "I don't know what I can do to prove to you that our intentions are good. But my village and Violina's village were brought to ruin at the hands of our enemy. We have come a long way and we have spoken with a Concertmaster named Fortissimael who taught us tunes and melodies of purity and light."

Tenor interrupted Lutcas, "You spoke with Fortissimael?" Tenor paused and stroked his thin facial hair, "Very well show me what you learned."

Lutcas took his Lute and played a pure tune of light. As he played the strings on his Lute began to glow and suddenly a great light flashed from his Lute. Tenor was taken back at the light and at that moment he believed them.

Tenor spoke to the group, "This is sufficient proof. I will tell you where to go my young friends. Travel southeast from here and you will find a cave entrance. The cave will take you deep into the earth and there lies the Theater of Eres."

Before they departed Pan studied the chest that held the armor and sword. Pan began taking out the armor and sword observing it.

Violina approached him and asked him, "Pan what are you doing?"

Pan answered her, "This stuff is used by the knights, right? It is basically a tunic of steel. It can protect them against many things. But what are they afraid of that makes them wear this?"

Violina, not sure where he was going, asked, "I don't think I understand. What are you trying to say?"

"We can give them something to be afraid of. We can use their own equipment against them. We will be able to deal with them safely since we will be protected and more dangerous with this." Pan said.

Violina felt uneasy about using the tools of their enemy. Even more so when Pan put on the armor. The armor was made of black plated metal that covered his entire torso. Unfortunately, there were no gauntlets or helmets. But there was also some protection for his legs and feet. The armor bore the same symbol that the Knights wore, a man standing on a podium.

Pan studies the armor he wore and said, "I will make this my own. Though I will be changing how it looks. I don't wish to bear the same symbol that those knights do."

Violina studied the armor concerned and said, "Well, let's hope you never need to use it."

Shortly after, the four began their journey to the Theater of Eres. The trip required them to go inland away from the river. So, they were unable to use the newly acquired boats. The armor that Pan wore was heavy, which made everyone understand why the knights always traveled on mounts instead of on foot. But Pan was stubborn and determined to press on with the armor. The landscape was pretty like what they have seen for the past few days. Tall pines and evergreens littered the base of the tall Rocky Mountains. The wildlife, however, was different. They saw various kinds of birds, moose that towered over the deer, goats that scaled the mountains almost effortlessly, and large birds that soared overhead. Like a well-assigned orchestra, they all had their place and role in the land.

It was almost sunset before they reached their destination. The four found themselves looking into the mouth of a cave they led into the belly of a mountain. Already they could hear a tune that was deep and strong, just like the ground, rocks, and mountains they all stood on. The four pressed into the cave a bit nervous about what they might encounter in its depths. Pan played a tune of minor flame, barely illuminating the cave around them. As they went down, they no longer needed the flame, for they encountered many glowing crystals that emitted a humming noise like that of the music coming from The Theater of Eres. Along with the strange stones, there were rivers of lava that slithered through the ravines of the cave. Fortunately, the group didn't need to traverse such dangerous terrain, but they still felt the immense heat being generated from the molten rocks.

Eventually, they found themselves in a large dome-like room. Around the room were the glowing humming crystals that illuminated the area as if it were day. The floor was smooth and consisted of various kinds of stones that had many different properties such as texture and color. Surrounding the entire room were bleachers made of these various kinds of stones but in a sorted manner. In the center of the room was the String of Eres which hovered over the podium of stones. Note, like the other times, was affected by the strings. But rather than run around and play, this time he walked in circles and began to lay down and rest. The other four approached the String in fascination.

Chornelious breaking the mystical moment asked, "So what do we do with it?"

Pan responded, "As we planned. We take the String. But will it be safe to do it?"

Lutcas studied it and said, "Well when my friend Guil took it he was unharmed and so was the String. If we don't let it fall into the wrong hands, they should still be fine. We just need to figure out who will take it and tune the string to their instrument."

Violina spouted out, "Lutcas, I think you should take the string!"

Surprised Lutcas asked, "Me? Why?"

"You have seen more strings lost than I have. It seems right that you take it. Besides, Pan doesn't have a stringed instrument and we both know it can't go on that hurdy-gurdy."

Chornelious crossed his arms, "Never before have I been offended by such a reasonable decision." he responded jokingly.

Lutcas looked at the String and found hope. He could rest well knowing that this String would not fall into the hands of the Knights of

Orchestrasus. Now the earth wouldn't meet the chaos of the rebellion against the conductor. Lutcas grabbed the string and pulled it from its pedestal. The deep tune the string emitted became quieter, but still active. The humming crystals around them dimmed their humming as well. But there was still sound and there was still harmony. Lutcas then readied his Lute to put the String of Eres on. Before he could do anything, the string latched on to the Lute and became one of its Strings. The String emitted a brown aura that distinguished it from the other strings on his instrument.

The group was relieved until Note began barking at the entrance of the Theater. They turned to see Tubiat, the hulking knight, walking into the room. He looked the same as before but with no other knights.

Tubiat bellowed out a laugh and said, "Well! I didn't expect to see you two again! I figured I had told you not to get in our way. But for a moment I had thought you had joined me with that knight right there escorting you in. That or I was betrayed."

Pan narrowed his eyes, "I am no Knight of yours."

Tubiat began stroking his handlebar mustache, "I see. Well, nowadays it wouldn't surprise me to see a knight go after the string before I could get it. There has been such a power struggle back at Orchestrasus ever since the String of Ahaba was pulled. A shame, with your stature it would seem you could make a fine warrior under my command. At this rate, it will only be a matter of time before trust is completely broken and people turn on each other, and it will come. I will persevere through since I have gained so much power under the leadership of Emperor Anthropo and Prince Lyle. That is why I possess higher mortality than my other men, I possess loyalty."

Pan snapped at him, "Loyalty to a false cause. Because of your ideals my people were all slaughtered and kidnapped with their bodies laid out for the birds to claim!"

Tubiat looked a little confused, "Well that certainly wasn't any of my knights. After my Lord claimed the String of Nepes, he gave us direct orders to try and not kill if possible and if we did to take the bodies back to our grand city!"

Lutcas heard this and was confused, he now understood where the bodies were going but didn't know why, "Wait why are you people taking bodies back to your city?"

Tubiat rolled his eyes and said, "Enough! I don't have time to explain this to you stupid kids. Now I will tell you this and tell you this once. Give me the string or you will all die."

Lutcas recalled Guil and his encounter with Tubiat and how they fled. With anger that Lutcas never had before he shouted, "How dare you! You took my friends from me! I will die rather than give you this string!"

Tubiat readied his Tuba and said, "Very well. Then die like the rest of them!"

Tubiat blew into his Tuba creating a great and terrible blast of wind. Lutcas saw this coming and played a tune of moving earth to shield him from the wind. When he played the tune, it was easier to play than ever before. Not only did the earth shoot out of the ground quickly but in a larger portion than he expected. With this tune a thick wall of stone moved up from the ground and shielded the party from the blast of wind. Quickly Lutcas kept playing the tune to move the wall of stone at him. Before the wall reached him an explosion blasted through it after a Tune from the Tuba was heard. The others saw an opportunity to charge in the cloud of dirt and smoke.

Pan drew his sword and charged at him while playing his flute. He played a tune of minor flames which shot small balls of fire at Tubiat. Tubiat saw this and answered it with a major tune of flame, making a large ball of fire shoot out of the tuba, consuming the incoming fireballs towards Pan. Pan could feel the heat of the fireball, but it was stopped when Chornelious played one of the new melodies learned from Fortissimael, the pure melody of force barrier. This made a barrier appear in front of Pan, dispersing the fireball. Chornelious saw that he had played music from his Hurdy Gurdy successfully and was filled with joy.

Over Tubiats head was another fireball that came from Violina's violin. Tubiat could see that everyone was closing in on him and he blew into his Tuba again creating another blast of wind. Everyone was hit by this except for Lutcas who was able to quickly respond with a tune of moving earth doing the same thing he did before. Everyone else was thrown against the walls of the room, but Note was only thrown towards the back of the room. Before Lutcas could do anything else the wall he made was destroyed by a great exploding fireball from Tubiat. The impact threw Lutcas to the ground.

Tubiat marched up to Lutcas and said, "Well it seems your friend over there knew a unique song. Well why don't I show you one of mine!"

Tubiat began to play a horrible melody. The song was not a song that moved the elements or created anything. The melody had no structure but only emitted chaos. As the melody played Lutcas began to lose control over his body. All he thought about was taking the string off his lute and giving it to Tubiat. He tried as hard as he could to resist but he was losing the struggle. This was the discordant melody of Unnatural control.

Chornelious saw this and was still dazed from the blast. He panicked and tried to play something on his Hurdy Gurdy, but it went haywire, and it was just flinging gusts of air and dust around. Before Tubiat could reach the Sting, Note leaped at him and bit his arm which was only protected by a leather glove. Tubiat yelled in pain and tried to get Note off him. Lutcas felt exhausted and couldn't move. Violina got up with her Violin still intact and played a pure tune of light once Tubiat faced in her general direction while struggling against Note. The bright light blinded Tubiat, and he was now on rampage trying to get the dog off him. Lutcas looked at Tubiat as he finally was able to loosen Note's and throw him off his arm. Before Lutcas could do anything, he saw a blade shoot out from Tubiat's neck. This was Pan's sword. The blade was removed from his neck and Tubiat hit the ground with a mighty thump. Lutcas felt weird since he normally was repulsed at death but was now satisfied when he saw it befall his enemy. Tubiat now laid on the ground as blood oozed from his neck onto the floor.

Lutcas was shocked that they were able to defeat him. But there was no time to celebrate. Violina went over to Lutcas and helped him up, since he was weak from that strange music. Pan was in shock studying the blood covered blade he was holding and Tubiat's corpse that laid on the ground. This was the first human he would kill.

Chornelious went up to Pan and said to him, “Pan we gotta get out of here! We got the String but there could be more knights!”

Lutcas was immediately checked on by Note who was wagging his tail glad that Lutcas was okay. Note only seemed to have minor injuries like bruises from where Tubiat tried to remove him. The party wasted no time and they raced out of the cave. To their surprise they encountered no knights and only saw Tubiats bull that was standing near the entrance of the theater. Once they made it out of the cave they decided to keep moving until they were some ways away from it in case any knights were following them.

After making some distance the group sat down to catch their breath from not only the fight but the rush out of the cave as well. After gaining back their breath they began to laugh and celebrate since they had secured one of the Seven Strings of Harmony. This was the first real victory against their foe and to celebrate Lutcas played his special song.

CHAPTER 5 ANGER

After the party stopped fleeing from the theater, they set up camp in the forest. For once they had a reason to celebrate. They played music of happiness and joy that they have picked up over their lives, music that their peoples would dance to and play along with. When day came, they proceeded back to the town of Siderous. There they told the news to the town, and they rejoiced because they knew that one of the Seven Strings of Harmony had been saved. Out of gratitude the town gave them traveling supplies such as rations, bedrolls, and more. Chornelious took a toolbox with him so that he could tune and repair instruments if needed. Afterwards he said goodbye to his family, which consisted of many little brothers and sisters and departed with his group of new friends.

According to the map they received from Harper, they would need to go down the river to get near the eastern swamps where the String of Aman was. The journey down the river was much more relaxed than the one on foot. It gave them a chance to rest their sore legs and feet from the long walks of their journey. They also didn't need to look for water since they were always surrounded by it. Their victory gave them a peace of mind knowing that they have something that the enemy needed to have before fulfilling their plans. The risk now was being spotted by knights who were patrolling the river. But Violina, if needed, could create fog to hide them and escape.

During the time they were sailing down the river the group grew closer together. They would exchange tails of their homes and of their friends. They would practice music and help guide each other when practicing. Of course, everyone began to like Note and his innocent and upbeat spirit that any good dog would provide. But as they would talk, they began to raise questions about all the chaos happening in the world. Even though they knew what they had to do and why, there were still a lot of things that weren't clear to them.

While traveling down the road further, the group saw what appeared to be fields that once belonged to some farmers. The field was not covered in lush green grass but rather dry colorless grass. Scattered in the field were the corpses of numerous livestock. Most appeared to be cattle of some kind that looked different from the ones Lutcas saw at home with their longer horns and greater amount of fur. Along with the cattle there was what was left of the sheep and horses that maybe once before could move around the once green landscape. The group was greeted with the smell of rot and the sound of the flies before laying eyes on the silent and motionless beasts of the fields. Like the animals, the crops that once stood tall and proud were withered and fallen.

Violina looked at this with disgust and asked, "What happened here?"

Lutcas replied, "It's like at my home. We didn't have so much livestock though. But it looks like the absence of the string even reaches way out here in the east."

Chornelious added, "Well at least we got one of them. What were the ones we lost already? I may or may not have forgotten already."

Lutcas answered, "We lost the String of Emet, Nepes, and Ahaba." He then remembered the odd string on Prince Lyle's Lyre, and he mentioned, "Lyle also had one of the strings. When he played it, my village believed everything he said. They know better than this and I don't think they were being controlled. But what was clearly false was uncanny to what was true."

Pan curious asked him, “What was Prince Lyle like? You are the only one out of all of us that saw him. Was he fierce? Did he wield an instrument stronger than Tubiats? Did he carry a sword?”

Lutcas answered, “Well Prince Lyle isn’t too much older than we are. He was equipped with fine clothes and wielded a Lyre that looked very strange to me.”

Pan said, “So that is our adversary. Do you think if we killed him then all this damage would stop?”

The comment brought some discomfort to Violina, “I don’t know about that. It seems too simple.”

Soon another town appeared on the east side of the riverbank. This town was known as Yubal and was about as large as Siderous. Yubal was mostly constructed out of these white stone bricks that made their towers, walls, as well as a bridge that arched greatly over the river. The townspeople were hostile at first with the group, since they had recently been attacked by bandits. But Lutcas and the others proved their intentions and the people welcomed them in. Yubal had been experiencing a famine and were unable to provide much food or water for their guests. But they still offered what they could along with information about the southern route. Pan, however, was very curious about the bandits that had been giving them trouble. The locals said that they were west of here past the farmlands in fortified structure. Pan wanted to go, but the Violina disapproved along with Chornelious.

While sleeping at the town inn, Pan woke up Lutcas, “Keep quiet, I need your help.” he whispered

Lutcas arose from his sleep and with drowsiness asked, “Pan?” he let out a long yawn, “I’m so tired. Is everything okay?”

Pan asked Lutcas, “I am going to this fortified building to investigate the bandits. I need you to come with me.”

Lutcas, confused, asked, “The Building? What?” he rubbed his eyes, “Pan I thought the others disapproved.”

"I know, but there is a lot at stake here. What if my brother and mother are there?"

Lutcas hesitated, "I still don't think the others will think lightly of this."

Pan sharply responded, "They don't understand. Chornelious's village is safe. Violina's village for the most part volunteered to go with Orchestrasus. My entire village was killed, and my family captured!" Pan took a deep breath to calm himself, "I'm sorry. I didn't mean to get angry. But I need to do this. If you want to be a good comrade and come with me then please. If not, then I'll have to go by myself."

As Pan was preparing his things Lutcas was pondering. He remembered how he had lost all his friends back at home. This saddened him and he did feel that if he could do anything to save any of his family he lost, he would. Lutcas also valued his companionship with Pan and didn't want to do anything to tarnish it.

Lutcas began gathering things as he whispered to Pan, "Fine, but we mustn't take too long. I may need to leave the string of harmony here."

Pan stopped and said to Lutcas, "Though it is risky that string's power may be what it takes to save our lives. Plus, it could get stolen if we leave it here."

Lutcas didn't want to lose the string but also didn't want to die or for Pan to die either. So, he brought the string still attached to his Lute. After preparing, the two began to head west towards the fortress.

The road towards the fortress was anything but beautiful. The moon was full and lit the night sky up brighter than usual. This allowed them both to move without the use of torches. What the moon revealed under its light was a vast portrait of death. Lutcas and Pan hiked down a road that led them between fields of dead livestock that wielded a wretched stench. Further down the road this continued for some time along with rotted crops along with abandoned homes. The two would occasionally check homes to see if anyone was there, but they either found no one or the eerie and familiar stench that already gave away the vacancy of the cottages.

Finally in the distance they saw a fortress resting on a hill. The two never saw anything like it with its high walls and gate. Its distinction with all the other buildings told them that this was the place. So, the two approached the fortress with a great measure of caution. Lutcas was anxious because he knew that the people in this fortress had caused great destruction and hardship across the land. These people have pillaged, killed, and kidnapped so many innocent people and they could be the next. Distracted by these thoughts Lutcas wasn't paying attention to where he was going and tripped over something, making him fall. Lutcas recovered from his fall and looked to his side as he got up only to see a face looking back at him of blood and bone. To prevent himself from yelling Lutcas covered his mouth and scooted away from the body that scared him. As he scooted away, he bumped into yet another body that had fewer remaining features than the first. This caused Lutcas to begin panicking.

Pan noticed and walked over and put his hand over his mouth as he whispered, "Lutcas shhh. Keep calm, the last thing we want is to make noise and blow our cover."

Lutcas closed his eyes and took a deep breath and said, "Pan, what is this? Why did their flesh become like this, and these bones exposed? Is this what happens to us after death?"

Pan looked at the corpses in disgust and fear, "Well if this is what death holds for us then let's not become dead."

Lutcas, not able to disagree with the blunt philosophy, answered, "Fair enough."

Lutcas got up and studied the silent and decaying people around him. After closer examination he found that there were not only those two, but the field they were in by this stone fortress was littered with what was left of those who once lived. Lutcas noticed that the corpses varied in clothing. Some had common tunics and leather armor while others wore metal armor that resembled the knights of Orchestrasus.

Lutcas pointed this out to Pan saying, "Pan some of these people may have been knights."

Pan looked at the corpses more carefully, "You're right. But that doesn't make any sense. The townsfolk said that this fortress was controlled by bandits, not by the Kingdom of Orchestrasus."

Confused and afraid, the two pressed on and approached the fortress. As they got closer the amount of carnage thickened and more sharp metal instruments with them. When getting closer they found large banners hanging from the side of the castle. Upon closer inspection, they saw the symbol of a man standing on the Podium.

"I don't like this place. Pan let's turn around. There is nothing but death here with more people than I can bury. Let's turn back." Lutcas requested.

Pan looking at the fortress said, "No. My Mother and Brother could be there. I will not leave here till I know they are not here."

He then pressed on ahead of Lutcas. Lutcas looked once again at the carnage around him and feared that Pan would find something he would not want to find. As they continued to approach the fortress, they tried to stay low and quiet. Fear began to grow into Lutcas' mind as he could only imagine if he would share the same fate as those who once were. The night was a very quiet one. The only noise was the buzzing of the insects that were swarming the corpses. But the two had heard so much of it as they traveled that it was essentially white noise at this point. As far as they were concerned, the night was as quiet as it could be for this was a symphony of death.

They sneaked around the wall of the fortress and made their way towards the front of the large stone structure. This was where most bodies had piled up and the means of death was a bit clearer. It seems that some used the power of music to kill others as seen with sharp rocks coming from the ground and impaling the men. More commonly it seems the cause of death was the metal tools and the arrows they discovered. Lutcas never saw an arrow before nor the tool it was launched from. But the Bow held somewhat of a resemblance to the ones he saw used with instruments.

The front of the structure had a massive gate that was destroyed, leaving the entrance unprotected. Near the top of the gate seemed to be corpses of archers that were slain while guarding the fortress. Past the gate was the fortress courtyard which was littered with more carnage. When going through the gate Lutcas and Pan jumped as a loud crash sounded behind them breaking the dreadful silence. Pan drew his sword and Lutcas grabbed his instrument. When they turned to see what it was, they found what was once an archer that had fallen from the top of the gate. The crash of the body nearly gave the two a heart attack.

After crossing the gate, the two made it through the courtyard of the fortress. At the end of the courtyard, they were able to enter the main stone structure of the fortified facility. The inside of the fortress was cold and dark. Lutcas found a torch and Pan lit it using a tune of flame. The building had steps that led down and down into the ground. Finally, they reached the bottom of the stone steps. Suddenly there was a mild rattling of chains. Pan held up his hand to signal Lutcas to stop, but Lutcas bumped into the wall and a stone fell from it creating an echoing sound through the chamber.

The voice of a small boy sounded from deeper into the darkness, "Hello? Who is there?" the voice asked in a frail and weak voice.

Pan recognized the voice as a boy that used to be in his village, "Piper?" he asked.

Pan ran down the hall with a torch looking through the prison cells to see a young boy chained up to the wall with only a loincloth covering his malnourished body. The boy's body was frail and barely had any flesh to go with his bone. The poor thing could hardly be distinguished from the carnage that littered his cell.

Pan went up to him and exclaimed, "Piper! Piper, what happened to you?"

Lutcas caught up to him and was frightened for a few reasons. First when Pan spoke, he sounded choked up and more vulnerable than he had ever seen him before. The second was the horrific sight of the child he was looking at. His body was covered in wounds, dried blood, and the tracks of where tears had run down his face. The third was because of the numerous other corpses in the room who all shared those similar features. Pan played a song of shaping metal to set Piper free from the chains while Lutcas caught him and set him gently on the ground.

The boy coughed up some blood and exclaimed, "Pan! It is you. I am glad to see you."

Pan's eyes began to rise with water, "Piper what happened where is everyone else?"

Piper closed his eyes and said, "They brought everyone here. My mom is somewhere in this cell. They did terrible things to her and me. We heard a big battle erupt upstairs then guards were moving out and fleeing. They took away some of the moms with them as they fled. I saw your mom with them, Pan."

Pan widened eyed said, "What about my little brother? Tell me what happened to him!"

Piper spoke what would be some of his final words. "Tuner is in one of the cells. I think he is further down the hall." After that Piper became silent and died while being held by Lutcas who gave him the last bit of warmth he would ever feel.

Pan out of fear moved down the hall to search for his brother. Lutcas was deeply moved by the pitiful state of the poor boy. Lutcas laid him down gently and put him in a more dignified position. After a while Pan finally found the cell with his brother. Similarly, Tuner was hung up on chains like Piper was and had a similar state. Tuner looked very similar to his brother except younger and now paler and more malnourished. Pan tried to invoke a response from his brother. His brother slowly opened his eyes and smiled at Pan but couldn't utter a single word.

Pan smiled and tears began to roll from his face as he released Turner from his chains with his metal manipulating music, "Alright Tuner, let's get you out of here."

Pan tried to help Tuner walk but Tuner could not stand, "Down please." Tuner uttered quietly.

Pan set him down and upon closer examination he saw that certain parts of Tuner's legs have been sliced off so he could not walk or stand. Pan sat him down and his face casted a face of despair. Tuner's eyes began to close and open as if he was trying to fight off a deep sleep that could finally be bestowed after seeing his older brother.

Pan couldn't maintain the strong and stout personality as he cried, "No Tuner please stay awake. I have finally come to bring you home."

Lutcas was in the cell and Tuner noticed his Lute and he pointed at it, "Tuner, do you want me to play the tale mom used to play for us." Pan asked.

Tuner nodded his head up and down to say yes as a grin emerged from his face. Lutcas handed Pan his Lute and helped Tuner sit up.

Pan then began to play the one tale that he knew how to play on the Lute, "Long ago there was nothing. No music or sound or anything. But out of love the conductor with the power music played the world into existence. He made the sea. He looked at its vastness and depth and said it was good. He made the fields and the mountains, and he saw how strong they were and said it was good. He made the creatures that joined his symphony of creation and he said it was good as their sounds echoed throughout the land. Finally, when he made humans, he said they were very good and would rule the world beside the Conductor who loved them so much. Because he loved them, he gave them dominion over all the creatures and power to spread life and goodness across the expanse of Symphonia. Now we spread goodness, life, and love with our music."

Right before the last part of the tale was sung Piper passed. This made Pan do something Lutcas would never see him do again. Pan embraced his brother's cold body and rocked him as he wept. Though this was the most vulnerable he ever saw Pan, it didn't last since there was sound coming from down the chamber. This scared the two and they readied for battle.

Pan whispered to Lutcas, "Do you know what direction that came from?"

"No, do you think it was one guy?" Lutcas asked

"Hard to say. Lutcas I'll go see what it was. You make a break for the entrance. The last thing we need is a bunch of those scum down here and they take String of Eres. If I don't come up when the moon gets low on the horizon, then leave without me. If you see people other than me, come out of here, you run back to the town. Got it?"

"I don't like leaving you here. But I know we can't risk losing this String. Just try and get out of here safely please. I don't want to see anymore death than we already have."

Lutcas left the dungeon and went out of the fortress. Pan pursued the noises that he heard. A part of him wanted to be killed after witnessing so much evil that came from mankind. Another part of him was bloodthirsty wanting to avenge the blood of his brother. As he pursued the shouting of a man, he found himself at the front of a large wooden door. Carefully he opened it and found a large chamber with a man sitting in a chair. The man had all his fingers removed and appeared older with long gray hair. The man's eyes were narrow, like the people of Siderous.

The old man cried out, "Ah look a Knight of the mighty Orchestrasus. A servant of Emperor Anthropo! Tell me, have you come to slay me? Bout' time your stubborn puppet!"

At first Pan was confused but he had forgotten that his armor bore their symbol, "No this is not my armor. I am an enemy of these people."

The old man answered, "Interesting. You wear armor, wield a sword, you're not here to kill me, and you are an enemy of the empire. Interesting. Tell me what has made you an enemy of the knights?"

Pan took a deep breath and answered crying and angry, "Well if you must know old man. They are the ones who threw the world off balance. Death now sweeps the land and has reached my own home. The influence of what they had done created bandits that have pillaged my home, murdered my brother and father, and kidnapped my mother."

The old man chuckled a little under his breath showing his growing madness, "Well I suppose this is my lucky day. I am afraid I will not live much longer. You may not know who I am, but I am Gong, the wandering swordsman. I once was a seer and I saw what would happen to this world. I made the blade and trained with arts bestowed upon me. But as I traveled east these bandits kidnapped me after I killed twenty of them. They found my scrolls where I record my research on the art of the sword and have tried to make me teach them. I refused and they held me in here for days. I have seen them bring in people from all over the northern and eastern lands of Symphonia. Their desire for love has been mutated to rule over and torture those under them. I have even seen the battle where the bandits tried to defend the fortress they stole from the knights. Those who were wise took all the treasure and women they could and fled south. Everyone else here who stayed died. They abandoned most of their prisoners and even me. Now it seems that fate has brought us together."

Pan, confused by the copious amount of information, asked, "Why are you telling me this Gong? What do you want?"

"Well, I will not let my wisdom go to waste. These buffoons didn't take the scrolls I had with them. I casted a Key over the scroll where no one can comprehend its content without an oath from me. You come here as an enemy of the very people that I wish to kill. Grab the scrolls from over there and bring them to me. Bring them and I'll give you the ability to avenge the blood of all who died in this grave" Pan did what he said and held the scrolls in front of the man, "Young man do take this oath to avenge me, avenge your family, and to avenge the very ground beneath us that has been done by the rebellious forces of this world?"

Pan thought about it. He remembered his village getting raided, he remembered telling one last tale to his brother, he remembered his family all together, and he remembered the other stories told by his friends on what had happened to the places they once called home.

Pan looked Gong in the eye and said, "As an enemy of the rebellious forces of this world, I Pan will put these enemies to the sword so their influence may no longer spread its wickedness."

Gong smiled and said, "Yes! Now go forth warrior and do what you have sworn to do. " This was Gong's last breath.

Suddenly Pan was able to understand the contents of the scrolls he held. After he took the oath, he left the chamber and went back to the surface. When he reached the top of the steps, he saw Lutcas waiting for him.

Lutcas noticed that Pan carried a few scrolls with him, "Pan what are those?"

Pan answered, "I'll explain it on the way back."

After coming to this Fortress Lutcas noticed that Pan was changed. His heart became harder than the steel that he now wielded and colder than the night he found his dead brother.

CHAPTER 6 TRUST

Lutcas and Pan arrived before the sun rose up from the horizon. When arriving back at their living quarters no one seemed to be up except for Note who was eagerly waiting for their return. Lutcas reached down and patted his loyal dog to calm him. Lutcas was glad that Note didn't wake Violina or Chornelious while they were absent.

Lutcas and Pan laid down to get back as much sleep as they could before they continued traveling. Sooner than they would have liked the local rooster began to crow and morning was upon them. Lutcas and Pan were exhausted. But regardless, everyone packed their things up and went back on the river. Before they left, the local townsfolk said that once they got to the swamps they would need to go on land and head to its very center. There they will find the String of Aman. So, the party began heading down the river south.

As they headed south the mountains began to decline till, they were only hills. Now all the mountains rested behind them up North. Only one mountain was visible in their path south. Very far away was a mountain that seemed to be a part of the sky itself. The party recognized that this was going to be their next stop after the swamp. There was a decreasing amount of farmland as they went further which limited the sight and smell of death that they all had been heavily exposed to. Along with less farms, villages and towns became less common to see as well.

When they were going down the river Lutcas fell asleep and fell overboard. Without hesitation Note dove in after him. This scared Chornelious and Violina, so they helped the struggling Lutcas back on the boat. They got him back on and noticed that Pan was barely staying awake even though everyone else was startled by what happened.

Chornelious looked at Pan and said, "You guys look exhausted. Did you not rest well last night?"

Lutcas did not answer since he knew that they wouldn't be pleased if he heard what they did so Pan answered, "Me and Lutcas were not able to sleep. So, we took a walk around town and came back."

Violina skeptically added a question, "So is that how you got those new scrolls?"

"Yes, a merchant gave them to me. He wanted to help us anyway he could." Pan answered

Violina looked suspicious of Pan and replied, "Alright then. Well, you two should rest before we get there. We need to be ready for the worst."

So, as they floated down the river in their boat the two took a nap. Soon they came across the swamps they had heard about. The trees were thick and not nearly as tall as the ones the four grew up in their homelands. The trees created a canopy that hid the land beneath it from the sky, creating a blanket of shadow. The sheer number of trees and their roots prevented the party from taking boats into the swampy waters, so they had to tread through it on foot.

The thick water and dark atmosphere made Lutcas nervous. But there was also beauty to be seen in the swamp. When proceeding further they found bugs that would glow and then stop glowing and glow again. There were such a great multitude of these bugs that they almost appeared as dancing lights. Lutcas was in wonder of how even in a place like this that the conductor's creativity and artistic prowess could show.

The terrain was a bit rough to navigate. Often, they would need to find islands of dirt and tree roots to walk on to avoid the deep water and mud. Often, the group would mistake large creatures moving in the water as logs or rocks moving around. They probably wouldn't have noticed if it weren't for Note barking at them. This made the party proceed with much more caution as they threaded through the dark lands.

Eventually the group made it to a massive clearing in the swamp which granted them sunlight after what seemed like forever. The clearing was almost like an island of nice dry and flowery land that stuck out from the rest of the swamp. In the middle of this island was a huge mound-like structure that radiated a tune that hummed through the air. The tune was inviting and brought comfort and peace. However, as they investigated the clearing, they saw a great number of horses outside the mound who bore the symbol of Orchestrasus along with their riders. One of the nights was much more decorated than the others and Lutcas recognized him as Prince Lyle.

The party stayed low as the knights walked into the huge mound covered in stone, dirt, and various vegetation. The party circled the parameter of the large clearing and found a path leading up to the near top of the mound. This entrance appeared to lead up instead of down like the front entrance did. It looked like the knights were not aware of this entrance since none were patrolling this entrance. So, the group moved in and went up the entrance and managed to make it to the large mound-like structure undetected. When inside the mound they saw it was a large opening with a theater that was much more attractive inside than outside. The dirt mound's interior was full of smooth stones that were almost gold like. Right in the middle of the opening was the String of Aman that was surrounded by what appeared to be a large drop into dark waters below. The party, due to the way they entered, were at a much higher place in the mound that allowed them to see what was going on undetected. The group quietly peaked over their high place to see what was happening. Unfortunately, there didn't seem to be a way down from where they were at. Additionally, the knights below didn't seem to have a way to cross over to get to the string. So, the knight discussed amongst themselves with Lyle on how to cross. Lyle seemed to have some notes with him that he was looking through to find answers. The group up on the high place gathered close and tried to come up with a plan. Lutcas was making sure that Note wasn't making any noise like barking or growling while they spoke. However, Lutcas was still sleepy from his loss of sleep and travel, so he began to get drowsy.

Chornelious whispered to the group, "Okay, this isn't good. We need to get the string and get it fast."

Pan drew his sword and said, "We could also try and kill Lyle. That way this madness can be over, and we won't even need to look for the other strings."

Violina responded to Pan, "No, we are outnumbered. Even if we did kill Lyle, we would be too overwhelmed to handle everyone else. We need to have a different approach. Lutcas any ideas?"

Lutcas was dozing off but was fighting the sleep as he answered, "...no I don't think I have anything clever. I could use my string to create a land bridge to get over the drop around the string. But they might see me as I make it and counter my tune."

Chornelious thought and said, "Okay I have an idea. It is like what Violina did before. Violina can play a melody of mist to use the water in that drop to make a fog. While you do that Lutcas can play a tune to try and make a land bridge to cross the chasm. Due to the low visibility, they won't even know what happened. Meanwhile me and Pan can create as much chaos up here as possible to add more to the confusion. Then we go out the way we came and take their horses."

Violina was impressed with the plan, and she complimented him," Wow Chornelious. You have a pretty good head on your shoulders. But there is one thing I don't understand. I'm sure they know earth tunes. Why wouldn't they do it now? It should be simple enough?"

There was a silence that the group noticed, and they became quiet to blend in. They looked over the edge again to see what was happening to cause such a silence. They saw Lyle walking over the drop as if there was an unseen bridge allowing his passage. Lyle made it to the string and grabbed it from its place. As soon as this happened, Note began to act strangely whimpering.

Lyle then crossed back over and said to his group, “My loyal knights! Today we have claimed another String of Harmony! Due to the reluctant cooperation of my brother and the knowledge of scholars we have been able to find the String of Aman. Now we are one step closer to erasing the hindering song forced on us by our creator and choosing to make an image of ourselves and the world we live in.” In response to this the knights cheered his name and then Lyle continued and played a tune while he spoke, “But my brothers we have much to do! My best commander, Sir Tubiat of the Tuba, is now dead with the String of Eres missing. We have enemies who want to take away godhood from us. I, Prince Lyle, will take initiative and avenge our commanders and reclaim the strings that were taken from us!”

After hearing all this Lutcas began backing up nervously and stepped on Note’s tale. Note yelped and then turned to Lutcas with a nasty snarl on his face. Lutcas was frightened at Note like he was never frightened before. A strong tension of hostility and betrayal now radiated from Note. Lutcas felt bad that he had stepped on Note’s tail, which normally he would be more on alert, but his drowsiness made him clumsy. But now he was more awake than ever before.

Lutcas said to Note, “I’m sorry boy. I didn’t mean to.”

Suddenly Note lunged at Lutcas pushing him off the highpoint and onto the lower level with the rest of the knights. The fall wasn’t high enough to have killed them or to have broken any bones. But the two struggled when they hit the ground, resulting in Note biting Lutcas on the leg extremely hard, which drew a great deal of blood. Lutcas was in great pain and had to get Note to stop. So Lutcas hit Note with his Lute in a desperate effort to make it end. On impact Note let go and darted out the main entrance of the theater. Lutcas couldn’t stand up well after that attack and he called out to his dog as he ran off far out of his vision.

Then Lutcas’s attention turned towards the more immediate problem. The baffled knights that surrounded Lutcas. The knights drew their swords and were studying Lutcas carefully. Lyle had glared at Lutcas. He couldn't tell if he was looking at him with concern, sympathy, surprise, or interest.

Prince Lyle then spoke, "Interesting. I thought I recognized you. You are the one that was with my brother when he ran off from Zoi. Tell me what your name is. "

Lutcas, confused and on high alert, answered, "Uhm my name is Lutcas."

"Ah Lutcas. So, you must be the one that took the string and killed my commander. I suppose I can't blame you after what happened at your home village. But just like them, if you stand between us and godhood, I will strike you down. Now hand over that String."

Pan slid down the steep slope from the high place with his sword drawn and his flute ready, "Actually the pleasure of killing your commander is mine and I will have the pleasure of killing you as well!"

Lyle was unphased by his threat but seemed confused, "So you weld metal and armor of Orchestrasus. Yet, you oppose me. Are you a traitor?"

Pan held his sword up and pointed it at the prince, "I was never on your side! You and your family have started destroying the order of the world! Now because of you my family was kidnapped and slain. I will kill you for that!"

A smirk appeared on Lyle's face, "As if! You think you can challenge me and all my men here and survive? I admire your ambition and fierceness. It is this sort of initiative that it takes to walk the steps me and my family have made towards our way to Godhood. So much so that my father and mother battled each other to secure power over one or another, with my father being the victor. Now I will secure my place by defeating my father once I return home with this string." The knights around him nodded their heads in agreement to what he said, "This is how to live. Not to Be sheep but to be wolves and take what belongs to us by force and make the world in our image instead of following the image of another! For I Lyle, future king of Orchestrasus will grant everyone the freedom of achieving Godhood in my kingdom!". Lyle looked at Lutcas and continued, "Now my friend allows me to lift you up from your lowly state of being. You have brought me the gift of the String of Eres, a feat which not even my strongest commander was able to do. Join me Lutcas! You and your friend here are welcome to join me in my grand vision. Don't live a life of fear and flight, be conductors with us! I understand the pain that you each had to go through, in this process I had lost my mother and my brothers to my father's action. But I know what my father did had to be done and so will be what I do to him."

Suddenly from the side of the slope Chornelious had rolled down with his hurdy-gurdy. Lyle looked at him a bit confused as did the rest of the knights. Before he could say anything Chornelious began to play his hurdy-gurdy winding the wheel and mashing keys. It was clear that he didn't know what he was doing in his panic. During his panic strange sparks and blistering cold winds emitted from his instrument. The knights and Lyle weren't sure what to think of the display. Lyle readied his Lyre to play something to counter what he was doing. But before Lyle could react a great force of energy burst from the hurdy-gurdy blowing everyone back except for Pan and Lutcas while also stirring up a large amount of sand and wind that clouded the area.

Joining them in the chaos was Violina, who grabbed Pan and Lutcas as she shouted, "Let's go!"

Pan resisted, "Not till I kill him!"

Chornelious stopped and pushed Pan, "We need to go! He will get what he deserves!"

Reluctantly Pan fled. Chornelious and Violina knew what general direction they were supposed to go in. The path was clear of personnel except for a couple of guards who must have rushed in from the entrance to see what was going on. While running Lutcas bumped into one of the guards running back in, causing both to fall on their butts. While the guard fell, his unsecured helmet fell off revealing the face of Bendzo. Lutcas couldn't believe what he saw as he looked at the face of his best friend.

Lutcas said questioning what he saw out loud in disbelief, "Bendzo?"

Bendzo drew his axe quickly but looked at Lutcas in confusion, “Lutcas?”

He was confused but Pan came back for him, grabbed his hand, and took him. Lutcas understood the urgency and didn’t struggle. But he did look back at his friend who was just as confused as he was.

Suddenly a tune could be heard from within the theater though they were far. The music was unnatural and discordant. This tune echoed as a voice in Lutcas’s head. This voice was Lyle’s.

Lyle's voice said, “Adversary hear my echoing voice through the String of Emet and hear what I have to say. Trust has been plucked and so will the trust in the world. Just as your people abandoned their land, your friends will abandon you. Discord and conflict will ripple through your relationships and will be brought to rubble. You will be left with heartbreak, and you will wish for death. This is so unless you join my quest.”

. At first Lutcas knew that those words weren’t the truth. But they would continue to haunt him for some time. The four made it to the knight’s horses that were outside of the theater. They mounted the horses and fled the theater heading directly south.

Navigating the terrain with the horses wasn’t as difficult as before. Due to how tall they were, treading through waters and leaping over obstacles wasn’t too bad. However, Pan and Chornelious were struggling a little bit since they weren’t very familiar with riding. But Violina instructed them the best she could.

Eventually they came across a small town that seemed to be over the swamp with various wooden structures. The locals were very hostile and different than what the kind of people they were used to seeing. These folk seemed to make their clothes out of many leaves rather than cotton or wool. Their weapons also were wood and stone rather than bronze or iron.

Violina and Chornelious were able to talk them down and convince them that they were not Orchestrasus. The main convincing came from Lutcas’s wound and their willingness to lay down their weapons. As soon as the villagers understood they were no threat, they began to house them and treat Lutcas's wound. But they could not treat the internal wounds inflicted in his heart. Eventually evening came and there was still no sign of Lyle or his knights anywhere. This put the town and party at ease. Lutcas, Violina, Chornelious, and Pan were all placed in the same living quarters due to the lack of space in town.

Nightfall, but Lutcas couldn't fall asleep, only being kept awake by what had just happened that day, despite his previous exhaustion. Unable to sleep, he went out for a walk around the village. The village was beautiful at night with the wooden walkways being lit by the orange aura of the torches around it. In the darkness far from the village were the dancing lights coming from the fireflies. The frogs kept ribbiting in the night, creating a flow of music that harmonized with the crickets. Lutcas wanted to view the fireflies closer, but unlike before the lights stopped whenever he was near.

As Lutcas was walking he thought of what happened and what Lyle said to him. He felt that he would detect any conflict or discord, like Lyle suggested, amongst his comrades. However, Lutcas understood that there was no tension with Note, but still Note was hostile and fled from him. Thinking of Note made Lutcas sad. A part of him expected to look out in the wilds and see Note running to him in a jolly manner. But no such thing happened. Regardless, Lutcas still leaned over the wooden rails to await his beloved dog's return.

Almost making him jump, Violina approached Lutcas and said, "Hey."

Lutcas, startled, answered, "Violina? What are you doing out here? Shouldn't you be resting?"

"I could say the same about you. I saw you were missing and was worried."

Lutcas understood and was concerned that he woke the others, "I didn't wake the others, did I? I would hate to do that."

"Not everyone is asleep. As usual Chornelious is snoring loudly which is drowning out the sounds of night. But I am worried, why are you out here?" she asked.

“I've been thinking about today. And a lot about Note. I just don’t understand why he had to bite me and run off like that. I want him back.”

Violin Shared his sorrow, “I suppose I hadn’t had time to think too much about it. We were running for our lives back there and I am worried about the effect of the string that has just been removed. But after we got here, he has been on my mind. I’m sad too, but maybe we will find him on our journey.”

Lutcas doubted this though he liked her encouragement, but there were other worries he wanted to get off his chest “But when we were leaving the theater, I could hear Lyle’s music playing in my head. His voice was in my head, and he said that my friends would abandon me and there would be discord amongst my relationships.”

Violina was skeptical hearing this and said, “I'm certain it is Lyle trying to get into your head.”

Lutcas responded, “I know but, Note abandoned me anyways. There was also when we were fleeing from the theater. When we were running out, I bumped into somebody. When I saw it, I found it was my best friend from back home, Bendzo.” Lutcas’s emotions were beginning to pour out a little bit and his voice began to choke up as he continued, “But what does this all mean? Why is Bendzo working for Lyle? Why did Note leave me? And what if you guys...”

Lutcas stopped for a moment. He could feel the tears building up, but they have not begun to pour down from his face. Though prior this thought would never cross his mind, Lutcas thought that perhaps crying would repel Violina. To avoid showing this weakness, he attempted to compose himself and hold it in.

Violina heard him and wanted to bring reassurance, “Listen Lutcas I can understand this. I know you're hurt right now but I want to let you know that we wouldn't leave you. But we should make sure that there is no discord between us so what he said doesn’t come true.”

Lutcas nodded his head in understanding and asked, “What can we do to prevent this?”

“We can start by maintaining honesty with each other. If we are totally open with one another then there is no reason to have mistrust.”

Though this didn’t give Lutcas one hundred percent confidence he replied, “I suppose you are right. We must be open and honest with one another.”

After talking the two stood silently for a moment enjoying the performance of the nighttime wilderness. However, it didn’t take long for Violina to bring up a topic that she was concerned about for a while herself.

So, she took a breath and spoke, “Hey Lutcas, I need to ask you something. I've been worried about it for a while now.”

“What is it?”

“When we were at the village I woke up and you and Pan were gone. When you guys came back Pan was different than before. I don’t believe I heard the full story from Pan. I have been worried about him, could you tell me what happened? I have so much to worry about and I'm tired. It would be a great help if you could ease my mind.”

Lutcas was stressed when he heard this question. It wasn’t that he wanted to lie, but he was hoping he could never talk about it. Pan however intended to deceive Violina from the first question, which Lutcas knew. But Lutcas remembered that Violina wanted transparency and he didn’t want to do anything to jeopardize the group. So, he told her everything. He told her of how they snuck out to investigate the fortress and how they discovered Pan’s dead brother. Violina listened carefully to Lutcas and all he requested was that this not be brought up with Pan yet.

After hearing the story, Violina was upset with Pan and a little bit at Lutcas. However, she did not allow this to show. She knew that showing hostility to Lutcas wouldn’t be a good idea and that bringing such a touchy subject up to Pan could also cause discord. So, she agreed to not bring it up. So, the two went back to their quarters to sleep.

In honesty Lutcas needed more than some words of reassurance. Lutcas desired more comfort and love to replace what was taken from him. Lutcas thought that Violina was beautiful and kind, so receiving this sort of affection from her would be nice. But Lutcas knew she was in union with someone else and he did not want to violate such a sacred bond. But then Lutcas thought about Sonare, the girl he found himself falling for. He remembered her long blonde hair and her smile. But then he worried about her fate. If Bendzo turned, did Sonare turn as well? These sorts of thoughts plagued Lutcas's mind and heart. He thought burdening his friends with these thoughts would repel them from him. So, he bottled them up.

As they were preparing to rest Violina made her way into her sleeping sack. While getting in it she took a moment to study Pan who was asleep, hugging the sheathed sword to his body. Violina pierced him with her eyes with a watchful glare of mistrust.

CHAPTER 7 SKY

The next morning the party began preparing for continuing their journey. They asked the villagers for directions to traverse the swamp. They told them that they would need to head south towards the Mountain that touches the Sky. There they would find the Theater of Sahaq to find the String that lies within it. However, the townsfolk said that the horses wouldn't be much use in the south side of the swamp, since the swamp was so thick and there were reports of more hostile animals in that area from some of the village hunters. This was an inconvenience of travel for them since they would have to travel on foot for a considerable distance.

Nevertheless, the party pressed forward heading for the String of Sahaq. The journey through the swamp wasn't as pleasant as the trip heading in. This area of the swamp was much more dangerous with thicker waters and great and terrible creatures. Without Note it was tricky to detect hidden animals such as the large alligators that traversed through its waters. Nights were difficult as well since as it got darker the insects got bigger. The only thing that would ward them off was fire. Fortunately, Violina and Pan were exceptional at playing Tunes of Fire, so with a little work the bugs didn't become much of a problem.

As they were going on and whenever they caught a break Pan would be restless, trying to practice the skills he was learning from the scroll. Despite being exhausted, Pan would talk either Lutcas or Chornelious into sparring him with sticks. Most of the time it would be Lutcas, since

Chornelious would spend his time tuning instruments and testing cords. Violina would always refuse and often watched Pan with a careful look in her eye. In time Pan was already a decent swordsman with Lutcas also picking up a few tricks, despite not possessing a blade of his own.

Eventually the swampy land became dry, and the vegetation was less thick, allowing light to enter the landscape, eventually leading to a regular forest with large and scattered trees. They knew that this was a sign that they were heading in the right direction. The villagers told them that they would eventually hit a forest and then a large open valley. This part of the world was known to be exceptionally beautiful. One of its beauty's is the Mountain that touches the sky, with it being the only mountain that stood alone surrounded by relatively flat land.

The party was excited to see such a site after treading through such terrible landscape. Eventually they made it through the forest and saw something they didn't expect. It was like the forest had suddenly ended. For a long stretch of land there was nothing but fallen trees reduced to almost nothing but ashes. The lack of trees now allowed them to see further ahead at the fields they had heard so much about. The valley was not rolling hills of green but rather crater filled mounds of mud. Behind this ugly site was the massive mountain, that suggested in the name, seemingly stretched all the way towards the sky. However, the peak of the mountain could not be seen with the smoke and cloud cover.

The party was confused at the sight of this. They pushed forward into the ruined muddy landscape. Chornelious who was studying the landscape saw a silent motionless body sunken in the mud. This scared Chornelious and with a burst of energy he propelled himself from the ground out of surprise. However, for Lutcas and Pan this was just a familiar sight to them. As the party looked around, they saw more bodies, broken instruments, and tools lying around everywhere. Pan picked up one of the tools that were lying on the ground and studied it. The tool was a large stick with a piece of oddly bent and warped metal at the end of it that resembled a spear or glaive, which also had dried blood at its tip.

Chornelious approached it and inspected it as well, “This is odd. This used to be a scythe of some kind. But it is all warped at the end of it. Not going to be good for reaping anymore.” he said.

Pan surprisedly answered, “Strange. I would have guessed it was some poorly made spear of some kind.”

Lutcas looked around and noticed that a lot of the strange tools resembled farming equipment, “Now that you say that Chornelious I think a lot of this stuff used to be farming tools. But why would they do this to them?”

Chornelious answered, “Well it looks like they may have needed weapons and needed them fast. So, they took all the tools with metal on them and warped them into weapons.”

Violina lowered her head and said, “They have beaten instruments of life into ones of death. These things that were once designed to cultivate life into this world are now used to take it from it. I guess it's kind of like what people are doing now?”

The party continued to press forward. Eventually they made it between two large hills that were far apart and made a wide valley. The valley wasn’t deep necessarily, but the two rises that besieged it prevented any from seeing it over its height.

The party stopped suddenly as they heard the faint sounds of music. It was distant but growing ever so closer. The party couldn’t tell which direction the sounds were coming from, since it seemed that it came from every direction. The party was unsure of what this music could mean, and it didn’t sound like they wanted to find out. The music gave a strong, deep, and uniform sound, almost as if it were marching closer and closer. The group tried to move faster but the sounds were getting louder and louder, eventually it became clear that the music was coming from drums of some sort.

Soon the party saw what these intimidating sounds came from. From over the hills there were major tunes of fire that sounded like war trumpets. Following these sounds and from over the hills rained balls of fire that went over the opposing hill sides. Shortly after the first volley, hundreds of people charged from over the hills. One group coming from the hill on the east and the other coming from the hill on the west. Each group was charging with various metal tools or instruments brandished. The party, who was heading south and caught in the middle of the charge, tried to escape. However, there was no chance that they would escape this crossfire.

The group had to think quickly, and the two armies were closing in. Lutcas afraid to get in the clash play a major tune of moving earth with his lute, which held the String of Eres. Doing this created a large stone dome of solid rock to shield them from the charge and from the various elemental projectiles that flew across the field.

Though the wall did protect them from the more immediate danger, it didn't protect them from the horrific sounds that came from outside. The various kinds of music being played with the intention of harming another began to clash till it created a torrent of discordant sounds. Along with the music the battle cries of many contributed to the chaotic music as well as the clashing of metal and the screams of the damned. The forces of music attacked the wall with great power, giving only the party a limited amount of time before they had to move.

Knowing they had limited time Pan spoke, "Guys we can't stay here we need to get out of here!"

Violina protested, "I'm not sure about that. If we go out there, we will get wrapped up in the chaos and we will perish."

Lutcas had an idea while trying to comprehend the chaos, "Hey wait a second. Maybe if it is a group fighting against Orchestrasus then we could help them!"

Chornelious, who was pressing his fist against his chin while rocking back and forth, responded, "No. None of those guys were wearing armor like the people of Orchestrasus usually do. I would suspect that if they were Orchestrasus they wouldn't need to be beating farming tools into weapons anyway."

Pan, frustrated, drew his sword and said, "Well, time is ticking! We need to go, or we are going to die here!"

Chornelious quit rocking and let his arm down while looking at his Hurdy-Gurdy, "I have an idea. If we are heading to that mountain across this valley, then we can make a path to get over there. If Lutcas can use the String of Eres to make two walls for us to run between then we can navigate through the battlefield safely.".

Pan responded, "Good thinking. That way we have a straight shot from here to there safely."

Violina, knowing danger was still present in this idea, asked, "So what if by some chance we get separated?"

Chornelious answered, "Well in the event we do get separated, we need to head to that mountain, nonetheless. The best we can do is all head towards that point and hope not to die!"

The three agreed to the plan and began to act it out. Lutcas used the String of Eres to play a major tune of moving stone causing massive rocks to shoot up from the ground making a seemingly endless stretch of path. The group left the crumbling structure they were in and proceeded down the path. Though they were without incident for a few moments, the plan eventually began to fall apart. Various elemental attacks began to shoot left and right through the walls and eventually combatants were finding themselves in the walled off path as well. Suddenly a major tune of water was heard which caused a great deal of water to pour into the passage they had created. The party saw this and had to bail out of the path. Pan and Lutcas both played a tune of moving rock to escape. However, the party became separated since Lutcas and Chornelious went through one side of the wall and Violina and Pan went through the other.

Shortly after the party was split the rock walls that Lutcas erected collapsed, creating a wave of dust and dirt that already contributed to the chaotic and barely visible battlefield. The sight of the battlefield was frightening, with bodies and parts being flung about as well. Battle cries and cries of pain and loss made horrible sounds to pair with the orchestra of chaos around them.

While Violina was getting her bearings together she stood up and saw a warrior in front of her. The warrior was about her size with a slim body. The warrior wore metal armor that appeared silver with elaborate decorative carvings on them that flowed throughout its design. The armor, along with anything underneath it, made it where none of the warrior's flesh or face was visible. The Warrior also wielded a bow and a violin, but the bow was different from a regular bow. It had a handle and on the side without the hair appeared to be a metal blade. Violina was intimidated by the warrior who was approaching her in the chaos, so she readied her bow and prepared to engage. The warrior took its bow and violin and with it gave a strange respectful bow before getting into a stance. Violina, caught off guard by this, tried to return the gesture to the warrior though sloppy due to the current conditions.

Quickly the battle began between Violina and the Warrior. Violina tried to play a pure tune of light to blind her foe. However, the warrior seemed unaffected by it, possibly due to the strange helmet that covered its face. The warrior rushed at her while playing tunes of fire that manifested small fireballs at her. Violina began playing tunes to use the water from the ground to douse the incoming fireballs. Though she was able to douse the incoming balls of fire she wasn't ready for the warrior's up-close rush. Immediately the warrior swung at Violina with its sword bow. Violina tried to dash out the way but was barely grazed in the arm. Pain shot up her body, but the adrenaline was keeping her moving. A design flaw from the warrior was that the instrument seemed to make the attack unbalanced. Violina noticed this and looked for an opening to do something. However, after a volley of odd attacks that were performed to compensate for the imbalance, the warrior fainted and hit Violina with the violin itself rather than the sword. This hit Violina in the head causing her vision to blur and for her to fall. The warrior rushed towards Violina in her state and tried to strike her weapon. However, a tune of moving metal could be heard, and Pan's sword flew at the warrior. But the warrior was quick and deflected the now floating sword's barrage of attacks.

The tune changed and the sword flew back to the hand of Pan. As Violina looked at Pan he appeared to have been caught in skirmish while she was busy. Pan held out his hand to help Violina up, which she took and tried to get back her bearings. The warrior, for whatever reason, allowed Pan to help her up in some fashion of honor.

Once Violina was up and ready the battle continued. Violina launched a volley of water blasts that turned to ice using a melody of freezing. The Warrior played a tune of fire to counter the blast and evaporate the projectiles. Pan took advantage of the distracted warrior and thrusted his sword at his foe, but the blow was deflected with the odd armor his adversary was wearing. Pan tried again with a slash but was blocked by the bow sword. The warrior then hit Pan with its metal violin, knocking Pan to his back and his sword out of his hand. The Warrior then tried to finish Pan off with its bow sword, but a spear of ice impaled the armpit of the warrior where there was no protection. In pain the warrior's attention shifted to Violina, who created the ice. Pan, noticing this, played a tune of moving metal to move his sword in the air, launching it into the neck of the faceless foe who promptly fell to the ground.

Pan took note of the fine metal work of the armor and suggested to Violina, "Hey, you should take this armor and the violin. I bet that would make you a lot dangerous."

Violina had no desire to wield instruments of death and was confused about how Pan could think of this at a time like this, so she replied, "I must decline. That is all too much for me. Besides, we need to figure a way out of here. I can't tell which way is were anymore."

Pan studied the armor and said, "Suit yourself. I think I will take it."

Pan played a melody of moving metal to make the armor he was wearing fall off him and then warped the new armor off the warrior onto himself. This armor protected Pan much more and even though Pan's face couldn't be seen, some musical property allowed him to see through it.

When Pan took the armor off the foe, Violina noticed something. That this was one of the girls that learned under harper with her. It was clear that she had the distinct features of a woman from her region. She didn't know how she ended up here, but it broke her heart to see her friend in such a state. Guilt, sorrow, and confusion all swarmed her mind during the bloodbath.

Pan, paying only attention to the surrounding battle, turned to Violina and said, "There is no way we are getting out of this mess like we planned. Looking at all this makes me sick! They are all contributing to the very forces that got my family and village killed. I will instead carve my own path out of this mess and make them all pay!"

Pan remembered a particular music piece that was on the scrolls he was given. The piece could be played with many instruments which included Pan's flute. Many warnings came with the song on the notes, though this piece wasn't too complicated to play itself. All that the song required was that you played it with a fiery passion that caused you to channel animosity.

Pan began to play this piece and as he played it, he imagined all he lost, experienced, and witnessed. As he played the piece his body began to shake violently, barely able to hold the flute and his sword. When the song was completed the once blessed flute Pan now carried lost its glow and was shattered by the might of Pan's hand. Pan now possessed unnatural strength, paired with inhuman movements like a beast and roars of anger. This was the discordant tune of rage.

Violina watched in fear as Pan now uncontrollably leaped from person to person killing them mercilessly, without compassion, and with such brutality it was like that of a beast. Though Violina was scared, she followed Pan's path of ruin since she was concerned and didn't want to lose another friend.

On the other side of where the wall used to be was Lutcas and Chornelious. Lutcas was instantly rushed by a man with a pitchfork-like tool. Lutcas, not having much time to react, tried to rely on his Lute for some protection. However, he was pushed away, and the Lute was tangled and thrown aside with the pitchfork. Lutcas then was tackled by another who brandished a knife and stabbed him in the shoulder. In pain and panicking Lutcas searched for something to help him. In the mud next to him was a bloodied sword, which he took and stabbed the man killing him.

Lutcas arose with a stinging bleeding wound while looking for his Lute and the String of Eres. He saw Chornelious wrestling the man with the pitchfork over it. Lutcas went over to the man and sliced his throat, causing the man to choke on his blood and die. The man dropped the tool, which was now tangled in the stings. Chornelious panicked and played a pure tune of force veil from his Hurdy-gurdy to cover himself and Lutcas in a veil. Lutcas's vision became blurry, and he was dizzy, for a good deal of blood was leaving his shoulder.

Chornelious was panicking and murmuring to himself in an out-of-control manner, "I've failed us! My plan failed! I've killed us all. Come on Chornelious, creative, think of something! Come on! You can't play this tune forever, come on!"

In his panic he was no longer winding and pressing keys as the pure tune of force veil would have. Instead, the barrier began to flicker, and random elemental blast shot out from it. Chornelious did something no one else had done before. Suddenly, by accident, he played a constant melody never played before. He played the first melody of lightning. Out from Chornelious in many directions shot forth powerful lightning bolts that were followed with claps of thunder. The Lighting seemed to hit at random varying places adding to the chaos of the battlefield. As Lutcas saw this, his consciousness began to fade, and he passed out.

When Lutcas awoke he was not on a battlefield. Rather he was now in a bed in a building that was somewhat structured similarly to buildings from Chornelious's village. His wounds were bandaged, and he was cleaned. His instrument and the sword he picked up from the battlefield laid next to his bed on the floor. There was a window near the bed, but when Lutcas looked outside of it he saw what appeared to be clouds and the sky with no land in sight. Across the room from the bed was a door with a man sitting by it.

The man was sitting on the floor with his legs folded over the other. His head was cleanly shaven of any hair, making it shiny. The man also wore yellow robes, and his eyes were narrow like Chornelious's. While the man was sitting, his eyes were closed, and he was humming some sort of tune. Shortly after Lutcas woke up the man took notice of him.

"Good morning young man," said the Monk.

Lutcas sat up in his bed tired and weak and asked, "Who are you? Where am I? Where are my friends?"

The man smiled and said, "Allow me to answer those one at a time. I understand that you are confused and scared. First, I am Cymbai of the sky monks. I live at the top of this mountain with my other fellow monks. Here we study sound and music in incredible depth. Recently with dance and the movement of the body with the flow of music. Which has come handy for us and you."

Confused by Cymbai's statement he asked, "Wait, how did that come in handy for you and me?"

"At the ends of the mountain there are two different peoples. Each is both large and advanced with many talented musicians. But when the Strings of Harmony began to be ripped from their places and the flow of the world music was interrupted, hostility arose from the towns. Eventually they each went up to us to try and side with them to take out the other, but we refused. So occasionally we had to defend ourselves with our dance and music, which increased our strength. We used these techniques to navigate our way through the battlefield and rescue you and your friends."

Lutcas was grateful for this, but was still confused, "So wait why did you rescue us? We don't know each other."

The monk answered, "I received a vision in a dream of your arrival. In fact, I know that many of the places you've have a seer that foretold your arrival. This is because your company has been chosen to retrieve the strings of Harmony. When me and my scouts saw the power of your earth tunes, we knew it had to be the company foretold."

Lutcas thought of his friends and was worried, "Wait how many did you rescue? Where are they?"

The monk stood up and said, "Young man you must learn to ask one question at a time. We rescued three others. One somehow found the secrets to lightning, one we have tried to master but failed to achieve. He is in the courtyard right now allowing us to study him. You had three other friends who we brought in. One was violent and animal like, only supervised by a girl who pursued him as he tore his way through countless men. He was gravely injured and did not know it. But we were able to calm him and retrieve him by the request of the girl who saw us retrieve you. He is in recovery down the hall right now. Your third friend we saw was fighting both sides and was trying to follow you as well as he could. He was very formidable and played his banjo well. But he was als injured and we took him in. But he makes us nervous since he bears the symbol of Orchestrasus."

Lutcas was scared when he heard him mention the one who plays the banjo. He knew that he had to be Bendzo. Lutcas did not understand why Bendzo would have followed them or if Prince Lyle was far behind him.

Lutcas told Cymbai, "Listen I may know of the last one you mention but I think he may not be your friend. If you can please let me speak to him."

"We figured that may be the case. He isn't in our traditional care area. Right now, he is in a holding cell with his wounds getting treated. We were going to do it to the one who slaughtered so many, but the girl insisted that he was friendly. Please allow me to take you there."

The monk let Lutcas follow him after he gathered his things. Once they went outside Lutcas got a look off the mountain. The mountain was unmatched to any other mountain he had ever seen before. It was clear that he was near the top of this mountain due to the great amount of distance he could see. He could see the winding river they took from the north as well as the mountains where the String of Eres was. He could see the swamp they went through to get to the String of Aman. To the east was a great body of water that stretched as far as the eye could see. He could even see the great grasslands in the west. But a dark shadow was casted over the far east portion of it. As for the land right below the mountain he could see the battlefield and the two towns that were in war. Both towns were large but seemed to be burning with pillars of smoke rising from them. In the east Lutcas could see a large army heading from the west towards the two towns.

The monk noticed Lutcas studying the land and commented, "It is a shame really. I used to enjoy looking off the mountain here at the artwork and majesty of our creator. You could even see the kingdom of Podiem from here. Now it is gone and in its absence is a shadow at the scar of the world. The grasslands are now teaming with death, the river with blood, and now the valley full of carnage that will be claimed by the marching black knights of the rebel kingdom."

Lutcas was hurt looking at it and asked, "Cymbai you are a scholar. Can you tell me why this is all happening? How could our good creator allow such evil and destruction to happen?"

Cymbai looked at Lutcas with sympathy and understanding, "For someone who has journeyed around the world and witnessed its tumble, this is a reasonable question. To answer this, we must look back at the origin of the world. When the Concertmasters were still here with us, they told us what they saw or were told themselves. Essentially, they say that the Conductor was love and when he made the world the world was of love as well. But Love is a choice, a choice that we as creations of love must make. Though we have great potential and design to be images of love, we also can refuse it and weave chaos in this world of love and order. To answer your question, young man is that part of the established flow of music in this world comes from free will, it is like the lines in which music notes can be written. But we have fallen because of our rejection of that. But be wary, for I believe that there is more to this than mere human rebellion."

Though Lutcas was intrigued by what he was saying, he had a hard time understanding all of it. After talking Lutcas was taken to the cell where they were holding the banjo wielding warrior. When Lutcas saw who it was he recognized it to be Bendzo. Bendzo's armor, instruments, and two battle axes were outside the cell. Bendzo was in the cell only with his tunic, a bed, and some food. Bendzo was a bit bigger than when Lutcas last saw him. He was more muscular too with some ungroomed facial hair and scars on his arms.

Bendzo noticed Lutcas and said, "HEY! I thought I saw you! It's been a while Lutcas."

Lutcas was nervous but couldn't hold back the excitement to see his old friend, "Bendzo it's been a while! I thought I saw you back at the Theater."

Bendzo was excited and said, "Yes, I couldn't believe my eyes. I'm sorry we had to meet like that though. But I am surprised that you are without Note. Where is he?"

Lutcas didn't want to think about Note, since the bite scar on his leg reminded him of that often, "I don't wish to talk about Note, I am glad to see you but there are more important things to discuss. The monks here need to know if you are against us or not. In honesty I am confused too so maybe you could help clarify things with me?"

Bendzo understood Lutcas's confusion, "It started after Lyle pulled the String of Nepes. He used the String of Emet to convince our town to move into the new kingdom replacing Podiem. It was great living there at first, but things got rough. Disease and civil war became more active than before. During the time I was already a soldier who bought into Orchestrasus Ideology. But I wanted out and I found you. After I saw you, I told Lyle I could follow you and report back to him. But Instead, I was hoping to be with you to get away from this all."

Cymbai answered his story with a question, "Well Bendzo it is nice to see that you have corrected your path. But may I ask if you could show us if you're telling the truth."

"Well, you will have to take my word for it. But if you look at my body you can see the scars from the wounds inflicted on me. This is the product of the path of Orchestrasus. A path I would like to walk away from. Now I have come to ask if I could join your company."

Lutcas felt that his friend was genuine, and he said to Cymbai, "Cymbia I am allowing him to join my company."

Cymbai trusted the one sent to find the strings, so he released him from his cell. Bendzo grabbed his weapons and instrument, but he didn't bring his armor since he no longer wanted to bear the symbol. After releasing Bendzo the party went down to the courtyard to meet Chornelious. Lutcas, Symbai, and Bendzo walked to the courtyard of the monastery grounds and found a surprise when they made it there. When they made it in, they were greeted with bolts of lightning shooting out from the middle of the courtyard. Many of the monks were on the ground or behind cover avoiding the lightning bolts. When the lighting was over Lutcas saw Chornelious in the middle of the courtyard with some monks taking notes.

Chornelious's face was full of excitement, and he ran to Lutcas, "Lutcas look! Look! Look! I can play a melody without it going haywire! See! See!"

Bendzo confused commented on the display whispering to Lutcas, "Wait he said that wasn't going haywire?"

Chornelious's chest was full of pride as he spoke, "The monks here are so impressed with my lighting melody that they wanted me to display it! Best part is they know my master and they said that he was here before us and was on his way to Orchestrasus."

Lutcas replied to Chornelious, "That is great! But before we go off track Chornelious I want to introduce you to Bendzo. He is my best friend from my home village."

Chornelious greeted him and was astonished, "Wow that is wild! How did you manage to run into each other?"

Bendzo not really wanting to explain everything again now replied, "It is a long story. But it looks like you guys will have me as a new traveling companion."

Shortly after Chornelious was introduced to Bendzo, Violina and Pan could be seen making their way towards them. Violina had a great look of concern and seemed to have a couple of small scars on her face. But she was given new clothes and supplies. Pan's wounds weren't noticeable, mostly due to the armor that covered his neck to his toes. His helmet was being carried in one arm and his sword was sheathed on his hip.

Chornelious took notice of the two and exclaimed, "Pan! Violina! You two are out of the infirmary. How are you holding up? You missed the lightning show!"

Violina distracted by her own thoughts replied, “That’s great Chornelious”

Lutcas noticed this but still felt that he needed to introduce Bendzo, “Pan, Violina, this is my friend from my hometown. Bendzo.”

Pan’s face went from his cold and serious face to an amused one, “Wait your village? But everyone was taken from there?”

Violina realized who this may be, “Lutcas, is this the friend that you ran into at the Theater of Aman?”

Lutcas nodded his head to confirm this, and Pan’s face became serious, “That must mean you were part of Lyle’s men.” Pan marched up to Bendzo and continued, “How do we know we can trust him?”

Bendzo wasn’t scared of Pan, but he still wanted to show his intentions, “Listen Warrior. I did serve under Prince Lyle. But I wanted out. I saw Lutcas and thought if I fled and followed then I could escape.”

There was an awkward silence between them for a moment then Lutcas intervened, “Pan listen. I know what you are feeling. But I must urge you to trust him. He is a very good and old friend of mine and I believe him to be genuine.”

Pan backed down and said, “Alright. I don’t like Orchestrasus. But there are only a handful of people I can trust in this world anymore. Lutcas is one of my best friends that I can trust. A friend of his is a friend of mine.” Pan extended his hand to shake Bendzo’s, “Welcome to our company.”

Bendzo shook his hand and replied, “I appreciate it, warrior. I will be sure to earn your trust.”

Violina’s face was relieved after seeing that exchange. After the group introduced themselves, a couple of monks rushed to Cymbai. They gave him an urgent message speaking of their enemies preparing to scale the mountain. Symbai sent them off with instructions of preparations. He then gave Lutcas and his friends instructions for where the String of Sahaq was.

The group understood the urgency of the situation and followed his instructions with haste. The String was atop the peak of the mountain. The group took the passageway of rocky stairs that winded up the mountain's sharp peak. Lutcas was surprised to still see plants growing at this altitude. The leaves on the odd trees were pink and as the wind blew through them, it made a sound like that of music. This same sound matched the tune now echoing from the mountain's peak. Eventually when reaching the top of the stairs they found a pond besieged by rocks that stretched the last bit of the mountain to the sky. In the pond there was a small land bridge stretching from the stairs to the podium in the middle of the pond. Floating above the podium was the String of Sahaq, glowing a bright pure white color.

Chornelious observed the Sting and spoke, "Well here it is. Who is going to take it?"

Pan answered, "Lutcas already as one. Might as well allow him to have the second. Besides, it is just like we said last time. He has been on this journey longer than any of us. I trust Lutcas with the String."

"I have no objection to that! Let him have it!", added Bendzo

Violina also added, "It seems we all agree. Lutcas go ahead and take it."

Lutcas approached the Podium and reached for the string. He could feel a breeze swirling around the string as it floated above the podium. Once he grabbed it the wind stopped and so did the tune. But the tune began to quietly play again. The tune had an energetic and flowing sound to it, almost like a dance. Lutcas was pleased to retrieve once again one of the Strings of Harmony. He held it up to his instrument and it warped into the place of one of its strings. After doing this the group returned to the base of the monastery.

The monk Cymbai approached the group and told them, "Before you all head down the mountain there is something I must tell you." The monk took a breath and spoke, "A messenger Concertmaster had given me a vision. He told me that you all must head to the far west part of Symphonia with the strings. Afterwards they told me of a vague prophecy of a man who could speak music, but I could not make much sense of it. But doing this I would assume will keep the rebel prince from getting the strings." Lutcas and the group were confused by the prophecy portion of what he said but the monk added, “But listen to me carefully. There was a warning. A warning to follow the instructions carefully and to not stray from them. Do not stray from the path.”

The group did not hesitate to oblige the warning. Soon after they were resupplied and were escorted down the mountain by some of the monks. For Lutcas this was a victory to not only have gotten back an old friend but to have also retrieved the String of Sahaq.

CHAPTER 8 BALANCE

The party was escorted down the mountains by a couple of the monks from the monastery. The mountain was so high and steep that traversing it by foot would be greatly challenging. However, the monks used some sort of pulley system that took them down from one ledge to the next. The system seemed to be made of rope, stone, and wood. But this was too complicated for Lutcas to really understand, but Chornelious studied the system with great interest though he had seen it before when being rescued. Eventually the party found themselves at the south side of the towering mountain. The monks wished them protection and scaled back up the mountain face.

After studying the map, the group began to head southwest towards their next destination. The road was long and Bendzo was trying to find ways to get to know the others. He then remembered the lightning display that Chornelious showed with his instrument.

"Hey Chornelious!" said Bendzo, "I am curious about the lightning thing that you were doing in the monastery courtyard."

Chornelious was very excited to talk about this and Bendzo didn't realize that he had just opened a floodgate, "Oh you're wondering about my lighting melody? Well, I didn't know I could do it till I panicked on the battlefield! Then I saw what was happening and I just kept trying to do it again and then I finally memorized something and just kept doing it and now I can play an actual song on this thing!" he said at great speed and without breath.

Bendzo was taken back at how much he said so quickly, "Wow okay. So that is great. But wait, you say you didn't know how to use your own instrument?"

Chornelious inhaled and exhaled as he spoke, "Well if you must know this it is because this instrument doesn't belong to me. It belongs to my master who went missing and created this. But it is so complicated and wild that I don't know how to play it. That was till we received the blessed tunes from a concertmaster. But now I figured out how to make a melody like this."

Bendzo didn't want to drag on the conversation due to Chornelious's excitement becoming draining, "Well that's great pal. It sure does seem like a powerful melody. Even one that may be able to catch Prince Lyle off guard."

Chornelious seemed to ignore everything he said, "So you're probably wondering how I was able to make it happen. Well, the monks said that due to the ability for this instrument to create one or more tunes, it can create a positive and negative energy which destabilizes and causes heat which..." Chornelious continued speaking but every word went out one of Bendzo's ears and went out the other, for Bendzo couldn't understand his words or the contents of what they formed.

Out of pity Pan intervened, "Well you did it now, you got him started on his excitement rants. He gets like this when he is thrilled."

Lutcas added, "I would be excited too. He learned how to play that stupid thing finally and now he has a lead on where his master is."

Bendzo responded, "Oh so he is trying to find his master that made that thing. So do you all have your own personal missions on this journey?"

Lutcas answered him, "Well our general mission is to collect as many of the Strings of Harmony as we can and go to someplace to the far west. This will prevent Lyle from getting more strings and ruining our world."

Violina added, "While I am on this quest, I also keep an eye out for my husband who is a rider going from town-to-town warning about Lyle and his Knights."

Bendzo was intrigued by this but knew something she didn't, "I hate to bring this up to you, but it seems that it may be for naught. The towns that I visited under Lyle were quickly won over by his influence."

Shocked, Violina responded, "Wait, what do you mean that the towns fell to his influence?"

Pan chipped in, "We shouldn't be too surprised. Humans are so miserable and filthy that it wouldn't surprise me that even with a warning they couldn't resist him."

Lutcas was taken back at Pan's harshness. But he understood what led him to feel this way and it would be hard to say humans aren't this way. Violina was upset by the comment, since it made Tekoa's riding seem vain. But she tried to compose herself and tune out Pan's comment.

Bendzo was curious about Pan and asked him, "Tell me then warrior, what is your personal mission?"

Pan took a breath and spoke, "My family was kidnapped and slaughtered by bandits. My brother was found dead, and my mother is probably dead too. If you asked me earlier, it would have been to find them. But now it is to bring them to my sword and set things right by spilling their blood."

Impressed, Bendzo responded, "Now that is something I can get behind. I like how you have brought it to yourself to set things right!" Violina looked back concerned for both Bendzo and Pan as he continued, "I too am handy with a blade. Maybe you and Lutcas will be willing to spar with me later? I would like to see what you got."

"Sure. It may be helpful since I broke my instrument on that battlefield. I would like to see how they taught Knights of Orchestrasus to fight more carefully."

Chornelious who had finally ended his rant found himself back into the present state of the conversation, "You know Pan I did bring some supply to make you another pan flute. But I can't bless it like that concertmaster did."

Further down the road the party kept getting to know Bendzo more. Bendzo would share some of his stories from the village, some being embarrassing stories of him and Lutcas. They all laughed not out of bullying him, but because of how wholesome and comedic the stories were. Bendzo, unlike Lutcas, was a very funny guy who could deliver punchlines and stories like no one else could.

Often during stops Pan and Lutcas would spar with Bendzo. Pan and Bendzo were similarly skilled with their fighting. Pan was curious about the axes that Bendzo carried. He learned how to throw them and wield them properly, which was different from what he was used to.

During their sparring, Chornelious was working on Pan's new flute. All the parts he had obtained he got from atop the mountain, all he had to do was assemble them. The monks studied many instruments including the Pan flute, which they had great knowledge about. The one Chornelious was making consisted of special metal found only on that mountain, which the monks said could amplify the music that came from it. While the others were sparring and constructing, she was practicing music. Lutcas would sometimes join her due to him being exhausted from the walking and sparring.

The further the party went south the more the landscape changed. The grasslands became less green but taller and browner. The party stayed close to a nearby lake which was teeming with large creatures. In fact, the tall grasslands were full of creatures far bigger than the ones they had ever seen. There was yellow spotted horse like beasts whose necks stretched above the oddly shaped trees below it. There were large gray beasts whose noses drooped down their face to their toes. There were even large birds who did not fly but ran at unimaginable speeds. On top of the strange wildlife, it became hot unlike they ever felt.

Eventually the party stopped once more after several stops, this one for the night. The wildlife was intimidating and dangerous, so they had to rotate look out on duty. Violina was on duty but was in a vortex of thought thinking of her husband and Pan whose violent path was bringing her worry. She wished the thoughts would leave her mind as they ate at her, but she couldn't find peace. Soon Violina's duty was up, and she was to rotate out with Pan.

When she woke Pan she said, "It is your time to watch. But I must speak with you."

Pan agreed and the two went to where they watched, "Pan I must be honest with you. I have been worried about you lately."

"Why are you worried about me?"

"I know at the beginning of the journey you were upset with those who did your village harm. But I am beginning to think you are changing and your hate is spreading. I don't think it is healthy."

Pan narrowed his eyes trying to see what she is getting at, "I don't think I understand."

"Well for instance. I know back at the riverside village that you and Lutcas didn't wander around town. I know you two went to that fortress despite me and Chornelious's disapproval. Because of your behavior you put Lutcas, yourself, and the String of Eres at jeopardy."

Pan, frustrated, knew that it may come to this, and he didn't agree with her criticism, "What of my behavior? Want to know why me and Lutcas had to sneak out? That is because you and Chornelious didn't understand what I felt or what me and Lutcas went through."

"That isn't true!" she began to raise her voice, "I lost my village too Pan. Everyone I know and love is gone because of Orchestrasus."

Pan's anger grew but he did care for Violina so he said sternly trying his best not to shout, "Violina, you could walk away from your village without seeing a single dead body. With hope that they lived and went to Orchestrasus. I return to my village to see the blood of my people spilled on its streets. Which by the way, if you want to know what I found at the fortress..." Pan's voice began to change as he teared up, "...I found my brother naked, tortured, violated, and surrounded by the dead. I barely made it in time to tell him his favorite story before he died!"

Violina had forgotten this detail when arguing and found it difficult to respond to this, so she answered him gently, "Pan, I am sorry that you had to see that. I didn't realize that was what happened. But please try to understand Pan, I care about you and the others. You have been scaring me ever since that night. You broke our trust and you have become violent. Pan, you slaughtered so many on the battlefield in such an inhumane way. You were like a beast scattering blood everywhere. Please, you are becoming more like..." She stopped herself not wanting to make Pan angry by comparing him to his enemy.

Pan's sad demeanor changed, and he became angry, he spoke with great frustration and hatred not at her but at everything, "What Violina? Like the Knights? Your cowardly ways of thinking are in the realm of fantasy. Look around you Violina we are in a world of wolves? Can a sheep survive in a world of wolves? No! Only a wolf can survive in a world with other wolves while a sheep just stands there and is slaughtered. Unlike the villagers and my family, I will not be a sheep Violina."

Violina realized this wasn't going anywhere. She found it hard to argue against him but knew that deep down he was wrong. She had no desire for the violence that Pan had fallen into and was worried that Lutcas may do the same thing. So, she let him be and rested.

Eventually morning came and Violina was the first to wake up. She was not well rested after her conversation with Pan. So, she got up and walked to find Lutcas on watch. Lutcas greeted her and she saw that he was wearing the sword on his waist like Pan was.

She approached Lutcas with a saddened look and she said, "Lutcas why do you carry your sword? Do you carry it to slaughter your enemy?"

Lutcas replied, "If this is about Pan, I understand how you feel. But I carry mine only as a deterrent or defense. A last resort if you will."

Violina then requested, "Lutcas I can only hope you don't fall on this path either. Please just promise me that you will not use this to kill in cold blood. That you do not use this to slaughter your foes but to protect your life only."

Lutcas was on the same page as Violina and said, "I promise Violina you don't have to worry."

Shortly after this the party began to pack up and head further west. The next village wasn't far, and they were quickly approaching. The heat wasn't as bad due to the heavy overcast. The group was exhausted and needed more rest than they had been receiving.

Eventually the village came into view. All the buildings in the village seemed to be made of mud walls with thatch roofs. There was a dirt road that weaved its way through the village. What caught the party's attention was what was behind the village. Though the village was resting on the grounds of the savannah, the land behind the village was tall rock like cylinder pillars that were in a massive canyon stretching as far as the eye could see. There appeared to be some land bridges between some of these pillars as well as man-made wooden bridges.

As the party approached the town, they were met with what they presumed to be the village guards. The guards and the people of the village were unlike any they had seen before. The people's skin was very dark, darker than the people of the swamp lands even. They were also tall and didn't wear tunics like they did. The clothing they wore was loose and consisted of many patterns and colors. The weapons however were not of steel but of stone and wood.

Pan was hostile once the guards approached them with weapons. However, Violina assured that the party didn't come to do any harm and was only seeking rest and passage. The guards looked at each other and guided them back to the village. As they went through the village, they saw the residents were not benefiting very well. Many of the people were very thin and weak including the children. Eventually they made it to the chieftain's hut. The hut was guarded by more men who instead of having their wood and stone weapons carried metal ones instead. They were let inside the hut by one of the guards of the hut and they entered. When the party entered, they saw a vast amount of wealth, food and women scattered about the hut. The women were dressed in very little and were wearing many precious stones on them. The wealth was in gold and golden objects in piles that were guarded by more well-equipped warriors. At the other end of the hut there was the village chieftain sitting on a throne. Like the people of the village and the woman in his hut he was very tall, dark, but not skinny. In fact, he was quite a heavy set.

The Chieftain spoke in a deep booming voice to them, “Why do you people come here? Are you seeking the String of Mozane?”

The party was surprised at his guess which prompted Pan to ask, “How do you know what our intentions are?”

The Chieftain answered him, “That is what seems to be the popular thing to ask for around here. Many have come here in search of it and never return.”

Curious, Bendzo asked, “Who came before us asking for the string?”

The chieftain stood up and was looking at his gold, “Well there are many people who look like you of pale flesh or of bronze flesh that come looking for the strings. I used to trade with the knights that came down here asking for the string. But I would always tell them to go into the canyon and they never return. Though the last visitor was a rider, a bandit group from the north wanted to sell him, so I sold him as a slave for quite a nice price.”

Violina’s fear and concern spiked. She was left to only imagine that this rider may have been Tekoa. But she knew that knowing him in this situation may lead to hostility. The other members of the party thought of this as well and didn’t say anything. Pan’s face at the mention of the bandit group piqued his interest, but he did not lose his temper.

Lutcas trying to draw the subject away from the man who maybe Tekoa said, “Wait did anyone you send come back from the canyon with the String?”

The Chieftain answered him, “No. The previous ruler of the village understood that Balance was a delicate thing and should be left alone. I gave my word as a warrior after I killed them that I would guide all away from it. But that word means less and less to me, for me and my people thirst for water and rain. For we are in a drought, and I have sold to many of my people as slaves. So now we don't have anyone who can play water music."

Chornelious remembered that Lutcas had the String of Sahaq and thought that maybe they could help, "If I may suggest, if we were to give you rain would you tell us the correct location of the Sting of Mozane?"

Lutcas was surprised and stressed at Chornelious's suggestion, since he wasn't sure if he could do that, but the chieftain answered him, "Very well. If you can somehow make music that causes the rain to fall from the sky, then I will tell you the true location of the String of Mozane."

Bendzo didn't trust the chieftain and asked, "Chieftain, how can we know that you will keep your word and not deceive us?"

The chieftain seemingly offended at the accusation shouted, "How dare you treat my words as such! What arrogant reason could you have for mistrusting my word? I am the chieftain of the southern tribes! Owner of slaves, ruler of gold, and the mighty spear of the pillar valley!"

The room became ratted at the chieftain's booming voice. The party prepared for a fight and the guards in the room gripped their spears with two hands, ready for their leader's command.

But after that rant Chornelious spoke out, "With all due respect Chieftain. You said it yourself that you deceived those who came before us."

The chieftain looked at Chornelious and noticed how small he was not only compared to him but to the group. It did not make sense to him how someone so small could speak so boldly to him, for all in the south feared the chieftain.

The chieftain laughed and said, "HA! Well, your little friend has amused me with the boldness of his words. But I will say that if I now lie to you, you can take away that rain that you say you can give us. To prove my word further I will explain the String is in its true place and why it rests there."

Bendzo replied, "Then tell us so we can give your people rain." This idea that kept getting mentioned stressed Lutcas out, since he still wasn't sure of all this.

The chieftain then told them, "I send those seeking the String through the bottom of the Pillar Canyon. But it is a death sentence, due to the hazardous conditions of the canyon. In truth, the String of Mozane is atop the greatest of pillars in Pillar Canyon which is at the canyon's core." The Chieftain signaled his guards and spoke again, "Now let us see this rain that you can make."

The guards at his command lowered their spears and pushed them outside. The party complied and was escorted out to a field nearby. The sky was still overcast, which made the party wonder if this attempt was even necessary. But the chieftain said that for some reason it would be overcast but the rain wouldn't fall till it got further east.

Lutcas stood there with his Lute in hand and without a clue what to do, so Chornelious asked, "Lutcas can you actually make it rain?"

He replied, "I don't know. I don't know any water tunes or anything to make it rain,"

"I wished you had said that before. Oh well I can give it a shot." offered Chornelious.

The group said nothing but gave Chornelious a stare. For no words needed to be spoken to acknowledge the stupidity of the idea. Chornelious soon realized the danger of the idea and said nothing but looked down in shame.

Violina then offered, "I am familiar with water music. If you let me tune the String of Sahaq on my violin, then maybe I can do something."

This idea was much more appealing to the group, especially compared to Chornelious's. So Lutcas set down his Lute and let Violina take the String of Emet and place it on her Violin. After she did this she stood up and readied her bow. She looked at the overcast sky and concentrated on what she wanted to happen. She thought of the water in the clouds that she wanted to come down to the earth. Soon she moved her bow across the strings and the power of music began to move. When her tune was finished, a sound of booming thunder was heard from the Violin. Shortly after the sound was heard it began to drizzle which turned into rain. The town's people began to celebrate as water finally made it to their weakened bodies.

The chieftain after seeing this was curious about their intentions so he went up to Violina who was done and asked, "say that was very impressive. But it makes me wonder. Tell me, what is so valuable about the String of Mozane that draws you in?" his eyes began to sturdy the String of Sahaq on her violin.

Pan heard this and got between her and the chieftain, "Why do you ask?" he said with hostility.

The chieftain responded, "Just curious, go on your way."

After making the rain the party went on towards the Canyon of Pillars. Between Violina learning of her love potentially being sold, the history of the bandit group coming to town, and the hostility and deceit of the chieftain, they did not wish to stay longer than needed. So, at the end of the village there was a long wooden bridge that stretched from the cliff of town to the first pillar in the canyon. They continued from the natural stone bridges and wooden bridges from pillar to pillar throughout the Canyon. Eventually the canyon was so vast that it almost seemed that the pillars sticking out of the dark depths stretched for eternity. Eventually in the distance they saw a pillar that stood above the rest. Atop its peaks was a bright yellow glow. When they got closer, they saw that the theater rested on top of a large stack of rocks that did not rest easily on each other. Besieging the stack of rocks was a spiral stone staircase that led to the top of the rocks. Some of the pillars around the tall ones had natural rock formations appearing like seats gazing at the String of Mozane.

It took the party a while, but eventually they reached the tall pillar and scaled it. In Front of them floating above a stone podium made of a stack of well-balanced stone was the String. It glowed a gentle yellow color and its music sounded like two different pieces that always sounded at the same time with one being deep and the other higher. At the top of the pillar, they could see far above all other pillars and even the canyon wall. However, when the party turned back to see where they came, they saw the warriors from the village in their pursuit. They were much quicker than them due to their familiarity of the terrain.

Bendzo saw this and said, "Greedy dogs. We should have known he would try this."

Chornelious added, "Well in fairness, I am surprised that he still told us the true location. Maybe he is an idiot?"

Growing impatient of the situation and with no visible path forward Pan exclaimed, "That is it! We are not losing another String! Let's take it and go!'

Pan then grabbed the String from its place and removed it. When this happened, the music emitting from the string fell silent. But instead of emitting a quieter sound it remained silent in Pan's hand causing the small podium to fall. Suddenly the whole pillar began to crumble, and the stacked rocks slid out from one another. This caused everyone on the pillared to begin falling to the dark depths of the canyon.

Lutcas had never been so scared before as he investigated the black abyss that he was heading towards. However, Lutcas began hearing loud and powerful music being played above him. Suddenly a great wind lifted him higher up in the air and carried them all over to the canyon's edge, back to flat terrain.

After they landed Bendzo complimented Violina, "Wow that was a close call. I thought we would be eating the canyon bottom for sure. How did you do that?"

Violina looked at her Violin with the glowing string and said, "I just concentrated on what I needed to happen, and the bow's movements came naturally to me."

Pan was surprised at this power and commented, "So it is that easy. I am surprised that you didn't use this power to wipe out the village back there with great winds or a deep downpour from above."

Again, Violina knew that Pan was wrong saying this. But that temptation to do that was present in her heart. She understood how easy it would be to move the bow in such a way that could cause such destruction. But she knew that there were innocent suffering people in that village who would have died from such an attack. Yet she still found pleasure thinking of using the power against the village. As she thought this, the quieter tune emitted from the String of Sahaq flickered as if it stopped and continued.

Violina took off the String of Sahaq from her Violin and handed it to Lutcas saying, "Believe me that is what I wanted to do. But this is also why I am giving this back to you Lutcas."

Lutcas was taken back from this and said, "Violina are you sure you don't want to have this on your Violin?"

"Yes. It would be for the best Lutcas that you carried this power instead of me."

Pan and Bendzo were confused by this display but didn't bother saying anything. Pan handed over the String of Mozane to Lutcas as well who put it on his Lute. There were now three Strings of Harmony that were on Lutcas' instrument.

Bendzo then asked, "So what do we do now? All seven Strings of Harmony have been retrieved."

Lutcas replied, "We do what Cymbai instructed us to do. We head to the land in the far west. There we will know what to do."

CHAPTER 9 SILENCE

After the party retrieved the String of Mozane, they pushed further northwest. As they pressed on the savannah's grasslands began to fade into dryland. The grass became absent, and the land was covered in sand and dirt with only dry patches of grass remaining. To go with the dry land there were long stretching plateaus that were scattered across the desert. The party was confused since the map they carried did not say that there was desert here but said that this should be near the edge of the central grasslands.

As the party pressed forward, they did their routine activities while taking breaks. Lutcas this time decided to learn what he could do with the newly acquired Strings of Harmony, with the assistance of Chornelious and Violina. While they were studying, Pan and Bendzo continued to spar with their iron. After a couple of duels Pan and Bendzo sat down to take a break.

Bendzo curious about what Violina did earlier comment, “So Pan what do you think about Violina giving Lutcas back the String?”

“I don't know. It is confusing. She could have kept it and used it with far greater power than Lutcas could. Yet instead of using this power she was afraid of using it and gave it up. It doesn't make sense to me.”

"I think I must agree with you, my friend. There are too many people in this world that crave power to be giving it up like that. I like to think that with this world if you have power or the chance to receive power then you should take it so you can do your will." Bendzo paused to ask Pan a question, "Listen Pan. I am a little worried about our plan to just head west. We don't know what we are looking for and what the end game is. But tell me what you would do after we secured these Strings?"

Pan looked off for a moment as to ponder, "Well I would try and use the String's power. I understand that Violina may be trusting the conductor to do this. But in honesty I haven't seen him working much. If anything, it has been shown that the conductor has put this duty on our shoulders. So, I would wield this power to liberate the world from this evil. I would put the world to the sword and by their bloodshed make sure evil never resurfaces again."

"I agree! I think it is up to us to usher in a good world of our design! But it is a shame that the others may not agree with us."

Pan looked at the others and said, "Well Lutcas I think understands the need for force, but he is more moderate than we are with it. Chornelious is just not physically strong enough to effectively wield an iron weapon. Violina is strongly opposed to the ways of bloodshed, which to me seems naive."

Bendzo put his hand on Pan's shoulder and said, "Once we get to wear, we are going then perhaps they will understand the need of our ways."

While they were discussing Lutcas experimented with the String of Sahaq by attempting a tune Violina suggested. This caused a small spiral of wind to form and shroud Chornelious in a cloud of loose dirt. Once the wind stopped the dirt subsided revealing a small boy covered head to toe in dirt.

Lutcas apologized and Chornelious responded, "Now you know how I feel. Trying to do one thing and go haywire the next."

Lutcas and Violina laughed but Violina was reminded of something she meant to ask Chornelious, "Hey Chornelious, you said you were looking for your master regarding your instrument. What will you do once you find him?"

Chornelious now clapping the dirt off his attire replied, "Let me think. I suppose I would give him back his instrument and ask him to teach me. But now after seeing the power of this thing then maybe my master can use it to help resist Orchestrasus. But enough about me I am curious about the String of Mozane! Let's see what it can do!"

Lutcas wasn't certain what this String could do so he responded, "Honestly, I am scared to touch it. Even the village chieftain said that they used to respect the String so much that they always left it alone."

Violina commented, "But it is so strange to me. The String of Sahaq seems to have authority over the winds and weather, the String of Eres has authority over the earth and what comes of it. But this String is not as self-explanatory. It is like a repeating idea that one of the Strings of Harmony is a string based on balance. I mean, isn't harmony already perfectly balanced music?"

"I don't know. I know Harper back at the far north village described the Strings to us. But I can't remember what he said." Lutcas replied

Remembering a little bit of what he said Chornelious pitched in, "Oh wait I remember! I believe it was something to do with the stability of existence itself or something to that effect."

Lutcas heard this and remembered Harper saying this, "Oh my! That is intense!"

Sharing the same expression, Violina teasingly said, "Well we know who's instrument this won't be going on."

The two looked at Chornelious and he boasted, "You all are heard. I know I'm dangerous. But I can play Lightning and you both can't."

Studying the Sting of the Sahaq Lutcas wondered aloud, "Well you know maybe with this String I can play Lightning melodies."

Chornelious shook Lutcas shoulders as he begged him, “No! Don’t do that! Let me be special!”

Inconvenienced by the shaking Lutcas proclaimed sarcastically, “You’re SPECIAL. Alright mister wild music? Now quit shaking me!”

Pan and Bendzo approached the three and Bendzo asked them, “So! Any progress on finding out what the Strings do?”

Violina replied, “Not much. We already know the String of Sahaq can play wind music and weather music. But we are a bit hesitant to try the String of Mozane.”

Pan, concerned it had something to do with her naive thinking, asked, “Why are we hesitant to try it?”

Violina answered, “Chornelious brought up how Harper said that this String has something to do with the stability of existence. So, we thought even experimenting with this would be dangerous to us.”

“Well, that is all too complicated for me. So maybe it is for the best.” replied Bendzo.

Pan changed the subject, “The sun is getting low. We may want to push a little further ahead and rest for the night.”

The party agreed and pressed forward a little bit before stopping. As they pressed forward and were coming around the edge of a plateau there were smokestacks as if a town or a village was nearby. But when it came into view, they saw that it was an encampment of soldiers. Not just any soldiers but the knights of Orchestrasus.

Pan exclaimed, “Crap this isn’t good. What are the odds that they show up around here?”

Bendzo studied the camp, “No that is not just any encampment. That massive tent in the middle is Lyle’s. This is Lyle’s and his men’s encampment.”

Violina was worried and exclaimed, “We need to leave before we are spotted. We should turn back and find another way through these valleys.”

Bendzo added, "But here is something to think about. Prince Lyle never goes anywhere without his Lyre and his Strings of Harmony."

Chornelious put his hand under his chin, "Are you suggesting that we try and take the remaining Strings from Lyle?"

"That would fix your problem of not having the remaining four Strings." Bendzo added.

Violina didn't like this idea and protested, "Listen we received strict instructions to stay on our path and head west."

Bendzo responded, "And we did and look! How wise is the conductor that we happen to run into the man with the remaining four strings on our path?"

Thinking aloud Pan added, "On top of running into him. We are also the only ones that stand a chance against him. Lutcas over here now must be the second most powerful man in the world with three Strings of Harmony. Not to mention Chornelious's lightning."

Chornelious said, "They raise a good point. We have a lot of power with us."

Violina couldn't argue with this but still believed it to be foolish, "Guys we can't do this. We are putting too much at risk. Don't you agree with me Lutcas?"

Everyone's eyes gazed at Lutcas making him kind of nervous. He didn't realize it until Pan said something, but he may be one of the most powerful people in the world right now. Plus, Lutcas thought it to be an extreme coincidence that Lyle happened to be over there.

Lutcas responded, "Violina it is hard to argue against them. I may be the only one that can stand a chance against Lyle right now. Plus, the Strings are right there. This all may be in the conductor's design to happen."

Violina folded her arms and paced for a moment and said, "Alright fine I cannot argue against this, but that doesn't mean I like it."

Bendzo smiled in relief of her agreement, “Well you will not need to worry once we grab the Strings and put an end to all of this.” Bendzo turned to Chornelious and asked, “So Chornelious we need to think of a plan of action any ideas?”

The party discussed the plan which was mostly derived by Chornelious. The plan was to rest before the plan happened and strike when it is close to dark, but not too dark since they would have watch set up around camp. Violina and Chornelious would be away from the Camp and would cause a distraction. Lutcas, Pan, and Bendzo by the plan would use the distraction to enter camp and find the strings and get out. The party agreed with this plan and decided to put it in motion. So, before the plan the group rested well with Bendzo taking the first watch.

After a few hours the sun got close to the edge of the horizon. Bendzo woke the others up and everyone began preparations. Chornelious gave Pan am now finished metal pan flute. Pan put on his helmet from the battlefield and readied his weapons. Lutcas got his instrument and weapon together but began to worry. He knew that he was going to camp since if a confrontation happened with Lyle, he would stand the greatest chance of defeating him. Although the objective was to not let this happen, Lutcas knew that he still may have to do it. But he thought about what Lyle and his family have done to the world of Symphonia. He knew that if he had to be put to death he wouldn't hesitate.

The party climbed up the plateau that stood next to the encampment, scaling it with the music from the Sting of Earth. Below they saw a large encampment with many tents. However, they saw that the encampment was between two of the plateaus, the one they stood on and the one across the encampment. What was odd to Bendzo, which he shared with the party, was that Lyle’s tent wasn’t in the middle of camp, but rather the edge near the other plateau.

Chornelious who was studying the scene suggested, “Well this works to our advantage. Me and Violina will stay up here to cause the distraction and be on watch in case something happens. You three can find your way to the other plateau and descend on Lyle’s tent from there.”

Everyone agreed and Pan, Lutcas, and Bendzo treaded carefully around the valley encampment and made it to the other plateau. At this point, the sun was just below the horizon and the orange sky was a deep blue color slowly fading into the night sky with stars hanging above.

The three slowly worked their way down the plateau hiding behind large rocks to conceal themselves from anyone looking at the cliff face. The three awaited their signal and suddenly a rumble was felt, and a rockslide occurred on the plateau they were at previously causing a part of the encampment to be crushed. At this many of the soldiers in the camp panicked and rushed to investigate what happened and to rescue anyone one who may be heard.

The three moved at this signal and made their way towards the large tent that stood out from the others. The guards who were once guarding the tent drew their attention to the chaos coming from the other side of the tent. Pan used this opportunity to use the loud sound to play a tune of moving metal and cause his sword to float unnoticed. The guards now looking at the landslide from their post were almost shoulder to shoulder wearing the same helmet that did little to protect the fronts of their necks. Pan with his tune uses the floating sword to fly across the guards, cutting their necks open and letting them fall. Bendzo and Lutcas both went inside the tent, leaving Pan to stand back outside and keep watch from a distance. Lutcas and Bendzo entered the tent and in front of them was an empty sleeping roll, with a chest at the front of it.

Lutcas whispered to Bendzo, “He isn’t here. What if the Strings of Harmony aren’t in here either?”

Bendzo pointed at the chest at the front of the bedroll and said, “Go up to the chest. I doubt he would have guards standing outside for no reason. Lyle isn’t in here, so the Strings must be.”

Lutcas went up the chest and before he could even touch it, he felt something hit him hard from behind and his vision went black. When Lutcas opened his eyes, he felt great pain near the back of his head. He was tied up and was being dragged towards the middle of the encampment. Looking at him were the faces of armored knights whispering to themselves. Suddenly the knights made space and a knight equipped with grand looking armor looked down upon Lutcas and removed his helmet. Lutcas only saw his face a few times, but he recognized this face. It was Prince Lyle holding his dark lyre with four of the Strings of Harmony. Lutcas attempted to struggle moving but to no avail.

As Lutcas struggled Lyle smiled and said, "Alas the once sent to claim the Strings of Harmony has now been captured! But I must take a moment to thank the one who delivered them unto me. Bendzo of the north!" Bendzo marched forward with Lutcas's Lute and kneeled before him, "Bendzo has done me a great service. With my honest doubts he lured the enemy to us and because of his tested loyalty, will now replace Tubiat as my second in command and as one of my royal guards."

After Lyle took the Lute from Bendzo many of the knights around him gave him praise and chanted his name. Lutcas had no idea what was going on. His worst nightmare had been realized as he saw Lyle with all the Strings in his possession and Bendzo by his side.

Lutcas, frustrated, tearing up, and struggling in the dirt to move, cried out, "Bendzo why! Why do you do this?"

Bendzo leaned down to Lutcas and said, "Lutcas the world we know as been gone. Peace and harmony are gone. In this world I have learned that now we must take for ourselves what we want so that we can truly live. With power we can become like gods, conductors of the world and our fate to seize our destiny and make the world in our image."

Many of the knights praised what he said, and Lyle kneeled preparing to place the Strings from Lutcas instrument to his own, "Lutcas. Your friend's loyalty never rested with you. It rested with his concern of self. Just like your friend Harper who we found in the town of Mahase. With enough torture of him and his student, who I once called my brother, he told us where you would be heading. While you three were resting Bendzo warned me of you, and we set up our trap. Understand that no one was on your side dear Lutcas. I truly pity you; I feel awful imagining your existence like this. Now let your journey be at rest formidable adversary."

Once he said this, he began to rip the Strings from his Lute and began to put them on his Lyre. The first being the String of Eres, which caused a great shaking of the earth beneath them after it warped into place on his lyre. Lutcas Struggled hard on the ground as he was watching this happen. Lyle had Lutcas restrained by the guards so he couldn't wiggle his way near Lyle. Not far there were sounds of clashing metal and yelling of men, where Pan was now fighting fiercely against the many knights.

Lyle turned to Bendzo and said, "My loyal guard. I ask that you go forth and fight the one you called Pan. But do not kill him if you can." After he said this, he moved the String of Nepes, invigorating Bendzo with life and strength.

Bendzo compiled and rushed over to the sound of clashing metal ready to combat Pan. Lyle then took the String of Sahaq and when he placed it on his Lyre a great clasp of thunder was heard above, and a powerful gust of wind darted through the valley. Then Lyle reached for the String of Mozane and ripped it from its place. But before he could place it on his Lyre, a tune of fire was heard and Violina launched a ball of fire at Lyle. It was so fast and precise that Lyle could only barely move to avoid direct impact, but enough to burn the side of his face. Lyle yelled in pain and fell backwards. The Knights around him then made a circle around him trying to protect him from any other potential attacks.

Shortly after Lyle was hit by this Chornelious began to wind and press the keys on his hurdy gurdy and play a melody of lightning. Lightning streams then began to shoot from Chornelious's instrument and race around the camp, scattering men. Violina used the chaos to try and advance towards Lyle. Some knights came after her and she used many arts of music that she picked up from her companions she traveled with. She used water, wind, earth, fire, and light to try and make it to her goal. She moved elegantly to dodge any opposition while continuing to play her music all in advancing towards the enemy.

While Lutcas was restrained he could see Lyle on the ground putting the String of Mozane on the Lyre. When this happened many of the knights began to fall to their knees in pain. Limbs began to bend in directions they shouldn't, skin began to boil and burst, appendages started falling off the men. Some of the soldiers who advanced towards Violina succumbed to these things and fell before her. She noticed that the lighting around her began to fade, and she turned to see Chornelious lying on the ground covered in unnatural growths and boils that deformed him. Violina turned with frustration and readied to play a powerful melody.

Suddenly as a wave of unseen energy pushed all things around Lyle he shouted, "Silence!"

All the soldiers fell to this unseen force and so did Pan and Violina. Suddenly Lutcas could hear nothing. Not the wind going through the valley, not the battle cries of soldiers or their footsteps, nor the clashing steel of Bendzo and Pan. Lutcas looked around him confused and saw Violina and Pan thrown to the ground with Chornelious deformed.

Lutcas cried out to them but alas no sound came from his mouth. He tried once more, and no sound was emitted. But out of the unbearable silence there was a sound, footsteps of Lyle. When everyone was getting their bearings, the soldiers got up and restrained everyone. Violina reacted to this and began to glide her bow across the strings of her violin. But no music came from the violin, and she was quickly subdued. Pan in an act of desperation wanted to pick up his flute and play a melody of rage, but no sound came of it, and he was subdued by the mighty strength of Bendzo. Chornelious was so deformed that the men who approached him were afraid to touch him.

One of them knights drew a sword and was about to kill Violina, but Lyle said with his echoing voice, "No do not kill her!"

Lyle approached her and looked at her with half of his face burned, "I will be fair to you. You didn't kill me, but that still gave me great pain. Let me balance it out."

Lyle then droves his sword into her shoulder. Violina's face became an illustration of pain as her mouth opened to scream. Yet no sound came from her, and her pain could only be seen and not heard.

Lyle then walked over to Chornelious who lay deformed in the dirt with tears and snot coming out of his now unnatural face, "The one who wields lightning. I admire your talents and I pity your state of existence.

Eventually you will now die here slowly with your odd instrument. But I will end you as an act of mercy."

Lyle then took his sword and drove it into his heart. Violina, Pan, and Lutcas watched as what little resemble their friend was slaughtered by the enemy. Pan did not try to cry out; instead, he broke free of Bendzo's grip and charged at Lyle with a sword picked up from the ground. Lyle saw this and easily parried him. Pan tried again and this time Lyle disarmed him from his now sloppy attacks. Again, and again did Pan try this and over and over he failed. Eventually he stopped when he was too weak to get back up.

The prince leaned forward and said, "Bendzo spoke highly of you and from what I saw back at the Theater of Emet and of today I am impressed. Your journey has been for naught and now you can stop. But I offer this to you, as the victor of this world be my partner along with Bendzo. Together with our passion we can make the world in our image! But I will give you time to answer once you have healed."

Finally, Lyle approached Lutcas who was now laying down defeated, "My dear Lutcas. You of course have been a big part in me collecting the Seven Strings of Harmony. You, just as I, have been all over the land of Symphonia. With the influence of the String of Emet. I have influenced many to the path that was set before me. I have used the String of Nepes to choose for myself who shall live and die. I have used the power of the Strings to bring down my father after he killed my mother and seized all the power of Orchestrasus. Now I will return there and reassure my people that the power to become gods is before them. Then we can all play a song and make the world in our image!" he stopped and went on a knee before strumming both the string of Emet and Aman, "Lutcas I would value the mind of someone who has seen the world. Please join in my quart at the heart of the world, The Kingdom of Orchestrasus! Their will can be done, and you can make things how you want them in your image, Lutcas."

The music of the Strings of Harmony ran through Lutcas's mind. As if he was dreaming, he could see a world where everything was as it was before. But he was back at the village with Note. Bendzo, Violina, Guil, Pan, and Chornelious were next to him looking at the beautiful landscape around them. But Lutcas remembered that evil existed in his world, and it was his will to get rid of it all. So, he thought if he was the avenger of Symphonia defending its purity with iron. He thought that perhaps in his world he would take the evil of the world and put it to the sword. The more he thought of this the more he thought of how evil existed and how it would be purged, since all he wanted was for the world to be pure again as it once was. Then the landscape changed before him as he felt a tug on his leg. The hills in the distance changed from lush green to various assortments of colors with red mixed in with it. The trees became metal polls with corpses as leaves. The grass around him was red littered with warped tools and weapons. Beside him was Pan laying on the ground prompted up with thirteen blades piercing him from the ground. Bendzo laid next to him, slain with Pan's sword. Chornelious was lying deformed as he was but note gnawed on his remains. This was all horrifying, Lutcas knew what he wanted yet this is what it became. He finally turned to the tugging, and it was Violina bleeding out on the ground pulling at his tunic. Next to her was Lutcas's body pierced by the sword and slain.

Suddenly Lutcas was snapped out of the trance, and he saw Violina, not as wounded as in his trance, crawling up next to his leg and pulling his tunic to get his attention. The knights who were restraining her saw no threat to her for she was wounded, and her violin was shattered.

Lyle watched this and said, "Listen I value what your party has to offer me. I am sorry that I had to kill your friend. But if you want a future in the world we are about to forge together, the gates of Orchestrasus will be open for you. This I promise."

Lyle began departing as soon as he was finished speaking. The surviving knights in his company followed behind as they got their mounts and prepared for departure. Bendzo looked back at the three lying in the dirt and then followed his comrades. The knights, after gathering what they could, departed east where the Kingdom of Orchestrasus resides.

Lutcas and his comrades were weakened, beaten, and defeated lying in the dirt left alone to the muted surroundings. Only after a while was sound heard again once a single raindrop struck the ground. Following that raindrop was the rest of the drops from the sky hitting one another, as if the world itself began to weep.

CHAPTER 10 ELEGY

Violina, after she stopped her bleeding, took Pan's sword, and cut Lutcas's restraints. Pan, once he was able to move, stumbled over to his mutated and dead friend and wept loudly over him. Lutcas had never heard such weeping since they went to the fallen fort. Lutcas looked at Chornelious and what could be recognized of his body and grief swelled up in\him before fell to his knees and wept. Violina did the same as she too cared deeply for her Chornelious.

Fortunately, the knights didn't steal their supply. So Lutcas put the spare strings he had carried with him and put them back on his Lute. Violina looked at her shattered instrument and tried to match piece for piece, but it was beyond repair. She thought that if Chornelious were here, he may have been able to fix this. The thought overwhelmed her, and she crumpled to the ground silently.

With a face of sadness turning into rage, Pan asked Lutcas to bury Chornelious. Lutcas took his lute and played a tune of moving earth. He was spoiled from the power of The String of Eres. Now the tune was weaker and took more time and effort to perform its music.

Pan studied the burial site and noticed Chornelious's broken Hurdy Gurdy on the ground, "Lutcas, why didn't you let him keep his instrument as he went under?"

He answered him, "Before today and after he went on the mountain, he learned his master was in Orchestrasus. I thought you, as his best friend, would fulfill his wish if there was any chance of finding his master."

He took a deep breath and put a hand on Lutcas's shoulder, "I will honor him. But not by giving his more than likely dead master a shattered instrument. I loved him as a brother as I do you and Violin a sister. I will honor him by bringing death to the one who brought death to him. An equal exchange." Pan turned away from Lutcas, so angry that he began to tear as he marched away. Lutcas didn't want to press him further and he gathered what he could of the instrument and put it in his bag.

Violina seeking direction and comfort asked, "What do we do now? Do we go after Lyle and his men? Do we go into his kingdom?"

Pan angry said, "As much as I wish to do that Violina we can't. We would be killed. We must become stronger first. Only then will we be able to rip the Strings from that Lyre!"

Thinking, Lutcas suggested, "Maybe we must continue down the path we were set on. Maybe whatever is in the far west could be what helps us."

For the party, there was no other option. No other hope to cling to. Pan was right that they could not dream of challenging Prince Lyle now. So, with nothing but a gambit of chance, they headed to the land of the far west.

The night was already upon them, so after they rested before embarking. The journey however was tough, not only due to the lack of sleep at the party, but because of what was happening around them. As they pushed west great black clouds came from the east. From these clouds came ash that sprinkled over the landscape. These clouds came from the Theater of Eres, where the volcanic mountain was. Occasionally accompanying snow of ash was the violent shaking of the earth beneath them, as if it were a beast's belly rumbling. Whenever it wasn't snowing ash there was a great gust of wind that swept in from the northwest causing great chunks of ice to fall from the sky. The sky was now a battleground which resulted in great pillars of wind racing across the barren landscape. At night these were impossible to see, for the sky was now a veil of darkness. It was as if the moon and the stars vanished from this world. The only light to come of it was the flickers of lightning that struck the ground like a thousand blows.

Due to these things the journey was slow and every night they had to find a cave to seek shelter. The caves weren't pleasant either. The rumblings were always a test to the integrity of the cave's constitution. Finding food was difficult as well. The plants that Lutcas grew would sometimes sprout as rotten. When seeking plants elsewhere they saw that even the plant life was hostile. Some plants grew mouths and snapped at anything around them. Some grew dangerous thorns that would not allow them to be easily picked. Hunting was a dangerous option now. Many of the animals they saw now were mutated into much more massive and powerful creatures. There were lizards that would tower homes, birds that could pick up an entire man, wolves that would cannibalize their own in pure violence and savagery.

The sights were horrifying to them. Lutcas looked at them with horror and guilt as he walked across what may have been fields of grass. But Lutcas not only looked upon all this with fear, but of guilt. He began to remember many things said to him. He remembered Cymbai's message before they left the mountain, to stay on the path. Lutcas realized they didn't listen and due to their arrogance, it was their fault. But Luteas in his mind, pinned more of the blame on himself, for he could have stood a better chance if not knocked out so easily.

While the world was becoming a vortex of chaos, Lutcas's mind became a vortex of self-destruction. He thought about what Prince Lyle said back at the Theater of Aman. When he was told that his friends will leave him, and he will desire death. After discussing this with Violina back at the swamp village, he thought it was designed to mess with Lutcas's mind. But Lutcas saw this to be effective since it not only succeeded but was coming true. What he said was unfolding before him. He knew that Violina and Pan disagreed and would argue, the silence of their journey west displayed that tension perfectly. Chornelious was no longer with them due to his execution. Even Bendzo and Note, the two best friends Lutcas had hurt him and left him. Lutcas knew that it was only going to be a matter of time before evil crept into the hearts of his only remaining friends. He felt that there was nothing he could do to ensure his friends would continue to love him and stay by his side. The fear of what Lyle said overwhelmed his heart and he became afraid. Death at this point didn't seem like something to be afraid of, but rather it became something to look forward to.

After a few hours of silently traveling the group made camp in what used to be an oasis. Now it was a dried-up watering hole filled with dead fish. The vegetation besieged the empty pond and the campsite. After gathering wood from the nearby vegetation, Pan used a tune of minor flame to light it. In despair the group sat silently. They didn't play their songs of thankfulness, there was no sound of Bendzo and Pan sparring with each other, and there was no cranking and squeaking from Chornelious tinkering with the Hurdy Gurdy.

Remembering these sounds and acknowledging their absence made Lutcas want to cry. But instead, he held it in. He didn't want to show himself as weak Infront of his friends. He was afraid Violina would find him too dependent and move on. He was afraid Pan would find him too weak and leave him. But thinking about this cascaded into the previous thoughts he had in his journey and intensified them. His fear amplified, his feelings of loneliness increased, his feeling of strength dried up, his desire for death was unquenched. But he didn't cry, he just stared at the broken Hurdy Gurdy and did nothing as the flames flickered ahead of him.

Pan studied the Hurdy Gurdy and commented, "Lutcas I am not certain why you didn't bury it with him. You now must carry that with all its parts, that is if you have managed to keep them all. We should have let it die with him."

Violina had been holding in frustration until Pan said something, "Pan enough! How insensitive can you be to Lutcas and to Chornelious's mission?"

Now defensive he responds, "It isn't practical to be carrying around dead weight. Especially for something that should have been left with my friend and for something you want to give to someone we will never see."

She snaps back, “Practical? That's what you think you are! Saying that the way of the sword is the only practical way to live! Look where it got us Pan! Chornelious’s dead because you and Bendzo couldn’t know any other way to solve a problem!”

“My fault? You believe my best friend’s death is my fault!”

The arguing continued, but Lutcas turned it out. He saw what was foretold to him right before his eyes. He saw them grow further and further apart. This amplified Lutcas’s feelings to a high level. He wanted out of this conflict, out of this world that is now broken and defeated, out of the danger of losing the ones he cares about.

Lutcas then turned to see Pan’s sword near him. Violina and Pan, tired and defeated, were arguing very intensely. Lutcas unseen grabbed the sword and sprinted to what was left of the green brush of the oasis. He hid behind some brush as he looked at Pan’s sword and felt bliss and comfort. He knew that in a moment it was all going to be over. He would not need to fear abandonment anymore. So Lutcas grabbed the sword and stuck the handle out from him and pointed the blade towards his heart. He moved the blade towards his chest, but when it hit his flesh, he paused and hesitated. He thought to himself, come on and get it over with or there will be greater pain waiting for you.

Lutcas then took Pan’s sword, closed his eyes, and thrusted the blade towards his chest. However, the sword didn’t touch him. Instead, when Lutcas opened his eyes, he saw that it was forced out of his hand and into the dirt near him. Lutcas saw that it was Pan who kicked the blade from him. He was so concentrated on death that all sounds and feelings around him were silent, including Pan’s approach.

Desperate Lutcas crawled towards the blade. Pan noticed this and raced for it. Violina then tackled Lutcas who was still going for the blade. Lutcas was on his back with Violina pinning him to the ground. Lutcas still struggled looking only at the sword. Violina tried to hold him down, but he continued to writhe and crawl.

Lutcas with tears in his eyes and sad that his friend had to see him like this shouted, “No please! Let me go! It is right there!”

Lutcas was then rolled over on his back and Violina then slapped Lutcas across the cheek. The first blow didn't faze him but the second one and the third and fourth did. Lutcas's attention was now off the sword after Pan picked it up. Additionally, his face began to sting after three more slaps. But before the final one struck it landed softly on Lutcas's face. It couldn't really be called a slap, but more like the hand stopped and rested on his face with his tears running over her fingers.

Lutcas closed his eyes and felt more tears on his face, not from his eyes, but Violina's. Lutcas laid their widened eye and stared at Violina who was sobbing looking at Lutcas with a face of fear.

"Please let me go, Violina. I am tired.", Lutcas whimpered.

She desperately wanted comfort as well, but she shook her head, "I know. I know Lutcas. But please I have lost so many too. My husband, my village, and now Chornelious."

Lutcas, still pinned, requested, "Violina Pan, please don't leave me. I don't want to be left. I don't want to be alone."

Violina closed her eyes and pressed her forehead against Lutcas's, "Lutcas I know you're scared. I can't bring back the ones who left you. I can't bring back the ones who left me. But all I can do is say this Lutcas. You and Pan are all that I have left. Lutcas, I know what you told me about what Lyle said. But that doesn't have to be true. We can still be together, the three of us. Just know that I love you and Pan Lutcas, and I am not ready for you to leave us."

Violina allowed Lutcas to get up and Lutcas sat there on his knees trying to comprehend everything. Now he began crying but not for the same reason as before, but because he knew the weight of what he tried to do. The stinging slaps on his face couldn't match the pain of his guilt.

Pan who was deeply moved by this dropped the sword and moved in with them, "Lutcas I am sorry. You, Violina, and Chornelious all mean the world to me. Truly. But understand that even though we may have failed, our task may not be over."

At once the group embraced each other.

The next morning the group continued to push forward west. The plateaus were gone, and they came across a massive river that ran through a vast open field. However, unlike the other rivers they saw it was flowing. They followed it and soon on the other end of the field over a rise they saw an unforgettable sight. Before them was a small patch of land that was unaffected by the unharmonized chaos of the world. Past it was a wall of clouds that seemed to hide some sort of massive castle behind it. The party was relieved to see such a beautiful sight as they walked through the destroyed lands of Symphonia. As they approached closer, they felt invigorated and energized. They were able to see sunshine again and not the dark and chaotic clouds of the sky. Eventually they made it to the cloud wall. They could barely see what appeared to be castle towers above the cloud wall.

Studying it Pan asked, "What in Symphonia is this?"

The party looked across the cloud wall and saw that it seemed to go on forever, "This looks like the end of the world.", commented Violina.

Lutcas studied it and said, "You know before the knights called it Orchestrasus, I believe the Kingdom of the world used to be called Podiem."

"That is a name I haven't heard in a while. Do you think this is it?" Violina asked.

Impatient Pan said, "Only one way to find out."

Pan then moved into the cloud wall and suddenly walked forward out of another part of the cloud wall back into the field. Pan turned and tried again but with the same result. Lutcas and Violina tried some as well, but they kept appearing back where they started.

A voice echoed from behind them and laughed, "I am afraid that won't work."

The group turned to see a tall man glowing behind them. He was radiant and had lights swirling around them that appeared as musical symbols. But the group knew that this was no mere human, but a concertmaster, a higher being.

“Forgive me.” said the concertmaster, “I am Altiel. I am a messenger concertmaster from the one on high, The Conductor. May I ask what brings you here?”

The group was silent and ashamed of their failure, but Lutcas spoke up, “Altiel. We were the ones who failed to bring the Strings of Harmony here. We strayed from our path and because of that they were lost.”

Altiel with his oddly echoing pitch responded, “Ah that much is clear. The truth of the world stripped to allow evil to come in. Followed by the loss of life, which death runs through the world. Shortly after Love is lost and the desire for self-gained. Trust next, breaking peace and bringing hostility and fear. Next Earth and sky as the earth spits fire with smog and sky which spits out a hurricane. Finally balance in which the music in all beings is disrupted and makes things mutated and unnatural. This is the result of the loss.”

Pan, still impatient, comments, “We know this! We came here because we have no idea what to do next. Our fight for the Strings will be futile.”

“That it will be.” replied Altiel, “Now you are all confused. I understand this. You probably are wondering what this place is aren’t you?” The group nods yes, “This place you see before is the edge of the world. Past your world is the domain of the creator and my fellow concertmasters. Once it was one with your physical domain of existence. But humankind has rejected the Conductor. To honor their wishes the Conductor took his kingdom with him which is what you see before you.”

Pan became angry, “So that is it? You and the Conductor abandoned us all to die in our own cesspool of chaos,”

Altiel became frustrated at Pan, “You fool! You know so little, and you make such big claims. Evil cannot exist in the presence of pure goodness; chaos cannot exist next to the one who rid the world of it. His radiant goodness would overtake you like the heat of the sun. He has sent many prophets to the kingdom of man, but alas they have all been slain and failed. He has sent four of you three to bring the Strings back here, but you failed. You chose your own wisdom and strayed from the path and looked where that got you.”

Violina being hit with all this again cried out, “Well is there no hope? Has the Conductor given up on us and our failures?”

“I tell you all this. Be not afraid. There is a promised hope for the world. I cannot speak of all the details to you, for it is not my place and time to do so. But the Conductor sent a new prince who will challenge Orchestrasus and its ruler.”

Confused, Lutcas asked, “Conductor send us a prince? Who is this?”

“He is in Orchestrasus right now as we speak. He is filled with the wisdom of the Conductor and will be the one to defeat them. He will do things in ways you never would think could be done and will not reveal himself until the time comes. He will offer a new path for humankind and the world will be restored. That is all I can say. Now leave here, follow the river, and go to the city of humankind. Follow him and witness what will transpire.”

With a great flash of light Altiel vanished, “Well I suppose this sort of thing runs in all the Concertmasters. To be dramatic and then leave.” commented Pan.

Confused Lutcas asked, “So we go to Orchestrasus? The source of where all this started.”

Excited Pan responded, “Looks like we are Lutcas. Now let's head to the heart of the enemy! We are coming city of Orchestrasus!”

CHAPTER 11
ORCHESTRA

With a confusing new piece of hope the group pressed forward to the center of the world, where the kingdom of Orchestrasus spreads its chaos. As the party pressed forward, they saw more of the world fall apart. Grasslands become drylands, lakes become craters, the sky a blackened and thunderous shadow, the earth shaking like the surface of a drum being beaten.

Along with the everlasting cursed landscape of Symphonia, they came across many villages that seemed to be destroyed to the ground. It really could have been many different things to have done this. It could have been the Knights, could be powerful pillars of wind that race across the earth. But nonetheless it was clear that there was no life out there.

Finally, after a few days of traveling and looking at nothing but the face of death, the party finally came across a sign that they were getting close. In the far distance they saw what miles of field was slowly show jagged rocks that formed a basin almost as far as the eye could see. But there was a structure that stood above the jagged rocks that was hard to make out from the clouds in the distance. But it was intimidating, as it appeared like a dark shadow towering over the land illuminated only by the lights beneath it. They knew that this was the right direction.

As they approached the basin-like formation the landscape grew thicker with destroyed villages as well as various broken tools, weapons, and instruments that were shattered and spread across the fields. As the structure and the basin were getting closer, they saw more roads with travelers scattered about them. The closer they got the more travelers and dirt roads came into view. But they were all traveling in one direction, towards the dark tower.

Finally, when they reached the edge of the basin all came into view and it was an indomitable sight to behold. Before them was a deep basin besieged by jagged rocks that seemed as if they could fall any moment. The crater stretched for miles and miles. In the middle of the crater there was a city. Lutcas had never seen such a large populace before in one place. Leading from the edges of the basin were numerous roads with travelers far away enough to look like ants. The roads all led to the first wooden wall that ringed around the whole city surrounded by small structures. Past those buildings was another wall and higher towers. But in the center was the structure they were able to see from so far away. So tall that it stretched over the edge of the basin. At first Lutcas didn't understand what it was supposed to be, but now he did. This massive tower was an ugly attempt to make a podium, a symbol of the creator's throne. The tower was a behemoth and at its top it became much wider, giving it the appearance of a podium. On the walls, towers, and Podium Tower were the flags showing off the symbol of Orchestrasus, a man standing on a podium.

Looking at this all gave a perfect illustration of horror. At the background of the illustration, we see a mountain in the far distance creating the dark smoke and lightning above. On the margins we see the great pillars of wind racing across the landscape, but never getting near the basin. Sandwiched between the back clouds and the barren land, was the greenish yellowish sky given by the lowering sun. In front of this background was the kingdom that is the source of all its chaos, prideful enough to erect its own podium. It made sense to Lutcas now why Cymbai called this place the scar of the world, for it looks as if something was ripped out of this place leaving only a wound.

After beholding this sight, the group pressed forward on the road leading into the crater like basin. As they pushed forward the roads began to merge, and the travelers began to compact on the same road. The travelers were a hard thing to look at. Lutcas could tell that many were from many different places around the world. Some pale in flesh like he is. Others very dark like the people in the southern savannahs. Some with narrow eyes like in the villages in the east. Some with a softer brown color that lived in the eastern marshes. Most of them are dirty, exhausted, malnourished, and weak.

But Lutcas also paid attention to the knights that were examining the crowds entering the city. Many didn't wear helmets but held them to their sides. The knights mostly resembled Guil and Lyle with their bronze skin, dark curly hair, and large noses. But Lutcas saw many other people in the knight uniforms as well. Some pale, dark, brown, and narrow-eyed.

While he was studying the people around him Lutcas, Violina, and Pan found themselves in a line that would stop and move and stop and move forward a bit more. In view came a large wooden wall with wooden spikes on the side. The line seemed to head towards a large gate that made a way to get in the city.

As they were approaching a knight on a horse road up and down alongside the line and shouted while reading from a scroll, "Welcome weary travelers! Welcome to the grand city of conductors! The Kingdom of Orchestrasus! A place where you all can make conductors of yourselves and make the world in your own images! King Lyle welcomes all of you and wishes that you will share and be a part of the dream that he seeks. I know many of you are tired and many of you face the tragedy of this unbalanced world! But fear not! King Lyle soon after preparations will play a new song and save us all from this world and make a world where we can forge our own destinies!"

Many people on the road heard the words of the knight and they all shouted in joy. They clapped and cheered at the idea of hope the knights were selling them. Lutcas and the others however saw enough of the world to know the results of such ideas. So, they did not celebrate and clap like the others but remained silent.

The knight continued, “Now you will all enter the outer district of the city soon. You will stay in line after you are let in by the outer guard. Then the middle guard will see if you are able to pass through the second wall if you're assigned to live in the second district. Then if you are assigned to the upper district, you will receive instructions furthermore. Now rejoice! For I know the world outside is dangerous and cruel. But now you can build your lives here and forge your own destiny!”

After the Knight said this the crowd cheered once more and he rode further down the line to spread the message. Lutcas became nervous about all this. He found the systems and lines stressful, and he questioned if he heard the instructions of the knight correctly.

Ready to plan, Pan asked his two friends, “Alright so we are entering the city. What is our plan? Do we try to find the strings or what?”

Remembering what Altiel said, Lutcas spoke, “Remember Pan. We are to look for the prince that the concertmaster told us about.”

“Well, he didn’t give us much to go from. But he did say that whoever this is, he will defeat them.”

Violina added, “Well don’t forget that Altiel told us that this prince will not reveal himself till the time comes. Or whatever that means.”

Eventually the three made it to the wooden gate. The gate stood tall and guarded by knights. However, the knights did something that was unusual. The knights would kneel for all who would enter the gate, as if they were royalty. When the three made it to the gate the knights did the same to them. Violina stood confused, Lutcas embarrassed, and Pan ignored it.

Violina spoke quietly to the other two and she asked, “Why on earth did they do that to us? They bowed to us as we walked in?”

“Oddly kind for them considering that they destroyed the world.” commented Lutcas.

Pan folded his arms and he walked with thought, “Well they told everyone who was walking in that we would become Conductors.”

Shortly after they walked past the first gate, what they saw wasn't very impressive. Most of the buildings were not stone like walls ahead. They were made of dirt. It appeared as if most of them were for housing. What outnumbered these buildings were tents scattered across the barren and muddy landscape. It was sad for Lutcas to look at, but he also studied the behavior of those he passed by. Some he saw fighting in the mud over food or some object. Some just sat outside their tents appearing to not be able to do much. But some, especially the ones near the road, proclaimed out loud how King Lyle, their savior, will deliver them from pain and will deliver them to everlasting pleasure.

Finally, the three made it closer to the stone wall and another knight on a horse road alongside the road addressing those in line, "Alright congratulations future gods and conductors of the world, you have made it into the outer district. You will approach the gate and will be told where to go from there. If you are instructed to live in the outer district, please go to your assigned living quarters and begin your life here!"

This line seemed to move much more slowly than the previous line. Lutcas's anxiety was mixed with a pinch of boredom. But he did look at the poor state of the outer district around them and was confused on how these people were convinced they were being made into gods.

After a while the three made it to the stone gate. Infront of it were some knights, this time armed with a metal shield and spear. They didn't bow like the ones before, and they seemed to be guarding a man at a table in front of the gate. The man spoke with an accent that only came from the central lands of Symphonia and had bronze skin.

When the three stepped up he asked, "Okay what are your names?" They told the man, and the man began to frantic as he reached for some scrolls, picked one up and read it to Pan, "Well! What an honor it is to have you three here. Pan the slayer of hundreds, the berserker of the flute, the swordsman of the north! Welcome!" The knights that were guarding the man bowed and he turned to Violina, "Violina! Grace of the northern rivers! The master of the way of the Violin! Welcome!" finally he turned to Lutcas, "And last but certainly not least, Lutcas! Lutcas the loyal! Lutcas the wielder of three of the Strings of Harmony! Without you this dream could not be achieved so soon!"

Lutcas was surprised that they are being almost worshiped as opposed to challenged or executed. But Lutcas did remember that Lyle essentially invited them in. Embarrassed, Lutcas replied, "T-thank you?"

The man behind the table smiled and said, "Now you all must be tired from your journey. If you enter through this gate and stay on the southern road to your right, eventually you will have a road that will lead to the upper district. They will happily let you in as you are called by our beloved savior King Lyle."

The stone gates swung open and the three were let in. The middle district looked different from the outer district. In fact, there wasn't even any dirt ground. The streets, buildings, and towers were all made of stone. The chaos of this district wasn't too different. There were shops everywhere and the streets were always crowded. There were many alleyways with many people consuming strange substances. Knights scattered about, but most of the time they were drinking it seemed. Against the wall were tall stone towers looking over the outer district. In fact, many of the buildings in this district seem to tower over the road making Lutcas feel dwarfed.

There was no longer any line and now it was just a chaotic street of people and commerce. Due to this they began to discuss what to do next. They began walking down the street they were told to go down in hopes for some sign of the prince.

Lutcas spoke but his voice could hardly compete with all the sound around him, "So we made it in the walls. Do you think the prince is gonna be here?"

Violina rested her hand under her chin and observed, "Well the outer district is not where I would look for a prince. The middle district is a bit of a step up from the outer district. So, from what they told us, it seems that royalty would be in the upper district."

The reasoning was sound to them, and they proceeded down the road. The status of the street didn't seem to change. It continued to be an orchestra of many different noises. Most of it was coming from the sheer crowdedness and busyness of the roads. But there were some standing on boxes with instruments trying to gain the attention of others crying out that others in the city are preventing them from achieving godhood.

Out from one of the alleyways there was a guard in armor who took notice of Pan and grabbed him by the arm. Pan's reaction was instinct as he drew his sword and pointed it at the guard who grabbed him.

The guard laughed and took off his helmet revealing a young man who Pan recognized from Chornelious's village, "Pan it's me Ruanard."

Pan was astonished and he said, "What? Ruanard? Why aren't you back at your village?"

He answered Pan, "Don't you know? Anywhere outside of this place is basically uninhabitable. Disaster and chaos are everywhere. But man, I've heard stories about you. Warrior of iron! Slayer of hundreds. I heard your name when I was spying near the west gate."

Confused by why he was spying, Lutcas asked, "Wait spying? Who were you spying for?"

Ruanard leaned in and whispered to them, "The Zealots. We are hidden and we have not allowed ourselves to be indoctrinated by the ways of Orchestrasus. Orchestrasus is our enemy and we seek to defeat it and seat a new head of the throne by spilling the blood of those who sit on it."

Pan's eyes widened with astonishment as he turned to Violina and Lutcas, "Guys this must be what we are looking for. They said they will replace the head of the throne and defeat Orchestrasus just like the prophecy said."

Lutcas heard this and was frightened. He knew that this was appealing to Pan, but it didn't settle right. As they traveled, they used battle to power through situations. But he remembered what the concertmaster said. That this prince would do it differently. Everyone in the world seemed to attain things with brute force.

"I don't know about this Pan." Commented Lutcas.

Violina shared Lutcas's concern, "I am not sure that this is what we are looking for Pan. I mean we are looking for a prince not a warlord."

Pan titled his head in impatience, "Come on guys. This man may not be a prince yet, but he will be."

Lutcas had flashes in his head of the vision he had when Lyle played music to him. He remembers the mounds of blood and bodies. He knew that with the desire to destroy this by their own hands wasn't going to work as the world did.

Lutcas tried again, "Pan I really don't think this is what is going to work."

To Pan, his interpretation was clear, and he felt that this would go nowhere, "Fine, how about we split up. We didn't hear Altials' message the same. You guys can go search elsewhere. I'll let you know what I find out from these Zealots"

Violina looked at Pan, almost ashamed and asked, "Wait, are you trying to tell us goodbye?"

Pan looked up in thought and then looked back at them, "Just for now. The city is too big for us to search together anyway. Besides, this seems plain to me. I don't think we are going to compromise with how much we disagree."

Violina didn't want to split up, but she knew that Pan was right about not agreeing, "Fine after everything we have been through you are going to leave us?"

"You can come with me if you would like. But I firmly believe this is where we need to be."

Violina was angry with Pan, and she snapped, "Fine we will." she stormed off further down the street.

Pan looked at Lutcas knowing how he would feel about this and said, "Lutcas you are a close friend of mine. If you choose not to go with me and investigate the zealots that is fine with me. But know that this isn't goodbye for good my dear friend." Pan reached out his hand for Lutcas to shake.

With great sorrow Lutcas said their goodbyes after they shook. Lutcas left him and went to Violina who was making her way up the street. Just like that, Lutcas felt as if he had lost someone else who had traveled the world with him.

The Streets of Orchestrasus seemed as if they went on forever. It was miles and miles of stone buildings, walls, shops, and noisy people. Violina was stomping off in anger and Lutcas walked with his head casted down sad that he lost another friend. Slowly the noise around him began to muffle. Despite all that was said, Lutcas still ended up losing another friend.

It was getting late, which made Lutcas and Violina think the activity of the city would calm down. Rather the sound became louder, and more people filled the street. It was almost overwhelming for Lutcas to witness how the city streets transformed in the evening. There were women that danced seductively barely concealing themselves and their unmentionables. Lutcas saw one woman, who had seduced a drunkard, stealing the man's belongings from his bag and pockets. He saw another man, very large and burly, drag another woman by the hair into a dark alleyway.

In the alleyway Lutcas saw what appeared to be silhouettes of sleeping folk, except they seemed to not be lively with all the flies swarming what's left of them. Lutcas at this point was better able to tunnel out his hearing and concentrate on what he could pick up. He looked over and saw a Knight talking with a man who was next to a stabbed corpse.

The man defending himself said, "Sir my brother forced his thoughts on me. He told me what to do. He endangered my status of becoming a conductor of my own fate. He didn't make me feel like a god."

The knight who didn't seem to care that much answered calmly, "Well fear not he cannot attack you with ideas any longer. Just make sure you leave him out here for the body wagon to pick up soon."

Lutcas was astonished at how much of this was going on unchallenged. But after the justification of that man's death, Lutcas didn't say a word. Bursting out from one building was a man who had colored his hair, his face covered with metal that pierced his flesh, and who seemed to be drunk, "Look at me. All gaze upon me. I am happy! Make me happy! I am as beautiful as the most godlike among us. You all must say it to me! I am the conductor of beauty and majesty!"

Personally, Lutcas wouldn't have used those descriptions when addressing that man. But he dares not say anything. He thought maybe once this person did have the beauty that bared the image of his creator. But alas it was changed from a created image to its own.

Violina seemed as equally disturbed by these displays, "Look at this Lutcas. This is all madness. There is no order here. Those who run the city don't even demand order, they encourage chaos!"

Lutcas, trying to be careful, said to her, "I must admit it is overwhelming. But you may want to keep your voice down when addressing such things. We haven't drawn negative attention yet, so we must be cautious as we look for this prince." Lutcas then looked around at all the crowds and said, "That is if it is even possible to find him."

Violina stopped and put a hand on Lutcas's shoulder, "Why don't we take a break?"

Lutcas agreed. His feet were sore, and he was exhausted from the line waiting and all that he had taken in today. The two looked for a somewhat spacious place to step out from the moving crowds. They went next to a building that didn't look like there were many people entering and leaving it.

Violina learned against the stone wall and let out a breath, "Who knows how long this will take Lutcas. There are so many people here. If a prince were to campaign against this place, I would imagine him shouting and rallying others to his side. But so many feel as if they need to make noise here that it will be impossil..."

Before she could finish her sentence, a figure cloaked in white from head to toe appeared out of the building behind Violina. Before the two could react, the man put a cloth in his hand over her mouth and he pulled her into the darkness of the nearby alleyway. Lutcas shouted her name and chased the figure down the darkness. Lutcas made it into the alleyway and could barely see the figure. Before he could pursue further another figure dropped in front of him. Lutcas then took his Lute and played a tune of moving rocks. This caused numerous stone bricks to shoot out from the walls at the figure. However, the figure was nimble and managed to avoid each one. The figure even took a smaller one and threw it at Lutcas. Lutcas unable to dodge the rock and was grazed in the head by it causing him to fall and his vision become black.

Lutcas opened his eyes to see that the sky wasn't orange as it was when he was with Violina. Now it was dark, with only the orange aura of torches lighting the city. But this was only what he was able to see from the darkness of the alleyway. In a panic he got up and grabbed his instruments. But there was none there. He shouted her name, but no one was there and there was no answer.

Lutcas rushed out into the street and shouted her name. But no answer. He cried for help, but no answer. It was as if he were facing Lyle again, but instead of being muted with silence, he was muted by the sheer amount of noise around him. He shouted again, but this time his head hurt. He was dizzy and when he touched his head it stung, and he looked to see blood on his hand.

Lutcas, who was not paying any attention was hit by a stranger who in anger shouted at him, "Hey watch it pale flesh!"

Lutcas scrambled around shouting for Violina. But the more and more he went up and down the street the more and more he began to lose his voice, the more he became dizzy, and the more tired he became.

When his legs couldn't handle it anymore, he fell next to a building out from the street. He realized now that he was truly alone. Pan left him believing he found what they were looking for, Violina now taken by an unknown figure, Chornelious deformed and buried out in the west, note out in who knows where, and Bendzo serving this very kingdom. The realization of his loneliness hit him all at once and all he could do was weep. The taste of death began to seem enticing once again.

He thought of how nice it would be to see their faces again, to see his friends, his family, again. He thought of the days when he didn't have to concern himself with the safety of others who were safe in the perfect harmony of life. He also remembered the days when he could worry about pursuing the hearts of another, he thought of Sonare. Though he hadn't much time to dwell on the good memories, he thought about seeing her again back in the village with her hair woven with garden flowers. It was if her presence could heal the crater in his heart. Then he woke up, finding himself on the side of the city streets in the morning.

He was aching all over. His head, his heart, and his feet were in a chorus of soreness from last night's events. He slowly got up and did only what he could remember he was supposed to do. Keep going till he found a way to the upper district, where he assumed the prince would be. The city wasn't as busy in the morning as it was at night. It was a funny thing for Lutcas, he was used to his home village being busier in the morning and more silent at night. But this place was a reversal of his home. Not to mention no one seemed to work and work in this place. It is all sell and consume. Speak and be heard. Accept or die.

Slowly moving through the streets, he made his way down the road. Along the way he was approached by someone out the alleyway. It was a beautiful woman. Her hair was long and brown and braided in the back. Like many of the women out here she was not modestly dressed. But when Lutcas noticed her directing his attention at him his heart raced.

The woman walked over to him and caressed the side of his face gently. Her smile was radiant, and her deep brown eyes pierced his soul, "Hey there." She said, "You don't look so good. Perhaps you could take your things over to my place and I can make you feel like a god."

Lutcas hadn't felt this sensation in a long time. The last time he felt such excitement was when he was around Sonare or when he first met Violina. Lutcas knew that she more than likely had no good intentions, but with his friends gone and with him all alone he felt so drawn to her.

Suddenly a chaotic orchestra of music began to play up ahead in the streets. Which caused the beautiful pale woman to flee. The sound came from a parade making their way to them. There was a grand float covered in various decorations. On it and marching around it were those that appeared to have come from the southern savannah or the eastern marshes. They all held instruments and seemed to just constantly make noise, despite it not particularly being in harmony with any of the other music. The instruments were attached to contraptions that allowed the user to use many instruments at once. To accompany the chaotic music was the shouting, "We the dark flesh demand that we be elevated to godhood. We demand that we be treated like gods. We demand that we ascend despite the will of the evil pale flesh who try to keep us from being like conductors!"

Amongst the chaos Lutcas noticed an elderly man who was trying to cross the road before the parade made it. But he was too slow. Upon closer inspection Lutcas recognized this man. This man was Cymbai from the monastery of the sky. Lutcas, finally seeing someone he knew, rushed towards him.

Cymbai was pushed by one of the people in the parade who said to him, "Watch it narrow eyes. Can you not see that we of the dark flesh are trying to put ourselves in our rightful place! For too long the pale flesh has been our enemy. Now we seek to rule over them as we will become conductors of our own image!"

Lutcas didn't understand why the flesh was so important to them. But Lutcas also didn't want to see Cymbai hurt. So Lutcas rushed over and helped him up saying, "Sorry I will help him move please don't hurt him."

The man in the parade laughed at him, "Bah! What a strange one. Of course, a pale flesh comes to disrupt our coronation parade! Begone filth, you tyrant, you oppressor! Go before I call the guards and tell them that you are getting between me and godhood."

Lutcas at this point had no pride. He valued the safety of his friend rather than correcting this man. But Lutcas was so confused. Why was he being called these things? He never met them before, and they threw heavy accusations at him. It almost hurt his feelings, considering that he had spent his journey trying to save the world. But he quickly led Cymbai off the main road.

Weak and tired, Cymbai said to him, "I recognize your voice. I cannot see anymore Lutcas. But my house shouldn't be far from here."

Lutcas looked more carefully at Cymbai. He was malnourished and his eyes were hazy. Somehow, he had gone blind. He didn't want to ask him how this happened until he got home. Cymbai described that his living hold is under a red sign that shouldn't be too far up the street from here. Lutcas eventually found it and returned Cymbai home.

Cymbai's home seemed to be part of a structure that contained many other homes for other residents of the city. When he walked in, he saw a mostly empty house, illuminated only by the dim light from the front two windows sandwiching the door. The floor and ceiling were made of wood along with the other furniture. There weren't any rooms really, likely due to the cramped housing the building offered. Lutcas guided Cymbai to a chair and let him sit.

Shortly after being seated another man walked into the house. He was old like Cymbai but seemed to lack personal cleanliness. His grey hair and beard held lots of hair that went everywhere. He carried a large bag on the back of him and a belt holding a variety of tools that Lutcas had never seen before. The man had narrow-eyes, just like Cymbai and Chornelious.

The man dropped his bag to the floor and only when he turned around did, he notice Lutcas, "Cymbai who is this? Did you bring in a stray?"

Cymbai laughed looking at the man's direction, "Oh Hurdo, we do not call our guests strays. Nonetheless he is no ordinary 'stray' but an important young man."

The man laughed and asked, "Who would that be?"

"Lutcas, the chosen bearer of the Strings of Harmony!"

Hurdo's attention was captured by this, "Chosen bearer? You are the one who failed this task?"

Lutcas winced at the harmful reminder of his mistakes. But before Lutcas could reply Hurdo said, "Wait Cymbai is this the same boy who was traveling with Chornelious?" Cymbai answered with a confirming nod, "Please allow me to introduce myself. I am Hurdonius Gurdaius, the magnificent maker of instruments! Or at least I was once called that till the kingdom didn't need me anymore"

As per the pattern of introductions Lutcas began to introduce himself, "It is nice to meet you. I am Lutcas."

“That's great kid. I know. Cymbai just introduced you to me.” From somewhere he took out a flask and drank a sip of alcohol, “Since you are here Chornelious must be here as well! Tell me where my precious student is.”

Lutcas suddenly felt a rush of grief. Before him was a man filled with a face of joy that sang excitement and eagerness to see someone he misses. But Lutcas knew that this was about to be erased.

He looked away from Chornelious's master and said, “I'm sorry, please forgive me.” tears swelled up in his face.

Hurdo's face transformed from confusion, to pain, to anger. He took a swig of the contents in his flask, and he grabbed Lutcas by the collar of his tunic.

The blind man shouted at Hurdo, “Calm down old friend!”

“He had the Strings of Harmony on his own instrument. Yet he allowed my beloved student to die! Why! Some of the last good I held on to in this world is gone! All that is left to my existence is the damnable city. It divides peoples, portraying each other as enemies! It separates to obstruct vision! It destroys any who challenges its ways! It seeks to empower the very beings who contribute to the fall of a once beautiful world. I once bought the ideas of this place! I gave the rulers of this place various instruments to make unruly amounts of noise. Yet they toss me out once I question their ways.” he took a breath before finishing his rant, “Oh Chornelious. This world was too cruel for you.”

The water began running down Lutcas face as he choked up speaking to Hurdo, “I am sorry. I couldn't save him. But I would imagine that he would want you to have this.”

Hurdo released his collar and allowed Lutcas to remove his bag. From the bag Lutcas took pieces of Chornelious's Hurdy Gurdy and placed them on the table. Hurdo saw the pieces of his instrument and his heart melted. Hurdo took the pieces of the instrument and held them close.

“He carried it with him. I meant to teach him how to play this one day. Tell me did he learn anything from it?”

Lutcas wiped his face, smearing the tears and answered, "Well we encountered a concertmaster who blessed us with divine knowledge on how to play certain music. So, he was gifted with some knowledge on how to play. But he taught himself how to play the music of Lightning."

He laughed and smiled, "You're telling me that he figured out how to play lightning?"

"By accident." Lutcas answered, shrugging his shoulders.

He chuckled, "Of course he learned it by accident. I am so proud of him." he took a breath and regained his composure, "tell me Lutcas. You have lost all the Strings of Harmony and have been utterly defeated. What brings you to this terrible place."

Lutcas answered, "After our defeat, me and my friends venture to the far west. When we were there a concertmaster spoke to us about a prince who would come. He said he would be filled with the concertmaster's wisdom and would do things in ways we wouldn't expect."

Cymbai's head rose in attention, "Interesting you say this Lutcas. You may recall that I told you about a vision I received on the mountain." he rests his chin in thought, "Your timing is good. For there was something I wished to investigate. I am blind as you have noticed, and I was sitting by a window of the front door. But as I was sitting, I heard many philosophers and teachers from the city come and go. But there was one voice that I heard. When I heard it, I could see the sound? I could see things I can't describe, and it was beautiful. But it was a distant passing voice and the visions left me. I tried to follow the voice but got lost in the crowd. Which is why you had to escort me home Lutcas."

Hurdo looked up from the pile of parts he was studying and asked Cymbai, "Are you saying that whoever was speaking is the same person Lutcas is talking about?"

"Yes, I believe so." Cymbai stood up, "That is why I think you two should search with me around the city. To find this Prince.

CHAPTER 12 ARIA

Violina woke up in a large bed. Her dirty tunics were now exchanged for a sleeping gown that was made from very fine fabric. To accompany the large bed was a large room filled with massive paintings and plants in highly decorated pots. On the other side of the room from the bed was a large double door stretching from floor to ceiling. Shortly upon waking up a woman walked into the room through the towering doors. The woman was young like her and wore a black and white outfit consisting of an apron and a bonnet.

Violina didn't wake up in distress, since she was able to not only sleep cleaner than she had been in a while but also in a comfortable bed. It was only when the woman walked in the room, she became confused. She remembered a moment where she was looking at Lutcas and then she was grabbed and fell asleep.

Violina was now frightened as she shouted, "Where am I? What's going on?"

The woman spoke to her, "Do not panic. You are safe in the castle of Lord Sho Naham. He expects you for lunch and hopes you will attend. I will escort you once you are prepared."

Violina was confused but she understood that she wasn't in immediate danger. If she was to be killed, they would have done it by now. Knowing this, Violina decided to comply. She noticed a large wardrobe, so she got up and opened it and saw a beautiful dress. It glittered in the light and contained many beautiful colors. She put it on and left the room to meet the maid outside. The maid took her down great large halls with more massive paintings which led to a large dining hall with a long table full of complex assortments of civil war, glasses, decorative plans, candles, etc. Sitting at the other end of the table was a very handsome man. He was a dark brown color, slim yet muscular, wearing very fine clothing that drew out his features.

Violina sat down where the maid guided her and the man at the other end of the table spoke to her, "Wow you look spectacular this morning my dear Violina."

She did not recognize this man and didn't want to come off as hostile, "My apologies but who are you?"

"Oh no. Please permit me to apologize to my lady. I have failed to introduce myself. I am Lord Sho Naham of house Naham. Right now, you are in my castle in the upper districts of Orchestrasus."

Violina looked at the food before her and could not take her eyes off it. On their journey, they didn't get to enjoy large bounties of food every day. Only the villages in the east provided that hospitality. But this food looked far greater than any food she had laid eyes upon.

Sho noticed this and said, "My dear please eat all you like. One as beautiful as you have no business not enjoying luxuries such as this."

Without question she began to dig into the food in front of her. It was as good as it looked, with various dishes and ingredients that came from faraway lands.

After he gave her a minute Sho asked her a question, "So you are probably wondering what you are doing here in my castle, yes?"

Suddenly Violina stopped eating, now with her hunger sated and she asked, trying not to panic, "Where am I? Where is my companion Lutcas? And how do you know my name?"

Sho chuckled and gave a warming smile as he answered, "You are here because I rescued you. I will speak plainly to you, my lady. I am lonely up here in my castle. My parents ended up getting themselves killed and I was looking for a partnership. I sent my family servants to spy and look and then they heard your name and all your titles from when you were permitted into the middle district. Then we rescued you."

Violina studied him carefully, "So why did I need to be rescued?"

He took a deep breath before answering her, "One of my spies was watching you closely. That is to ensure your safety until you make it to the upper district. But Zealots, whom you and your partner Lutcas rejected, were going to kill you. My spy could only save one of you."

Violina, shocked in disbelief, stared at him, "No it can't be. She stood up and began walking to the door. But the weight of grief overtook her, and she collapsed and fell to her knees. The maid with a fan tried to provide her with some air. The man in the chair stood up and rushed over to her and embraced her. Violina, devastated, didn't resist the hug. When hugged she felt Sho's warmth and his soft fabric and hair. Broken and in great desire for any comfort, she hugged him back.

Sho spoked gently to her, "My poor Violina. I know the pain of loss and its sting. But despite my wealth and influence I cannot reverse what has happened. Let me take you back to your room so that I may comfort you.

Violina tried to compose herself. A great swarm of thoughts clouded her head. She thought of Lutcas being slain, Pan potentially betraying them, Note running off in the wild, and Crafty's poor deformed body. She could only imagine what this place could do to others. She remembered back in the southern savannahs that her husband was captured and sold as a slave. She tried to think it through, but she could only conclude that he must be dead too.

Violina wiped her face, accepted the worst possibilities, and answered, "Yes I would like to go back to my room."

So Sho Naham led her to her room. He often visited her with various treats and beautiful trinkets. Normally Violina wouldn't care much for these sorts of things, but she was defeated at this moment. Every bit of care that she received from this man and his servants gave her a sensation of security and affection that was previously only given to the one she was united to, Tekoa.

A few days had passed, and she now enjoyed her time in the castle. She did not need to worry about the chaos that resided in the middle district, she didn't need to look for a prince that could not be found, she didn't need to grieve anymore. Sho Naham gave her all she needed. They even bonded well since both knew the way of the violin. With this Violina allowed herself to be united with Lord Sho Naham.

Meanwhile Lutcas, Hurdo, and Cymbia walked down the morning streets of the middle district. It wasn't busy like the nighttime streets, but it still was noisy, nonetheless. Lutcas saw much of what he saw before. Just people spouting out how they are going to be gods and should be treated as such. One thing that was new that Lutcas caught sight of was people shackled who were being led like a small herd.

Lutcas saw this and asked, "Wait why are those people shackled? Isn't this a place where we all are to be made like conductors?"

Hurdo laughed and said, "That is if you believe that load of horse fodder! There are many reasons why these people are slaves. I couldn't tell you all of them, but the statement made by King Lyle is that these people once tried to strip everyone from achieving godhood. So, they stripped them of everything including their chances of becoming gods."

This frightened Lutcas, for he had seen people in the city accuse one another of stripping each other of this title. Even he was accused of such things for only being the way he looked. It seemed like there were a lot of customs and rules that were foreign to Lutcas.

"That is crazy. Is there anything else I should know about this place? "he asked.

Cymbai answered him, "No book could contain all the cultural rules of this place, Lutcas. It changes depending on where you are and who you are with. You will just need to learn to be adaptable and quiet."

He understood this, for he had seen the middle and outer districts of the city. But he wondered what the upper districts look like. When he made it through the middle district entry point, they instructed him to go there. Would it be better or worse he wondered to himself?

“Wait, so I've seen the first two districts. But what about the upper district of the city? What is it like?”

The old craftsman took a swig of his flask and answered him, “I used to live up there. That is until I started asking questions. It is the highest point of the city with castles and fine living resting at the base of the royal podium tower. It is a strange place filled with strange customs. Some people up there even carve themselves into an odd image of what they want to be rather than how they were created.”

A loud sound interrupted Hurdo as the upper district gate opened. From it was another parade float of people. Like the one Lutcas saw before, it was full of people screaming and shouting their demands for becoming gods. The people walking around the float also wielded many wild tools that attempted to play multiple instruments at once.

Hurdo spat at the ground and said, “Look how they have abused my work. I gave them devices that could play many instruments at once, as if one person was a whole band. But they go and reproduce as many cheap replicas as possible. But none will match my craft and serve only to insult it”

Lutcas couldn’t hear much of Hurdo’s spiteful complaining over how loud the instruments in the group were. But as quickly as the loud group showed up, they became silent. Lutcas couldn’t believe his eyes. Before him he saw a group of people who demanded godhood be silenced. On top of that they began to move to the side of the road to allow something else to pass through. In fact, everyone, not only them, was doing this.

He looked down the road to see what was coming. He thought that perhaps it was the prince finally coming through to make things right. But Lutcas could smell what was coming before he even laid eyes on it. It was a smell familiar to him since the beginning of his journey. Before this stanch lingered in the city, but now it was concentrated and strong. This was the smell of death. Coming into his view was a massive wagon being pulled by a few knights. The wagon was beyond capacity, baring a mound of rotting corpses. Everyone was silent until it came out of view. Once gone, the chaotic noise began once again.

Cymbai acknowledged what just happened, "Lutcas here is some information. I know what that sound was, that absence of music and talk. That sound was death, and only that can create that silence here in this place. Death is what rules this place. All get out of its way for no one can stop it. That is why it rules over us."

After a while of wandering around the city streets, Cymbai heard a noise that drew his attention. Hurdo and Lutcas guided him to the noise. Eventually they had to stop for a reasonable sized crowd that blocked their path. Lutcas could hear a little of what the crowd was there for since the sound of a speaker was distant. Lutcas expected to see attention drawn in this city by large bands and parades, but this entire crowd was captivated by one man. Lutcas tried to see above the heads of the crowd but was shorter than most so he couldn't see. Lutcas wanted to ask Cymbai if he could see but refrained since he almost forgot he was blind.

Hurdo wasn't very tall either and he went to Lutcas, "Hey kid. Why don't I hoist you up on my shoulders so you can see what the commotion is about?"

Skeptical of Hurdo's physical and intoxicated prowess he asked, "Are you sure you can hold me up?"

The old craftsman rolled his eyes and said, "You really have picked too much up from my student, including his bad sense of humor and occasional sass. Now hurry up before we miss it!"

Lutcas allowed Hurdo to lift him while he sat on his shoulders. Lutcas was now head and shoulders above the crowd. He searched where everyone was drawing their attention towards to find something peculiar. Drawing everyone's attention was an ordinary man! He was standing on a box and looked like most others who are native to this place. He wasn't much taller than Lutcas, but he was an adult man. Really if he was in a crowd no one could distinguish him.

Lutcas was able to catch some of what was being said by this man. One of the things being, "I tell you this. This place tells you that you all need to become gods and conductors of your own making. But they are missing the mark! Instead, I will tell you this. Do not seek to become conductors of your own making, rather seek to be like the conductor who made the world and each one of you! Seek to be like that and you will find what you all are truly seeking."

Lutcas was relieved to hear what he was hearing. But he understood that he was looking for a prince, not a commoner. This was discouraging to Lutcas, so he asked Hurdo to let him down from his shoulders. He complied and let him down. The two were getting ready to leave and both noticed that Cymbai wasn't around. The two began to panic. Hurdo lifted Lutcas once again on his shoulders, allowing Lutcas to see Cymbai's shiny bald head move between people. At once the two began to pursue him. But with them both being small, it made it difficult to press through the crowd. Before they could reach him, he was already up there with the speaker.

Cymbai fell to his knees as he pressed through the last person of the crowd and he shouted, "Oh it's you! But how can it be you? I am blind but I still recognize your voice as music that Ionce heard before the tumble of this world. Oh, I apologize... For I am not worthy of being in your presence. But please save us, for I have done evil and evil as gripped this place!"

Lutcas was very confused at what he was hearing Cymbai say. He talked to this man as if he was royalty and that he knew him. He was afraid for Cymbai. Drawing attention to yourself in a place that wouldn't accept what this teacher was saying.

The teacher went up to the man, deeply moved at the sight of him, "Oh Cymbai." when he spoke it was as if he was playing an instrumental note, "You have been through much. I know what you have done, but you must know that you are not out of my reach. Now go back home."

Observing this, Lutcas was the more confused. Cymbai, a poor old blind monk who asked for help is being told to go home? This made Lutcas feel bitter towards the man. But he wondered how this man made the sound of an instrument without using one.

Suddenly Cymbai sprung up with joy, "I can see! I can see! I can see again! I have regained what was once lost to me!"

As he leapt around the crowd was shocked and gave him space when he approached. He went towards Lutcas who didn't move back. Cymbai grabbed him by the hands and spun him around in a goofy attempt to dance. The spinning caused both to fall. This wasn't the same old blind man who he helped earlier today; it was like when he was at the monastery but with joy.

Cymbai full of energy laughed and said, "Lutcas my boy! I can see once more!"

Overtaken by his energy he simply replied, "Yes I know I can see that you see." This brought on Lutcas's face what he hadn't had for a while, as smile.

"Hold up some fingers Lutcas I can show you." Lutcas held up three, "Three! Ha! Three!"

Shortly after, Cymbai skipped down the street rejoicing. Lutcas watched him for a moment and then turned back to the man who did this. However, his eyes seemed to be locked on him anyway. When Lutcas felt his gaze, it felt like he was being beckoned. Lutcas could not avert his gaze in response. The man smiled and walked away with some others following him.

Hurdo broke the tension and said to Lutcas, "Welp, I say you might have found the man you're looking for!"

Lutcas dumb struck brought himself back together, "I don't know. I am going to spy on him. Will you come with me?"

The old man scratched his neck and said, "Nah. You have given me some work to do. I need to go and fix my student's instrument. But I do hope you find what you are looking for."

The old man went back home and Lutcas went in the direction the strange man went. Lutcas weaved between people who were still in amazement following him to his next destination. He managed to get a distance that he could still see him from afar, despite his lack of height. The man went on to do many teachings that day. Lutcas saw him do and say things he would not have the power or courage to say and do.

One of the incidents Lutcas witnessed was when a woman approached the teacher, "You!" she said to the man, "I did what you asked me to do. I went to the outer district of the city and now I am confused."

Lutcas vaguely remembered this woman. She had darker flesh and was dressed like the way the people in the small parades were earlier. To this she was surprised that she was even talking to this man.

The man smiled and answered, "Tell me, what has confused you?"

The woman continued, "I went to the outer districts with my parade, to show our righteous cause. To destroy those of pale flesh who seek to oppress us all. But when I got there, I saw those of pale flesh who suffered as well. A great number of them."

"So how does this confuse you?", the man asked her.

"They all are supposed to be the oppressor, not the oppressed. They aren't supposed to be the ones that suffer, we are the ones that are suffering. They are the enemy!"

The man shook his head in denial, "My dear. They aren't the true enemy. Some lord power over others and some suffer by the hand of it. Just as all do. This is a chaotic and repeating verse in this world."

Confused, she shouted, "Then who is my enemy? The knights told us it was the pale flesh that is responsible for all this. Of what flesh is the enemy? My flesh, your bronze flesh?"

He shook his head once again, "You think too much of whose flesh does what. My father always looked at his children not by their flesh but by their heart. Follow me and you will see that there's more to this than meets the eye."

Lutcas saw this from afar peeking from around a corner of a building. Yet after the man said this his gaze didn't fail to meet Lutcas's. Quickly Lutcas darted behind the building to conceal himself.

This was the last bit of teaching he was going to do that day. Lutcas stayed around long enough to hear talk of where he would go next. After hearing this, Lutcas went back to Hurdo and Cymbai's house for the night.

He knew he could go up to the upper district, but he was afraid, and familiarity was his only security at this point.

The next morning Lutcas arose very early and made his way to the northwest side of the city, where it was said the teacher would appear next. This part of the city wasn't much different from the rest. But it seems that the roles were reversed. Back in the southwest area of the middle district, it was darker flesh protesting the pale flesh. Here it was pale flesh protesting dark flesh, saying that they are the oppressors. It was confusing, Lutcas could not tell who was responsible for doing what.

Eventually the teacher arrived and Lutcas stayed out of sight while listening and observing him carefully. The teacher taught similarly to what he taught yesterday. The spoke of not seeking to make yourself a conductor, but instead to be more like the conductor as we were supposed to be. But the teacher elaborated more on the dangers of seeking to make yourself a conductor.

One of the things he said in his lesson was, "Dwell on this. We have been promised by this place to all be made like the conductor deciding and distributing justice. But in this city, everyone seems to want something different despite all claiming the same goal. If we all were like this, we would be in chaos! The agents of chaos, the true enemy, have taken a rock and thrown it into the pond. Now the water that was once calm is now disturbed and unsettled."

Lutcas did not hear him elaborate on this. He became nervous when he saw Knights listening in on what he said. But they seemed to not understand and therefore not care. But the confusion lured Lutcas into what he said. He wondered if the rock was orchestrasus or Lyle.

Shortly after the speech many came before him to be healed. They had various assortments of issues. Lost limbs, blindness, skin disease and more. But there is one thing that Lutcas saw get healed that frightened him. A woman charged through the crowd on all fours growling and spasming. The crowd scattered at the sight of her yelling that she had a Cacophony. Lutcas never heard of such a thing before. When she approached the teacher, the crowd went silent. In the silence Lutcas could hear a faint sound coming from her. It was like a violin was being harshly and poorly played, creating a wretched screeching sound.

When this woman spoke, it sounded like ten voices spoke as one, "You Prince! The bane of my existence!" the woman spasmed and she sounded normal, "Please! The only thing they fear is you. Please help me!" she shook her head and the voices spoke again discordant, "What will you do to us? Are you here to make us suffer by your hand?"

At once before the woman could speak again the man spoke as if we were singing, "Wretched rebels leave this poor woman and never return! Be gone!"

The woman spasmed one final time in a cry that brought a chorus of dread. At once it was finished. The woman stood up on two legs catching her breath. In tears she embraced the man who freed her, and he embraced her. The crowd was frightened at what happened and they began to talk among themselves. Using this to his advantage the teacher slipped between some alleyways with a small group of others following him. But Lutcas did not lose him.

Lutcas's mind was racing with more questions than answers at this point. He couldn't understand the illustration told earlier, he didn't understand what happened to the woman, and he really didn't understand why that woman called him Prince.

After it became late the teacher was settling down for the night at someone's house. He sat with the small group of others that followed him. Joining him was the woman he spoke with yesterday and the woman he healed today. They all were eating, and they all seemed happy.

Lutcas envied this as we watched from the window. It wasn't very well lit where he was standing, and the shadow provided some cover for him. Occasionally it seemed that this teacher would look in his direction. Immediately when the head turned, he ducked beneath the window. This happened a couple of times until one time he peaked back over the window, and he was gone. Confused, he looked around till the man jumped up from beneath the window on the other side of the wall and said, "Boo!"

This surprised Lutcas where he almost fell backwards. Lutcas knew now that he had been spotted and he was thinking about fleeing. But before he could the man walked out of the front door.

The man shouted to him over the volume of the city streets, "Hey Lutcas you must be tired from following me around all day. Why don't you eat some dinner with us?"

Lutcas was surprised at the hospitality he had been offered, so with hesitation he replied, "Uhh sure. I mean thank you." Only after he answered he pondered on how this man already knew his name.

The man opened the door and let Lutcas in the house. It was like the quality of Cymbai's living quarters, but something about it made it much livelier. There were candles over a long table with drinks and some food scraped up from what little food the markets had to sell. Funny enough there was already an empty chair that was ready for Lutcas to sit at.

Lutcas was still nervous, despite the warm welcome. He had now grown used to the hostility in the city and would try to keep a low profile and avoid trouble. But now he was in the spotlight. Everyone watched him as he walked toward the empty seat, next to the head of the table where the teacher was sitting.

As he approached the seat he asked the man, "Is this seat taken?"

He smiled, "No silly. There is no one sitting in it!" the group chuckled in response.

The man who seemed to own the place asked, "So who is this that joined us tonight?"

The teacher answered, "Well why don't you tell them about yourself my friend?"

Lutcas threaded his answer carefully, mentioning his journey could be risky for his safety, "My name is Lutcas." he said timidly, "I am from the northwest green lands. I was a farmer and then I started to travel the world. Now it looks like I ended up here."

One of the people at the table protested playfully, one who had narrow eyes like Hurdo, “Come one now! Could you be any vaguer? Why did you travel the world that brought you here? Why were you following us?”

Lutcas was scared when he pointed this out and he didn’t want to bring up The String of Harmony, so he said, “I guess you can say I was on a mission to help the world. But I failed and now I am here looking for some Prince that can change everything.”

The teacher looked at Lutcas examining him closely. Lutcas felt like that answer satisfied the others but with this man he felt as if he already knew why he was there. But the look he gave wasn’t a look of skepticism, rather it was a look of understanding and compassion.

In response the teacher said, “Well maybe if you would like to follow us, not in the shadows, you might find the prince that you are looking for.”

“What do you mean?” asked Lutcas

“I mean that I don’t want you spying on us. Instead, I want you to join me and my students and follow me.”

His offer rang through Lutcas’s heart like a bell. He did not know this man and this man, he assumed, didn't know him. Hearing this invitation stretched out to him like this was a vastly comforting thing. With his friends dead, leaving, or missing, he felt lonely. But it seems that this man and his students could not only fill that void but do much more. After what he's been through, trusting someone was not easy. Yet the mere melody of his voice only emitted comfort and peace. This feeling rushed through Lutcas’s body, and he smiled.

“You know what. I think I will join you.”

The man smiled at Lutcas, “I am glad. With a musician that has traveled across the world I’m sure you will have plenty of stories to tell.”

Now curious Lutcas asked, “You know I may be late asking this, but what is your name?”

"Coda. My name is Coda." said the teacher patting Lutcas on the back.

While sitting at the dinner table Lutcas learned many of the names of the students. There were about twelve students and two additional guests not including himself. They all appeared to come from different places. Some pale with red hair, some with narrow eyes, some with dark flesh. It was as if the whole world sat at this table. They were all very friendly with Lutcas as well. They teased him, encouraged him, and laughed with him.

After dinner they all sat around getting their instruments out to play joyful music and they invited Lutcas to join them. Lutcas grabbed his Lute, but when he did, he was flooded with emotions. The last time he had done this was a long time ago while on the road with all his friends. Thinking about it made him not want to play it anymore.

Coda noticed Lutcas's hesitation and said, "What is wrong? Why do you hesitate?"

He answered, "Sorry. The last time I played this tune was at a different time. But now it is hard for me to look back at that time. A time when things were better, and all my friends were together."

Coda felt compassion for him and said, "I know Lutcas, I know. But you know I think if you played it with us then you might feel better. It is hard to look back at good times when the times may be bad now. But we cannot go back to the past. I think it is best to remember those good times and to celebrate those times that you got to experience. Then maybe, just maybe you can make another good time to look back on."

Lutcas found it hard to argue against that. So, he played his music, his tune of thankfulness. The others loved it and they shared the music they played when they were happy. Sometimes Coda would ask to join in by hitting notes with his voice as if he was an instrument, something Lutcas never heard before. Hearing all of this brought back many good memories. He remembered playing fetch with Note. He remembered playing music with Violina. He remembered sparring with Pan. He remembered laughing at some stupid comment Chornelious made. He remembered running around his home village with Bendzo. He remembered the excitement of wanting to ask Sonare to be his lifelong partner. Overall, the session playing together was re-invigorating for Lutcas.

The next morning, they went to another part of the city. This part of the city was primarily occupied by those who look like Chornelious, Hurdo, or Cymbai. It seemed that this portion of the city seemed to be occupied by many skilled craftsmen and blacksmiths. Making many instruments.

Not long after Lutcas, Coda, and the rest of the students entered the district there was an incident. An elderly man covered in splatters of blood and populated with wounds crawled to Coda. The man mostly spoke in a gibberish that Lutcas didn't understand in a sound of many voices like a band of broken instruments. Coda, like before, took care of the man who had a cacophony. He spoke in a way that sounded like music releasing the poor man from his condition.

Curious Lutcas said, "Teacher I am confused."

"Tell me Lutcas, what confuses you?" Coda replied.

"I am afraid I do not understand what has happened to these people that are acting like this. What is going on?"

The teacher looked around and then spoke to him, "Do you remember when I spoke about who is the enemy? Tell me who you thought was the rock and the puddle in my illustration."

Lutcas pondered for a moment and answered, "The puddle is us and the rock is Lyle and Orchestrasus."

"Good, you are correct about the puddle. The puddle is the world and its people. But the rock answer you gave isn't complete. There is more to it than just Lyle and Orchestrasus. More accurately let me show you the one who threw the rock into this puddle."

Coda began to hum, and he put his hand over Lutcas's eyes, which now made him uncomfortable. But once he was done humming and his hand was removed, Lutcas was amazed. Floating around Coda appeared to be lines of sheet music swirling around him slowly and in harmony. Lutcas looked at himself and some of the others passing by and saw similar lines of sheet music floating around them like an aura. But rather than those sheets being like the ones Coda had, his and everyone else's were jagged, chaotic, and in discord. Lutcas saw some individuals who had a line of music stretching up towards the roof of a building. He followed it and what he saw frightened him.

Like a tree and its roots, the chaotic and terrible lines of sheet music that Lutcas followed with his eyes led him to a frightening being. It floated and had broken rings surrounding it. It had many eyes across each ring and music notes more chaotic and terrifying than any he found on a person. Lutcas's eyes continued to search, and he saw many of these chaotic hosts floating across the rooftops of the city, spreading the roots of their chaotic sheet music. Each took a form more unsettling, disturbing, and confusing as the next. But Lutcas vaguely could make out what these were. These were concertmasters.

Seeing this sight frightened Lutcas. Before the claiming of the String of Harmony, Lutcas understood the concertmasters to be agents of guidance, teaching, and power. Now these powerful beings, who no man would dare challenge, now stand with the dark tower of Orchestrasus.

Lutcas turned to Coda, who had his finger in a hush stance, and asked while heavily breathing, "Teacher. This doesn't make any sense. Why?"

He answered him, "Now you see the one who threw the rock. I know this would be frightening to show you. But do you know what I am going to do now that I showed you this?"

"What? What can we do against such an enemy? What sword could slay such a foe?"

Coda smiled, "Not with a sword my friend. Watch me and I'll show you how to beat them."

In the district, Coda continued to do his work. He healed, taught, sung, laughed, embraced, and did many other wonders. This time Lutcas watched more carefully as he did these things. The visions of the lines of sheet music never left him. In fact, he could see it woven in everything that he looked at. The earth, the sky, and the people around them wielded an aura of lines of music. Sadly, they were all jagged and unnatural, as if everything was now in the state of this mysterious aura. But when Coda interacted with one of the people he helped or spoke to, the lines would begin to organize a bit more. The lines that connected the people with the chaotic concertmasters would vanish.

In all honesty, Lutcas didn't understand sheet music well. He didn't understand many of the symbols he saw, but he began to understand something. He understood that these lines of music were embedded in all creation and that somehow this man could restore them to a state they were supposed to be in.

Not only did Lutcas gain more insight to his time with Coda. But time serving with the other students became very pleasant. He began to know many of their names such as Cellomen, Tubas, Mandolthew, Flutip, and more. He served them doing many things. Many impossible things. Sometimes Coda's students would argue if the teacher wasn't around. But after several days Lutcas learned to love them like brothers. Lutcas felt like he had family and friends again. Somehow, he also felt that the journey he took to find the Strings of Harmony wasn't yet over.

CHAPTER 13 TRANSPOSITION

In the morning, Violina woke up in her large comfortable bed with the lord of the castle with her. It had been several days since she had been in the castle with this man. But she made no attempt to leave, for she was comforted and had no desire to leave. Here the worries of anything outside the walls didn't bother her. All her attention was on the things in the castle and Sho Naham.

Despite the previous sense of comfort, she would every now and then feel disturbed. She didn't know why but she felt as if she should go out and do something. What that something was is unknown to her? But it made her pace and toss and turn.

Sho Nahim began noticing these patterns and asked, "My dear wife, what troubles you?"

At first, she hesitated but she answered, "Sorry. I don't why but I feel like I have some sort of cabin fever. Some restlessness. By chance could we go out?"

"Are you sure my darling? You have everything you could want in here. It is dangerous out there; may I remind you? But all I want you to be is happy. If your heart so chooses this, then we may go anywhere you wish."

This was exciting for Violina, and she pondered on what she wanted, “By chance are there any horses we could go see?”

Sho Nahim smiled, “Well that I can do. I inherited a stable in the middle district of town. If you want me and my guards can escort, you are down, and we could parade around the city on horses.”

This made Violina happy, “Yes please! Let's go at once!”

Shortly, two guards and Sho Nahim were escorted out of the castle into the upper district. This was one of the few times Violina got to lay eyes on the upper district. It was much more calm and nicer than the other two districts. Strange people walked these streets. Many mutated themselves to resemble others who they weren’t and even animals. But everyone, including Violina, was always dressed nicely here. The upper district consisted of many small castles that besieged the hulking tower that resembled a dark podium.

Eventually they made their way down to one of the access points to the middle district. Their Violina saw a parade float being prepared to be marched into the middle district streets. The people who prepared this spoke of being liberated from their oppressors who made it impossible to be happy. She thought it strange that this came from those who enjoyed the vast wealth of the upper district. Nonetheless they continued.

After making past the access point, they muddled their way through the crowds and noise of the middle district. Occasionally a cart full of corpses would pass by, muting the roaring streets of Orchestrasus. She was able to observe the middle district more carefully now that she had a sense of security. What was odd that she witnessed was many bodies being placed on the walls of the districts, away from public access. What made it strange on top of bodies not being disposed of was many instruments being placed near the bodies.

Soon they made it to the stables. Like any barn, it reeked of animals. But to Violina this wasn’t a bad smell but a familiar one that brought her to a once better time. This was apart from the surrounding chaos and the slaves that worked it. Sho Nahim showed her many of the beautiful horses that he had. They towered over the horses she normally saw and were well behaved. At one-point Sho needed to talk with the stable master, leaving Violina to enjoy the horses.

In the corner of her eye, she saw one of the slaves who looked very familiar. He was tall, but not very muscular. He had somewhat long curly red hair and tended to one of the horses. His face was populated with freckles and his eyes were green. Suddenly it hit her at once. This was Tekoa! She rushed over to the stall where he was working. Upon a second look it confirmed that this was indeed Tekoa!

She said in a loud whisper, "Tekoa?"

Despite it being a loud whisper, he could hear her voice through the chaos outside and he turned, "Violina? Violina! It's you! I can't believe it is you!"

Now in tears and unable to hold herself back she leaped at Tekoa and began to kiss him. He embraced her and did the same. This was the happiest she felt in a long time, more so than the time with Sho Nahim. After racing across the world of Symphonia she finally caught up to the rider of the north. She finally could see, hear, and embrace her one love.

However, this moment was broken rather quickly. Suddenly one of the guards ripped Violina from Tekoa and the other detained him. Joining them shortly was Sho Nahim, with a face full of someone who felt betrayed.

He said, "So after all I did for you? You decided to do this to me?"

Violina didn't answer, for now she was ashamed in front of Tekoa. Tekoa couldn't take his eyes off her. He was scared, confused, and hurt that she did this, for he knew what Sho meant. But his emotions were mixed with confusion, hurt, and joy.

Sho Nahim continued, "Come let us see what the public will make of you and your real love you wretched woman!"

Meanwhile, Lutcas and his fellow students were listening to a public lesson from Coda. However, the lesson was interrupted by some ruckus close to where they were. Lutcas looked to see some white cloaked men walking down the street beating a red-haired young man to the ground. He tried to fight back but it was pointless. Following this was the weeping of a familiar voice. There was Violina being dragged by the arm from a fine dressed and handsome man. The man saw Coda, who was standing on a box, and marched his way. The crowd made way for them as they approached.

Sho Nahim approached and shouted to Coda, "You there! The people gather to hear your wisdom do they not?"

Coda looked at Tekoa and Violina and felt sorrow, "Well I can only hope that it is really wisdom you are after. What do you seek?"

The angry lord shouted, "I'm glad to have run into a man full of wisdom, for I seek justice! Philosopher, I must know what to do with this woman."

Lutcas's heart began to race, and he was full of fear. Violina was being put on the spot. He was certainly relieved that she was alive, but he feared it wouldn't be for long. So, he watched what happened with great stress.

"Tell me more about this woman." Coda asked.

"She was in union with this man. Then she leaves him and comes to me, and I give her everything. But she goes right back around and goes to him. She has violated our union and she has made me feel less than a conductor. Now what should happen to her?"

Lutcas wasn't sure how much of what he was hearing was true. But he could tell Violina was in a state of powerlessness in this situation. Coda squatted down to look at Violina. She only gave a look that cried out for help. But after sitting there for a moment, Coda began to take a stick and draw on the ground. In fact, he did this for an awkward amount of time where people even began leaving the scene.

After a while Sho Nahim said, "Ha! I get it now! She is so wretched and pathetic that she isn't even worth the time! Come on men, let us return to the castle and begin searching for a new woman!"

Sho Nahim, his men, and the crowd, all left the scene. Leaving Lutcas, Coda, the students, Violina, and Tekoa. Lutcas was baffled about how that even worked, but he didn't question it. He simply went over to comfort Violina. Tekoa was just as confused, he was captive in the stables as a slave and now he is suddenly left out and freed. Without more fights he went to embrace his wife, and Violina embraced him in return. She was now in a place of relief, she not only survived that, but she got her friend and husband back in the process.

In tears she asked Coda, "What did you do? Who are you? Why did you help us?'

Not answering the first question he answered, "My dear Violina and Tekoa, I am glad to see you finally back together. I'm sure Lutcas is happy to see you too. You've been through a lot together. I am sure he would like you to stay with us for a while."

Lutcas whispered to Violina, "Yes please come with us. He might be the one we are looking for."

Violina glanced back at Coda and replied in a whisper, "What do you mean he is the one? He is no prince?"

"Trust me. You will see what I mean."

She looked at Coda again and thought, but then Tekoa intervened, "Violina. We owe this man our lives. I think the very least we can do is accept his invitation."

She pondered for a moment and then answered, "I think I would love to accept your invitation."

Coda smiled and said, "Very good! I'm so happy! Now let us continue our day."

The rest of the day continued like every other day with Coda. Many teachings and healings happened and Lutcas witnessed more of the lines of music being restored as they traveled. Violina was more studious and scholarly than Lutcas was, so she tended to ask more critical questions.

During one speech Coda said, “I tell you to love your enemy and those who seek to do you harm. For the enemy has fooled you into thinking that only peace and godhood can be ushered by eliminating one another. But it leads to the very opposite!”

But Violina replied, “Coda, there was a friend I once had. He would oppose this. He told me that in a world full of wolves, one cannot live like a sheep, or one will be slaughtered.”

Coda smiled and said, “It sounds like your friend wishes to live like a wolf. And yes, we are living in a kingdom full of wolves right now dear Violina. But we are preparing for a new kingdom, where wolves have no place. The world was never intended to be full of those who live off death, but in my father’s kingdom death will be absent.”

This was one of the few times that Lutcas heard this idea being teased. But Coda was very vague and mysterious about whatever this kingdom was. But since Violina’s arrival in the group this topic was touched on more by Coda.

As they traveled, Lutcas finally got to meet Tekoa. Tekoa didn’t meet Lutcas’s expectations. For someone as beautiful as Violina to portray him as a paragon of beauty, he expected him to fit more of the standards of beauty found in the city. But Tekoa, Lutcas, and Violina shared many of their tales from around the world. Tekoa had many stories of dashing escapes with his steed, beautiful views of the world, and more. He was also quite amused with the events that Lutcas and Violina went through together.

Violina ended up staying with the group, growing, and bonding with them. However, some nights when the others would play songs together, she couldn’t be due to her lack of instrument. Due to this she would often sit alone.

Coda noticed this and approached her, “Violina, tell me what is wrong. Why do you not join us?”

She replied, “King Lyle, broke my instrument. I have nothing to do music with you all.”

Coda, full of sympathy, responded, “Well allow me to show you something that I will show everyone else.” he grabbed the rest of the student’s attention and spoke, “Alright, so it is about time I showed you all this. Music is a beautiful thing that the conductor weaves the world with. It was given as a gift to allow creation to bring forward more life! But as you can see it is not always used for that anymore, some even choose to no longer play music, and some are even stripped of that choice. Like Violina here, she cannot play music without her violin. But I will show you a new way to play music. A way that can help restore the world to as it was. For this music is from the kingdom yet to come, use it and what was lost can be found again. It will not have its full power until the right time. But let me teach it to you.”

After talking he instructed them on how to make music with their vocals. It was strange for Lutcas, since he wasn’t used to speaking while playing an instrument. But to this and everyone else’s surprise, their voices sounded more and more like music. It was so great that for the remainder of the night they used the music of voice. Coda told them that with this they could heal others like he did, and they would spread out and play these songs one day.

Early the next morning Coda woke Lutcas up to run an errand. It was simply to go to the market and grab some supply. Lutcas noticed that it was only him and Coda, which gave him an opportunity to talk to him about something that was on his heart. A guilt that he hid from his fellow students and Coda. But Coda had earned enough trust with Lutcas for him to be vulnerable.

Lutcas with caution said to his teacher, “Coda I have something to tell you. Something that I hadn’t told any of the other students.”

“Go on.” Coda replied with great interest.

“You know how I said I was going around the world. That I was trying to find a way to stop all of this from happening? Well, I was trying to recover the Strings of Harmony. You see, me and my friends were on a divine mission. We were sent to retrieve as many of the Strings of Harmony as we could. But we often couldn’t beat King Lyle to most of them. We got three of them, but we didn't listen to a warning. In a moment where we thought we could grab the rest of them, we disobeyed and lost everything. It's our fault that the world collapsed like this Coda. The world was put on the shoulders of me and my friends. But we failed. I cannot hide this from you anymore. I am wicked and do not deserve to be your student."

Coda was deeply moved by Lutcas. Without saying anything he embraced Lutcas. He didn't understand why Coda did this. He thought that once people figured out what kind of failure, he was that he would be sent away. But he accepted this and allowed his tears to fall on Coda's tunic.

Coda finally answered Lutcas, "I know this. I know that once the burden of this world was on your shoulders. In fact, many were sent here before to share that same burden. But I want you to know that no one in my group of students is perfect Lutcas. The burden of the world is no longer on your shoulders, but I put it on mine instead."

Naturally Lutcas was confused, and he asked, "What do you mean it's on your shoulders?"

Coda chuckled and answered him, "When you first met me and my students you said you were looking for a prince. Lutcas your journey is not for nothing. I am the prince. Heir to the new kingdom of Podiem."

Lutcas was overjoyed. He followed him because he suspected such things. But to hear it come from him was such good news! Lutcas felt a sense of hope that overtook him with happiness.

"I will explain more of it later to the others. But go on and run your errand."

Lutcas obeyed and skipped through the streets. The chaotic noise and the evil around him no longer bothered him because he acknowledged that in the end this was all powerless. He began to imagine how everything would be once Coda fixed everything. In his thoughts and his speedy skipping he bumped into someone carrying a basket of flowers.

He apologized and began to help gather the spilled contents. When he looked up, he saw the most beautiful girl he had ever seen. Long blonde hair with northern flowers woven into it. Lutcas snapped out of the infatuation and noticed it was Sonare! Sonare didn't notice him yet due to her picking up the contents of the basket.

"Sonare?" he said quietly.

The beautiful girl looked up and said, "Lutcas? Is that you?"

"Yes! It's me Sonare! I am so glad to see you!"

"Where have you been all this time? Bendzo and I didn't see you when we were escorted here from our village. What have you been up to?" Sonare's eyes scrolled up and down Lutcas giving a not impressed glance at his clothes and cleanliness.

Lutcas, still overjoyed, said to her, "Sonare I have been on a crazy journey. I've seen the world of Symphonia and now I am working with the prince that will usher in a new and beautiful kingdom! It's going to be great!"

When he said this, Sonare's unimpressed expression changed, "Prince? New Kingdom? You mean King Lyle when he ushers in a utopia where all can be gods themselves?"

"No. That will pale in comparison to this kingdom! This will be far greater."

Sonare began to twirl her fingers through her hair, "That does sound marvelous. I bet you will be seated high in this kingdom since you are working directly with this Prince."

"I don't know. But I can't wait for it to happen!"

Now interested she gracefully rubbed Lutcas's arm, "Well why don't you tell me more about it tomorrow? Right here at the same spot? I'll be waiting to hear more from you and this new kingdom."

At the touch of Sonare, Lutcas was immobilized with love. He agreed and both went along to run their errands. Though he would often look back at the beauty of Sonare that he long hadn't laid eyes on. Now he was even happier as he ran his errand.

Eventually he did return, and the day was different from the other days. Instead of going out to the public and teaching crowds, Coda taught to his students specifically. The teacher finally revealed who he was, and the others were amazed. This sparked many questions from each student.

Off topic Violina was curious about something, "Teacher, the other day I saw knights place corpses on the rooftops and walls of the middle district. Do you know what that is about?"

Coda glanced at the walls and said, "Well I suppose King Lyle has something big planned."

One of the students Mandolthew asked, "Do we know what that something is? Do we have an answer to it?"

The teacher answered, "Don't worry. I have something far bigger planned."

Flutip, another one of the students responded, "Oh please tell us! Will it be how you will achieve victory over Orchestrasus?"

Coda's usual bright face became downcast, and he said, "I cannot speak of this yet. But I will tell you this much. We talked about living like a sheep versus a wolf. Soon I will show you how the sheep will overcome the wolf."

The next morning Lutcas was sent on another errand assigned by Coda. Lutcas without question agreed to run the errand, despite it being so early in the morning. Right before Lutcas ran off to do the errand Coda grabbed him by the arm.

"Lutcas, I want you to listen to me. I know what your heart has been troubled by. What I must do to be victorious will be scary. But I want you to stay strong for me, okay?"

Lutcas agreed with unquestioning loyalty and ran the errands, with joy causing his heart to be naive to what he said. He leaped across the streets full of energy and joy. He scanned the streets in case he was able to come across Sonare again. When he began heading back, he ran into Cellomen, who was in a panic.

"Lutcas!" he shouted, "Lutcas! Something terrible has happened!"

"Cellomen! What is it? What's wrong?"

“It's Coda! Our brother Tubas came back with a battalion of knights. They captured him. He is now in trial in the upper district public court! At the sight of this we were no match for the knights, so we fled.”

In deep fear and distress Lutcas asked Cellomen, “Can we get there? I need to get to him!”

“This court is a space between the walls of the upper and middle district. We can get there, but if we are seen we will have the same fate as him. That is if we are noticed as his students.”

“Fine but I need to get to him.”

Reluctantly Cellomen said, “Okay fine. I'll show you. But the odds are that he has been executed already.”

The two ran swiftly towards the court where Coda was being tried. Eventually they got to an almost dome-like structure. They didn’t dare take the main entrance due to the risk of being noticed. Lutcas took his Lute and played a tune of shifting stone. This allowed stones to pop out of the structure where they could climb it. Once they made it to the top of the dome, they saw what was below. It was almost like an arena with many civilians serving as spectators. In some of the higher seats were higher ranked officials of the city. At the highest seat was King Lyle watching this all with discontent.

It had been a while since Lutcas laid eyes on Lyle. He didn’t appear to be well. He was much paler than before and there was heavy baggage under his eyes. But Lutcas could see the notes and lines that enveloped Lyle like an aura. It was so chaotic and unnatural it made Lutcas want to puke.

In the middle of the arena there was Coda, shackled to a rod in the middle of the arena. Some of the higher officials would come forward and try to play music to execute him. They had large and powerful instruments that had to be wheeled in like Pianos, sets of drums, or the contraptions Hurdo made. They tried to play discordant melodies of death, torture, and confusion. As they tried to play these tunes, Coda writhed and yelled in pain. It was hard for Lutcas to watch, but he had to because he was waiting on him to just stop and say enough. But that didn’t happen.

After all the failed attempts to kill Coda, King Lyle finally did something. He brandished his Lyre, now strung with all seven of the Strings of Harmony. He didn't need to walk, since the power of the Strings allowed him to simply float over to him. He landed right next to Coda and spoke to him but wasn't heard from anyone else.

Then King Lyle turned to the crowd and spoke with a booming voice, "People of Orchestrasus. This one as valiantly withstood the test of execution. He is showing the strength of those who wish to strip godhood from you all. He even said himself that he wishes us to be sheep instead of wolves. Are we to be eaten like he says? No! I will make an example of the one who seeks to keep us from becoming conductors ourselves!"

Lyle then played what was only comparable to the most powerful piece of music ever done. A piece only done as an act during creation. A song. Lutcas looked up and saw all the chaotic concertmasters float over and join his song, with their lines of music entwining with this. This was the Song of Damnation.

In a torrent of chaos, Coda was lifted in the air, and he let out a great cry before his life ceased. Lutcas saw the lines of music vanish around him. Lyle continued to play the song and Coda's body was shot far away over to the dark tower that loomed over Orchestrasus. There we were hung up like a trophy. His blood could be seen trickling down the side of the mockery of a podium.

Lyle turned back to the crowds and said, "Alas, the rebel of my kingdom is no more. Look at my podium and see that my throne is built on the defeat of those who take godhood from us. Now you all go forth and anticipate the godhood I will soon bestow upon all of you."

Afraid, Lutcas and Cellomen fled. They did not even flee together in the panic they were in. All the hope that Lutcas had gathered was gone almost in an instant. Lutcas feelings began to resurface. He ran around the city looking for some sort of help or sign. He couldn't find Violina, Tekoa, or any of the other students. He was alone, left to a world that would soon devour everything. The prince that was going to save the world was now defeated. A hunger arose in Lutcas again. He hungered for the taste of death itself, so he didn't have to suffer this loneliness and despair any longer.

CHAPTER 14 ADAGIO

It was becoming much later in the day. Lutcas wandered the streets as if he were a husk of a once living thing. He was in such grief that it felt nothing mattered. As he walked down the street, he noticed that this was the part of town where he agreed to meet Sonare later today. A small spark of hope kindled in him. He thought that perhaps she could comfort him in this time of distress.

As it got later in the day, Lutcas saw more and more immodestly dressed women come out and try to seduce whomever they could. Soon Sonare appeared, who was dressed much like the other women he was seeing. She skipped over to Lutcas, who was trying to make his downcast face more joyful.

Sonare rubbed his arm and neck and spoke softly to Lutcas, "Hey there. I am glad to see you again, high servant of the new king. Now tell me more about the wonder of this new kingdom, the riches you will have, and the happiness that will usher from it!"

Lutcas was afraid that she would bring this up and he answered her downcast, "Oh Sonare. It was another false hope. The man who I believed could save us is gone. He was executed earlier today."

Sonare's face went from bright to disgusted in an instant, "Then we have nothing more to talk about your filth."

This was like a blade that ran through Lutcas's heart, "w-wait. Please Sonare, don't leave me. I have something to tell you. Something that I meant to tell you before everyone left the village." She turned and raised an eyebrow awaiting his answer, "Sonare, at the big harvest festival back home. I was going to ask you to be in union with me. You are so beautiful, graceful, kind, and caring in all you do. That's why I was so happy to see you again!"

Sonare sighed inconvenienced, "You poor pathetic thing! I will tell you this only once. I use my body and give love to only those who offer me security and power. Without any of those things, one can't live like a conductor. You will only drag me down to your dirt level. So why don't you get lost and drag some other poor girl in the mud with you."

She walked away and her last words were like the finishing blow of a battle. Lutcas fell on his knees and wept. If only he had a sword with him, would he drive through himself, a sorry excuse for a human. Thoughts raced through him, telling him he wasn't good enough. That if he was, he wouldn't have lost his friends, the Strings of Harmony, or Sonare's heart.

Another pair of hands began to rub Lutcas shoulders as he wept and the voice of a woman spoke, "Dear young boy. Why don't we get to my living quarters so I can make you feel better?"

Lutcas in a state of emotional defeat and weakness accepted. He turned to see a close to middle aged woman with blonde hair and pale skin. Lutcas wouldn't normally do this, but he was in such need for comfort and love that he couldn't and wouldn't refuse.

Suddenly a familiar voice sounded behind Lutcas, "Mother?" he turned to see Pan standing behind him.

Pan looked bigger than before and didn't wear his armor. Instead, he wore a large cloak concealing most of his body, yet unable to conceal signs of bulk. His face was painted in a portrait of confusion and hope.

His mother didn't share the same expression, "Pan. That can't be you're dead, aren't you?"

"No mother, I am right here. I thought I would be asking you that. I was certain that I would find you either a slave or dead."

His mother replied carelessly, "Well I would be one of those two if I hadn't followed the wisdom of our King Lyle. I simply did what I had to do to escape those bandits."

Pan had a bad feeling go up his spine and he proceeded carefully, "Yes, the great wisdom of Lyle. How did you escape mother?"

"It was when I was being held hostage at a fort. A group of knights tried to reclaim the fort from the bandits that took it. The knights managed to get some of us out, with me in mind due to my beauty. They gave me a chance to go back and get your brother, but I did what Lyle's wisdom would do. I left him to ensure my safety. At first, I thought it was bad, but the people here encouraged me and said that I just did what I needed to do to work towards godhood. Now here I am! A goddess of beauty!"

Lutcas couldn't believe what he was hearing. Pan's own mother blatantly stated that she ditched her own son, his brother, to save herself. It was clear then that this place erased any trace of guilt of what she had done. He looked to see Pan's face now a portrait of rage, far greater than any before then.

Pan spoke unsettlingly calm, "So that is it huh? You left my dear little brother to die to save your sorry self. You speak about this without guilt, without pain. Here let me give it to you."

Pan at lightning speed drew his sword and thrusted it into her stomach. Before she could scream, Pan covered her mouth with his hand covered in a leather glove. The place that she was stabbed wouldn't kill her instantly, and Pan knew that.

Pan then spoke, "I went across the world to find you and Tuner. I found him dying and I told him the story you used to tell us. But I see that you weren't there for that! My goal since I found him was to avenge him and save you. But I see that it would have been better for you to have ended your miserable existence then. Goodbye mother."

Pan quickly removed the blade from her and then used it to remove her head. Her body dropped to the road and the head rolled holding an expression of great fear. Pan then took a flask and poured its contents on the corpse. He then played a tune of sparking fire to ignite the flammable substance.

Lutcas was surprised to see nobody react. But death to them was such a common thing, that it wasn't worth their time to stop. Truthfully it was painful for Lutcas to watch. He knew how much he loved his family, even if that love manifested in vengeance. But Lutcas didn't know what to think of what Pan did. But it seems to be how they are different. Lutcas wanted to die after being betrayed, but Pan wanted to kill those who betrayed him.

Pan, after igniting her body, sat on the ground, and watched it burn. Lutcas sat next to him not knowing what to do.

Pan spoke to him, "Lutcas I am sorry."

"Why are you apologizing to me?" he replied.

"I made you watch such a terrible ending to my journey. But I'm sorry for leaving you and for what happened today with your teacher and I'm sorry about what happened about Sonare." Pan put his shoulder over Lutcas's to give some comfort, which really was an attempt to disguise his own need for it.

Lutcas accepted it but then thought to ask, "Wait, Pan how did you know about my teacher?"

"The zealots have been keeping an eye on him. They found his activity strange. When they reported seeing both you and Violina with him I was going to join. But I waited too long."

"Tell me Pan, what did you think of him?"

"No doubt he wielded amazing power, power that he gave to ya'll. But he isn't the prince that we are looking for. Sadly, like many before him he is still bested by death. But I guess I might be able to give you some good news. There is another who may be the prince you're looking for. Plus, he has a plan to defeat Orchestrasus. I've guided Violina and Tekoa there already. We are waiting for you there."

Without anywhere else to go and with a great desire to see his friends again. He agreed. Pan led him down a series of alleyways that eventually led into a tunnel. This was the entrance to the catacombs of the city. It was a series of complex tunnels running beneath its surface. Lutcas noticed that when he was in the tunnels, he heard a hum. Pan explained that a musical key was placed in some of the stones to conceal the presence of the catacombs.

After making their way through many windy tunnels, they made it to a large series of rooms. All were well lit with torches. Lutcas saw men who were training in the art of combat and those crafting weapons and instruments. Eventually Lutcas was led to a room that appeared to be a place of planning. There were a ton of people surrounding the table and they were all talking.

One of the people at the table was Hurdo, who turned to Lutcas and said, "Well! It looks like Pan is back and he brought back Lutcas!"

From the table Violina and Tekoa looked and moved over to embrace him, "I am glad to see you here. I was so scared after they took away Coda." said Violina.

"Me too", he replied, "But I am surprised to see that you have actually joined the zealots."

"Yes, I was reluctant to. But after what he told me, I knew that we had to take some action and fast."

"Who is he?"

From around the table came a very familiar face to Lutcas. It was a face that he hadn't seen since the beginning of his journey. In fact, one might say it was the one who was responsible for starting it all. It was Guil. However, Guil's body was by no means in good condition. He was missing an eye, some fingers, and was covered in scars that seemed to be caused by blades and burning. His body was now a product of the torture done to him by his family.

Guil opened his arms to Lutcas and said, “Well aren’t you a sight for a sore eye.”

Lutcas ran and embraced him ignoring his frightening appearance, “Guil! I'm so glad to see that you're alive. I am so sorry that I failed to succeed in the journey you gave to me.”

“It's alright, friend. We cannot change the past. But right now, we have bigger issues. Come join us at the table. There is someone you must meet.”

Lutcas approached the table and saw many maps and drawings of the city. But before Lutcas was able to study them Guil brought him to the man he was supposed to meet.

“Lutcas, this man’s name is Clarence. He is the leader of the Zealots.”

The man was tall, thin and pale, yet still resembled someone who was originally from the middle lands of Symphonia. He was aged more than most, yet he still seemed healthy. He was also smoking some sort of pipe as his face looked always skeptical of something.

He leaned down with his tall body and said, “Ah you must be Lutcas. Pan, my finest warrior, as spoken highly of you. Glad to see that he has such good friends. But come, we didn’t want to have this emergency meeting without you.” He grabbed everyone’s attention, “Alright everyone now that everyone is here, we can officially get started on the briefing.”

The room took a moment before it was quiet, “All right. I thank you all for coming to this dire meeting. For I understand that not all here are zealots and don’t agree with everything we work for. But as many of you have been told before you arrived, we have a reason to collaborate. Our intelligence says that King Lyle’s plan to recreate all Symphonia will begin the day after tomorrow.”

A rush of panic swelled in Lutcas. He wasn’t sure when Lyle would try something like this. But he had spent so much time in Orchestrasus that it felt as if it were never going to happen. But to learn that it would happen so soon was frightening.

Clarence continued, “Now for many of you understand that this is not good news. But the rest of the city would say it is. So somehow, we need to figure out a way to stop the process of this recreation event from happening. Guil here will brief on the details of what we know.”

Guil stepped forward and spoke, “Okay people this is what we could gather about this ritual that my older brother is trying to do. To do something to this scale he must play a song using his lyre and the Strings of Harmony. But despite that much power, it will take more than that. An entire orchestra of music on an unreasonable scale is needed. It is evident that they have the numbers they need, since rushed production of instruments has been halted. We also know that Lyle will be doing this on the top of the podium tower. It is reasonable to say that he will be guarded by his royal guards while he does this song. That is basically all we know and now Clarence will share what we have of our plan thus far.”

Clarence spoke up, “Thank you Guil. So here is our plan. During this time, it seems that Lyle will be vulnerable while playing this song. So, he will be guarded by one means or another. The trick is figuring out how to get to him. First, we will scatter our men in the middle district to push into the upper district. This will cause a diversion where we will send a swift team of our strongest to use the catacombs to get in the podium tower. We must count on this team being swift and decisive to infiltrate the tower, defeat the royal guards, and stop Lyle. After this we will place Guil in to fill the role of his brother and be the new king. So that is the plan so let us discuss.”

One of the members at the table, who Lutcas didn’t recognize asked, “Alright let's start with this swift decisive team. Who do you think should be on this team?”

Clarence answered, “Pan will be on this team without a doubt, since he is our finest warrior. He also personally recommended Lutcas and Violina since he has traveled with them and seen much of their skill.”

Pan added, “If I may add, after our observations of this Coda individual. Violina and Lutcas learned a new kind of musical power from him. If it's the same, then it should have many healing properties. Very useful in battle if one of us is wounded."

"Indeed", Clarence continued, "Along with Pan, Lutcas, and Violina we also think that Hurdo would be a good choice as well. This is due to his mastery of one of the most powerful instruments ever forged. Additionally, me and Guil will be joining them as well, although we are not the most formidable of fighters."

Hurdo then asked, after swelling up with pride from Clarence's first comment, "If you are not as fit for battle like you say you are then why do you go?"

Guil explained to him, "This is because of the Strings of Harmony. From what I have observed, they seem to go into their normal state based on the intentions of the user. So, if whoever will replace Lyle from among us is to grab the Lyre with the Strings of Harmony, then we assume it will help correct everything back into place."

Another unknown member at the table asked, "Well then who do we have lined up to take the throne? That is if the first candidate fails?"

Guil replied, "I am the first candidate, as I am in line next for the throne of my family. Next is Clarence, due to his leadership prowess over the zealots. Finding the next two candidates is tricky, however. Personally, I vote for Lutcas and Violina to serve as candidates, for they have seen the collapse of the world and the claiming of the Strings themselves. Though they lack leadership experience, I believe with the right guidance they would be great."

Lutcas was anxious about this. He looked at those around the table carefully to see the flow of musical lines and notes around them. Alas, none even compared to the harmony of Codas. Guil, Clarence, Violina, and himself were all surrounded by imperfect auras broken and discordant. Lutcas couldn't help but remember his frightening vision back in the west. But he knew Coda was gone and that whatever they could do surely would be better than what Lyle had done.

After this they continue to plan further. Though many of the details seemed to go over the uneducated mind of Lutcas. So, he tried his best to remember what he needed to do. They picked the order of candidacy as first Guil, then Clarence, Lutcas, Violina, and finally Pan. The group at the table refined that plan a bit further by organizing the attacks from the middle district. This allowed more opportunity for the small team to have received back up if they pushed through. After discussing the allocation of men and strategy, they went over what the inside of the tower was like and how they would go about it. This led to the idea of sending a team head of Guil's team, in order to help make a path if need be.

Before the meeting concluded Violina asked a question, "If I may, how certain can we be of the time of all this? Do we know for sure it will happen the day after tomorrow?"

Clarence said, "This intelligence comes from reliable spies. However, you are wise to question this since we may not be precisely correct on this. One thing we gathered is that for some reason they waited until after the execution of Coda to do this. After this meeting we will begin to organize posts at once in case this happens sooner than expected"

Not long after this question was asked the meeting concluded and everyone went to work. Before being taken to their housing quarters, Pan and some of the zealot soldiers showed them the place where they would be heading when the mission began. But they didn't go much further with risk of detection. Lutcas couldn't understand how someone could memorize directions in a place with such repeating hallways and corridors. So, he planned on relying on others' memories to navigate.

The living quarters were like that of a military barracks. With rooms full of bunks, not extremely well kept but the best it could be for an underground barracks. At Least they did have the decency to have a woman's barracks and a men's barracks.

Soon it was dinner time. Everyone that wasn't doing field work went into the dining hall. Like the rest of the barracks, it wasn't very nice, but the people there were able to give everyone some food. Lutcas noticed that some of the food served may have been rotten or bad, but he was so hungry that the bad taste didn't even bother him. What made dinner better was that he was able to talk to his friends again. Guil told him what happened after his capture and how he managed to escape. He did apologize to Lutcas though for not telling him of his presence when he arrived, since it was top secret. Pan shared all the training and missions he had to do after he met Clarence and Guil. Eventually he earned the title Pan, the blade master. Lutcas and Violina shared with Guil what happened around Symphonia on their adventures.

After dinner Pan took Lutcas and Violina to the forges to get outfitted. Lutcas once again was given a sword, since that was really the only weapon, he knew anything about. Violina was offered a weapon and a violin with the bladed bow. But she refused and took the regular Violina and bow instead.

After this Pan and Lutcas sparred with each other. It was a throwback to a time when he was on the road. Lutcas wanted to do this in case he needed to use his sword, despite him planning on using his lute more. Pan had reached a level of swordsmanship far beyond Lutcas now. It was clear that he had grown much stronger than before. So, Pan went easy on him to bring him back up.

After sparring everyone went to bed, except the zealots who were on night watch, patrol, or were spying. The barracks became full of the stench of sweaty, dirty, bloodthirsty, broken, and hurt men. Lutcas had a great deal of trouble falling asleep. This was not due to the conditions they were in, but due to the number of things Lutcas had on his mind. He was glad to see all his friends again, but he was stressed of the upcoming battle. The very world was at stake, and it would all be decided in a battle soon to come. He tried to comfort himself saying that it would all be fixed soon.

The next day was back to the meeting board. This was to go over the plan again and to station everyone to their posts to drill on the plan. Nothing much was changed about the plan. Just some troop and resource allocation decisions. Tekoa ended up being assigned to the group infiltrating the tower, who was also granted a place in candidacy for a replacement king due to how he witnessed the world. After the meeting was over, all the zealots were called in to do drills. Everyone practiced getting their equipment and running to their stations. Those who would besiege the upper district were led to tunnels and passageways that would take them to the middle district. The team ahead of them and Guil's team would head down a series of tunnels that would lead right to the podium tower.

After the drills everyone either resumed training, their post, or making sure they had everything they needed like armor or weapons. Lutcas went with his whole team to insure preparations. Everyone ended up getting armor of some kind. For the physically weaker, they were given lighter leather armor to allow faster movement. For the stronger, they were given a fair amount of plate armor. Pan still had his unique armor he picked up from the battlefield. What amazed Lutcas was how many weapons Pan carried. On his back was something that carried many weapons. Up and down his legs and arms were places to store either short swords or knives. On his waist he had two hand axes like how Bendzo carried him. On his back were two long swords and some javelins.

Lutcas commented, “Well you sure are prepared, aren't you?”

Pan smiled and said, “It's nothing much. You can't be two careful you know.”

Guil laughed and said, “It's nothing? They don't call you the master of blades for nothing Pan! I am sure that nothing will stop us from mowing down the enemy!”

Lutcas examined Guil carefully. He seemed to be wearing prosthetic fingers to help him play his instrument better, which was a guitar. But this Guil wasn't the same Guil that Lutcas knew before. He felt that if asked about it earlier, Guil would oppose such means of violence. But Lutcas knew that they had no choice but to use it. He only wished he could have seen Guil again where he was not tortured and cut up.

The day went on but with no sign of anything happening. They ate, trained, and trained some more. Lutcas wanted to be sure he was ready to go into battle. But he didn't want to physically wear himself out. So, after training with Pan, he would go back to play some music with Guil and Violina. It was impressive to Lutcas, since Guil and Violina were around the same level in terms of what music they were able to play. Eventually night came and everyone slept at their posts awaiting the signal to go.

It seemed that everyone was restless, knowing that this would happen soon. Lutcas wondered if it would even be the correct time. A part of him wished that it wasn't right. He wished this so that he could have more time to prepare. But he knew that no amount of time could ever make him prepared. So, a part of him wished to get it over with now.

It felt like it took an eternity to fall asleep and only a moment when he opened his eyes again to see Pan say to him, "Lutcas it is time!"

CHAPTER 15 RONDO

Energy surged through Lutcas. He heard these words, and he sprang to his feet, "Are you sure this is it?"

Pan answered, "Scout showed unusual activity in the city. Knights are mobilizing all around."

Suddenly a booming voice echoed throughout the city, it was Lyles, "My dear people! Salvation is upon all of you! It is right in your grasp! All that stands in your way is those who seek to take it from you. Now is your chance to claim salvation, liberation, and godhood for yourselves. Kill all who seek to take this from you as we play our song of recreation! Rejoice!"

The chaos above ground could even be heard from below. Lutcas knew that this really was it and he began to move. Shortly after joining his team Lutcas heard music coming from somewhere and a lot of it. The music was wretched and frightening to Lutcas. It sounded like a great orchestra of music from several participants vaster than the stars. Lutcas couldn't imagine what number of people were doing this.

They continued to sprint down the corridors of the catacombs until they saw a ladder. It took them up and brought them inside of a small stone room. There was no door to the small room, only a destroyed wall that led to the corridor. They stepped out to find themselves in a structure like the catacombs, but instead of regular stone it was a stone as black as obsidian. This along with the scattered bodies of knights showed that the team ahead of them was successful in their surprise attack. The music and the shouting and screaming was also louder showing that they were indeed closer to the surface.

Clarence shouted to the team, “Alright the advanced squad was successful. We need to push up now. Follow me!”

Right after he said this, the ground beneath them shook violently. Sounds of great heaps of earth could be heard around the city. No one had any idea of what was happening around them. This made the situation seem more dire. The team found the nearest corridor of stares and proceeded to the floor above them.

There the team made it to the ground floor of the podium tower. It was a long grand hall full of intricate lighting, red carpets, and portraits. But the floor was now covered in soldiers fighting to the death. Many Zealots and Knights spilt each other's blood on the floor. The advance team was however increased significantly in size, so the rest of them must have advanced further up. Trusting they could handle this, Guil’s team began going up a large flight of spiral stairs next to them.

Fortunately, there were windows to see what was going on outside the large tower. What Lutcas saw was hard to take in. The middle and upper district appeared to be lifting from the ground, as if it were beginning to fly. On the walls of the middle and upper district as well as the roofs of buildings were corpses. But they were not still or silent. It was as if the remainder of flesh and bone became alive. Some of the corpses were bone, some were decaying, and some were fresher than the rest. But they all shared one thing. They were all moving and playing the terrible music that swallowed up the city. It is as if a chorus of death now was giving the world its final song.

Lutcas saw this and thought of it when he traveled across the world. At his village the bodies were still present, but after that every destroyed or abandoned town never had a single human corpse left. At least those who were done so by the hands of Orchestrasus. Now he knew why they were gone. They were all gathered here to play this song for the one who rules the world with death. Lutcas's special vision allowed him to see more. He was strings attached to chaotic concertmasters that hovered above the chaos of the city. But something was coming from the chaos. Lines of music and jagged notes floating to the top of the tower, past Lutcas's field of vision.

The group made it to the next floor. It seemed to be cleared out. All that remained were what was left of some soldiers. So once again they found the next set of stairs and traversed them. Lutcas was astonished at how little progress they made up the massive hulking tower, despite going up so many stairs.

Guil shouted to his team, "Okay! Everything should be going according to plan. Only a couple more floors up and we should get to the lofts. That will take us really close to the top."

The next floor was a series of corridors and rooms seeming to serve as a workspace for those who served in the tower. Any knight who guarded this floor was killed. But it seemed that the advance team let the politicians and philosophers survive. Perhaps because they were begging for their lives with no means of fighting. Pan, however, gave none he passed any mercy. He got out his pan flute and with a tune of moving metal he sent the hidden blades he had out through their throats and back to their sheaths.

Soon they made it to the next floor where the last of the advance squad had advanced. Some of them were laid near the entrance of the stairwell injured. A line of zealots was clashing with a defensive line of Knights. This floor wasn't as open as the bottom floor. Like the previous floor, it contained multiple corridors to unknown and unseen rooms. However, they knew that this floor had the loft to take them further up. In fact, the loft was visible, since it rested on the other side of the corridor behind the knights.

Pan looked at Violina and Lutcas and said, "You two heal these wounded soldiers as quickly as you can. I'll take care of knights ahead!"

Violina as he was running off replied, "Wait don't we need to be quick?"

Clarence replied, "Trust me. We will only get in his way if we try to help."

Lutcas went ahead and began to play his lute as he hummed to some of the injured men. He used his voice to hit the notes just as Coda taught him. The men he sang to were revitalized, with their wounds sealed and healed. However, it troubled Lutcas to know that they will get back up only for this to happen to them again.

Lutcas turned ahead to see Pan leaping between knights at inhuman speed only to see flashes of metal and sprays of blood. It wasn't long until Pan made quick work of all the knights blocking the zealots.

Clarence shouted to Guil's team and the advance team, "Okay everyone, listen up! The plan is going accordingly. This loft will take us to one of the high levels of the tower. The lofts that would have taken us up to the top floor, as the scouts suggested, have been severed. We will advance together with this series of lofts and continue the planned route. I would suspect an ambush ahead. But once we run into trouble, Guil's squad cannot stop till we get to King Lyle."

The two teams went to the system of lofts in front of them. It was evident that the number of lofts showed a lot of traffic normally. But Lutcas could not wrap his mind around what they would need all this space for.

As they reached the next floors from the loft access it became quiet. That is apart from the horrid song that enveloped the city and the people who war beneath the tower. But they proceeded up a series of stairs that led up to the top. The number of stairs would make anyone exhausted, but everyone knew what was at stake and pressed on. Lutcas looked out at any window access he could. He could see that soon they would make it to the clouds. But what was also horrifying to see was the land below. As the tower's wind swept across the landscape, a great darkness was slowly making its way to Orchestrasus. It made the land crumble to dust like a burning paper and in its wake was a void of chaos and nothingness.

For a while they encountered no trouble or resistance. But finally, they came to what appeared to be the final floor of the tower. They were standing in a massive hallway. On the other end of it was a ramp that led up into a beam of daylight. Infront it was strange knights. Instead of wearing typical black armor like regular knights of Orchestrasus, they wore blood red armor. It was safe to assume that this was the royal guard. Without hesitation the two teams charged at the red knights. The red knights held their ground with some of their instruments and launched a series of elemental volleys at the charging zealots. Lutcas quickly took his Lute and played a tune he hadn't played in a while. A tune of Protective barrier. This stopped the projectiles from hitting any of the soldiers. Quickly Violina advanced and played a tune of light, blinding the knights who shot the volleys.

Now the group had their chance. They continued their charge and were close to the knights. But before they reached, a great number of red knights dropped from the ceiling striking many downs. One landed on Lutcas putting him on his back. The knight readied his sword to be plunged into Lutcas's gut. But before the knight could do it, Tekoa with a blast of fire annihilated the knight turning his head into ash with a major tune of roaring flame. Quickly Tekoa helped him up.

Clarence could be heard in the chaos, do not stop Guil's squad! Keep pushing forward. Lutcas and Tekoa got up and made their way forward. But a line of red knights was now charging at them.

Lutcas looked over to see Hurdo wind his hurdy-gurdy and he said to Lutcas, "Watch this boy. This is how to really use my beloved instrument!"

Spark of lighting came from Hurdo and with a great clap of thunder the lightning in a singular massive blast shot at the red knights. The lighting not only hit many of them, but the lighting leaped between them killing most of them.

Hurdo shouted at Lutcas and Tekoa, "Go now. The others are fighting the ones that jumped us. I'll help clear a path for you!"

Lutcas and Tekoa listened, and they sprinted towards the door. Following close behind was Pan, Violina, and Guil. As another group of knights approached, Pan began to play a tune of moving metal. This took some of the javelins from his back and launched them at the enemy. These ripped through the knights, piercing more than one each. Hurdo also continued to eliminate the upcoming knights with his melody of lightning. As Pan passed by his javelins he controlled, they returned to him as he continued to play.

Right in front of them was the ramp, leading them to sunlight. But before they reached it a hulking mass landed in front of them. It was by no means a living thing, but it was the biggest knight Lutcas had ever seen. Lutcas noticed the decayed fat and the wound in the neck. This was the recovered corpse of Tubiat. But it was as if it were alive. It was covered in some armor and wielded his signature tuba. In response Pan took one of the hand axes on his belt and threw it at him. The axe landed right between his eyes. But quite simply, the animated body took it and removed it from his face. The wound that Pan created sealed up back into the rotten shape it took before.

Pan shouted as they continued to run, "Great now what are we supposed to do?"

Lutcas responded, "I don't know what to do about this! This wasn't part of the plan."

Guil asked Violina, "I'm sorry to bring this on you two. But could you and Tekoa distract him while me and Lutcas and Pan slip past him."

"Yes! Just do what you need to do. They brought his body back. But if he has a corpse, he has got to be dumber than a pile of rocks."

Violina once again played her tune of Light blinding what was left of Tubiat. This seemed to work as Pan, Lutcas, and Guil slipped by. Lutcas wanted to help them, but he knew that time was of the essence.

Finally, they reached the top of the hulking podium tower. The top of the tower was so massive and flat, it was as if an infinitely flat piece of black land stretched across the horizon. This seemed this way since there was no land insight now. Only a sea of clouds around could be seen. Not even at the highest peak in the world did Lutcas see such a view. Above this was a twilight of stars mixed with the sun that was waiting to come over the eastern horizon. In the middle of this massive platform was King Lyle with his Lyre playing his instrument. And with him was Bendzo with red armor and his banjo which was modified to resemble an axe.

Lutcas looked at King Lyle, whose head was making unnatural twitches and spasms. He looked at the musical aura of him. All the lines of music coming from below seemed to all go to him. However, Lutcas felt something terrible just by looking at him. Something that made him want to vomit. But he could not see what it was.

Bendzo shouted to the three, “Hey! I didn’t expect to see you guys here!”

Pan said to Guil and Lutcas, “Okay let's kill him before they try anything funny.”

Pan took one of his javelins and threw it at Lyle. However, it phased right through Lyle. The three were astonished.

“Oh, come one now. Three against two isn’t fair. Here I was about to invite each of you to sit with me and watch.” He shouted, “Your majesty! I humbly ask that you assist me however you can! I will deal with the two pipsqueaks if you can assist me in taking down my greatest rival!”

The three walked forward and Lutcas spoke to the one he once called his best friend, “Bendzo please! We need to stop this!”

Bendzo said,” No you need to stop. You are holding everyone back Lutcas! You are my friend, but I have seen the providence of King Lyle. With him I have witnessed and participated in the growth of a kingdom. Now after this song is completed, everyone can be gods and we can live happy lives!”

Guil responded, “You think this will bring happiness? This kingdom was built on rebellion and suffering. My family is dead, and this ideology has brought only death and ruin!”

“I don’t want to hear a word from you! If it weren’t for you my friend would be here right beside me changing the world for the best.” he retaliated sharply.

“No Bendzo!", shouted Lutcas, “I am glad he found me. Because I would rather die than walk the same path you and the rest of this wretched place have.”

“So, you can play with your teacher Coda? Get real Lutcas you are asleep. Even if I must use force, I will wake you up and let you become a conductor with me.”

Pan began to charge at Bendzo shouting, “Shut up!”

Before Pan could get close, King Lyle appeared in countless copies. All walking around aimlessly. They began to all say different things as they wandered, “I miss my family.” “I want to bring growth to the world!” “I just want people to be free.” “Why can’t Guil see what im trying to do.” “I wish I could see mom again.”

While saying these things and more, they all turned and sprinted at Pan. Pan quickly played his flute and every single blade that he carried came out and swarmed him. Every second he took out countless numbers of these images of Lyle. But from everywhere they just kept coming. Though the wave of Lyle’s couldn’t touch Pan, the countless words of what all said would drive someone mad.

In the chaos Bendzo sprinted at Guil. He leaped high in the hair and came down with his axe. Guil rolled out of the way. Once Bendzo landed he took one of his hand axes on his waist and threw it at Lutcas. Lutcas ducked and wanted to run at Bendzo with his sword. But he hesitated, for he knew that he could not beat him like this, nor did he have the heart to slay his friend. Guil while he got back up played his guitar and played a melody of moving vine. This took a vine that Guil had with him and wrapped it around Bendzo’s arm holding the axe.

Guil shouted at Lutcas, “Okay Lutcas do something now!”

Lutcas then began to play a tune of light. However, Bendzo was familiar with this and didn’t look at him. He then took his banjo axe and severed the vine that grappled his arm. Guil in response threw out a vial of water and played a melody of ice, making the spilled water into an icicle. Then Guil played a melody to launch it at Bendzo. But with his unnatural reflexes he swung his axe and shattered it, sending the shattered pieces behind him. But Guil didn't stop playing as Bendzo marched towards him. He made the shattered icicles go back to their target. Lutcas saw this and played a tune of shifting rocks to take chunks of the black stone and hurl it at his friend. Bendzo heard Lutcas playing a tune and in response played a major tune of shifting rock to create a stone wall behind him. He then played another tune to launch it back at Lutcas. He narrowly jumped out of the way of Bendzo's counter, but what he saw made him afraid. There was now nothing between Bendzo and Guil.

Quickly, not knowing what else to do, drew his sword and ran at Bendzo. But Bendzo took his axe and plunged into Guil's chest before he could do anything. Lutcas shouted as he leaped at Bendzo, in anger of what he did to Guil. But before he could land the blow Bendzo turned around and caught him by the neck.

Bendzo then shouted at Lutcas, "Why can't you see yet? Your friends keep dying in a sad attempt to stop us! Why are you trying so hard? You don't even have the guts to use that sword against me! Just yield Lutcas! I don't want to kill you!"

Lutcas knew that Bendzo was right. He didn't have what it took to kill his best friend. But Lutcas only wished Bendzo could see what he saw. Then Lutcas remembered the humming tune that Coda made when he gave him his new vision.

Lutcas dropped his sword and said to Bendzo, "You are right. But before you must kill me, allow me to show you something. Look around."

Bendzo could see that he was no longer a threat and he looked as Lutcas hummed. Slowly Bendzo could see the lines that his friend saw. He could see the chaos and the jaggedness that overwhelmed him and Lyle and everyone else. Bendzo knew then that music wasn't supposed to be like this. He listened to more of the voices that the Lyle images spoke from which said, "It's too late to turn back now." "If I could redo this, would I?" "I wish I didn't kill my father." "I never should have listened to that thing."

Bendzo then looked at his childhood friend who he held up ready to kill. He knew what he did was wrong now. He knew that no good cause could drive him to such links. He thought to himself what sort of madness drove him to betraying and killing his own best friend. Filled with guilt Bendzo threw Lutcas away from him. He then took Lutcas's sword and fell on it, killing him.

Lutcas knew that this confrontation was possible. He knew that his friend may have to die. But Lutcas was hoping for another way. Lutcas yelled in sorrow and in rage at the fate of Bendzo. With tears running down his face he took the sword from Bendzo's corpse. Lutcas looked up to see all the images of Lyle coming at Pan as his storm of blades kept them at bay. But a few came over and walked slowly to the body of Guil. About three kneeled and wept over him. An echoing voice came from each of them. "I'm tired of this." "Oh no little brother. Not you too." "It doesn't want it. But I want you to end me." "Please be merciful and end my reign Lutcas." "I just wanted to help the world." "Now I am its adversary."

Lutcas looked at all the clones. Only one of them had the wicked musical aura he recognized. He obliged to the request of the images and struck the one with the aura. Suddenly blood gushed from it and the other images faded and their voices fell silent.

In Front of him was Lyle, wounded, who said his final words, "I am sorry Lutcas. Thank you… but beware the unharmonized…"

He finally did it. The one who helped plunge the world into chaos was dead. But something didn't feel right. He didn't feel good about killing Lyle. He had much frustration and hatred built up for him. Yet Lyle said some confusing things. The music the corpses were playing suddenly stopped leaving a deafening silence.

The others came up the ramp and saw Lutcas in front of Lyle's body. Lutcas didn't see Clarence with them. He looked down to see Guil's body with his brother's. This meant that it was his time to take up the mantle. So nervously he looked for the Lyre. To be expected it was right next to the Lyle he struck down. But the Strings of Harmony were not recognizable. They each gave off a black aura and didn't produce any music as they did before.

Pan shouted at Lutcas, "Lutcas! It must be you now! Take it quickly!"

Lutcas obeyed thinking that maybe he just needed to hold to restore the Strings, just like Guil said. As soon as he touched it, he blinked. When he opened his eyes, he found himself next to a tree in what appeared to be a beautiful forest opening.

An echoing voice, which sounded much like Lutcas, spoke to him, "Well Lutcas. I should have known you would find your way to me. It makes sense though since you have such a righteous spirit."

"Who are you? I don't see you?" he asked.

"Who am I? That is not easy to answer. I lost my name some time ago. But think of me as someone who was the royal advisor. One who held a high position. I suppose you want to know where you are?"

"Yes, actually. One moment I was standing on the podium tower and now I'm here."

"Yes. You are where all kinds of this world must go. Because you are now making a choice."

"What choice?"

"Before you are the tree of the kings. Once only at the Theater of Emet. But now it is here in this domain. For it has been destroyed and lost in west where it once was. But I will now present your choice. Will you take the fruit of this tree and become the king of the world ruling it with how you see good and evil?"

"What do you mean? I picked up the Lyre and I have the Strings of Harmony. The others have told me that I am to become the king."

"Yes, but you cannot wield them now without eating this fruit. With this fruit you will accept that you will bring forth what is good in your eyes and destroy what is evil in your eyes. You will rule over what is good and bad and decide what to usher into this world. Tell me what you desire."

"I want to destroy the evil of this world. Those who reject harmony and choose themselves over it have done evil. They must be stopped before all are caught up in it."

“Then I offer you this choice, oh King Lutcas. Take off this fruit and all the wickedness you see will be trampled under your feet. You will rule with such power that what you see as evil will suffer at your hand as you usher in freedom and righteousness with your wisdom of good and evil. Will you take the fruit?”

Lutcas thought the offer was what he was looking for. He could finally fix the world and make it the way he thought it was supposed to be. But then he remembered the vision he had when he looked at the fields of blades and bodies as his friends perished around them. He knew to usher in what he wanted would bring death. He looked at the fruit in his hand and saw the musical aura around it. It was jagged and chaotic. He knew he could not do this, for he now knew better to rely on his own knowledge of right and wrong. So, he casted away the fruit because he didn’t not want to wield power to be like a god. Suddenly a snake came out of the fruit and struck him in the neck.

He awoke and in a panic he fell and casted away the Lyre back at the corpse of Lyle. Everyone watched in confusion as he casted the Strings of Harmony away. But suddenly Lyle’s body arose and picked up the Lyre. Suddenly out of the Lyre, that all could see, was the great serpent. It grew and grew until it wrapped itself around the tower of Orchestrasus, constricting its prey. At this moment, hope died.

CHAPTER 16
OVERTURE

Everyone watched as this massive serpent slithered around the tower in all its terror. A dark aura consumed it. Running across its back were what appeared to be wings that were destroyed. Lutcas recognized the musical aura around this being. This was the aura that surrounded Lyle and his Lyre.

Violina, distressed and confused at the sight of the monster, asked aloud, “What? What is this thing?”

The creature spoke not aloud but in the minds of everyone present and with their own voices, “I? I am the monument of this world's sins. Once a beautiful concertmaster, far radiant and more powerful than any other. I saw the harmony of this world as a cage. I was honored with being the concertmaster of the kings of this world. But once I overstepped my boundaries and King Anthropo and Queen Thelys took the String of Emet, I was punished and claimed a rebel. Now I am the Unharmonized One!”

Pan shouted, “I'm tired of all this craziness! Lyle is back up and with his Lyre. If we take it, then we can stop it!”

The Unharmonized one spoke again, “You naive thing! You think you can beat me with the Strings of Harmony. Do you think salvation will come to you if the right person takes up this mantle? You are all fools! No one is strong enough to break my grip on this world. I am the most powerful being in existence, I am the conductor of the rebellion of this world!”

Hurdo shouted, “We need to do something. Lutcas couldn’t handle the Strings but maybe Violina can! We will take Lyle down again! Then we give her the Lyre.”

Pan shouted, “I’m on it!” Quickly he blew into his pan flute, sending every blade he had at Lyle.

What was left of Lyle, being moved like a puppet attached to strings, ran his hand across the Strings of the Lyre. This caused a shock wave and in its path was the deafening silence that Lutcas encountered before. Just like that time, no one could speak, and nothing could emit sound. But something else happened too. Everyone’s strength was sapped from them. All they could do was crawl on the ground.

The Unharmonized One spoke again, “I almost pity how finite you all are. No one can save you. Death will run its course and all Symphonia will be destroyed! Leaving only me as its conductor left. Now to teach you poor naive creatures something. I will break you and rip you apart in your minds with possibilities of you and your pathetic world. So, you can see what your human saviors will do.”

Lyle with his unnatural movements began to play the song once more. The orchestra of the damned could be heard below as the ritual continued. Lutcas tried crawling towards Lyle and made progress slowly. But before he made it much closer the serpent eyes shone a bright light.

When the light faded Lutcas found himself walking in a straight line along with hundreds of other people. They all looked like Lutcas and wore matching patterned shirts and pants. The walls were made of the smoothest stone he had seen. Soldiers wearing strange round caps and holding strange tools were standing on an indoor balcony looking down at them. Lutcas had never seen a building like this nor clothing and equipment.

One of the soldiers shouted, "Thank you for coming. You now have recognized how your race and your very existence have oppressed our nation. Now you may have the honor of being erased from this world. I bid you farewell."

Lutcas looked down and saw many holes in the floor beneath. Suddenly a wave of fire shot out of the holes, consuming Lutcas and all who stood on it to become ash. Lutcas opened his eyes and took a breath as if he was under water. He looked back up to see Lyle and the serpent again. Lutcas tried crawling towards him again, but the eyes flashed again.

This time Lutcas was in a trench holding a tool foreign to him. Like the ones the soldier was carrying before, it was a long barrel with a trigger and handle. Lutcas found himself wearing one of the round hats he saw before, which he now presumed to be some armor of some kind. The other men around him wore the same thing and carried the same tool.

One of the men shouted, "Alright men, peace is only a step ahead. Once we defeat them, we can return home to your families and war will cease to be!"

Suddenly, what Lutcas saw as some sort of flying metal bird swooped down near the trench. It shot hot rocks so many so fast that all who were in its path were mowed down, including him. Lutcas opened his eyes again and took a breath. His head hurt and his vision was becoming doubled. Once again, the eyes gleamed the light.

Lutcas now found himself on the side of a mountain overlooking a city. The clothes he was wearing were much nicer than any he wore before. The city below was like none he had seen before. The buildings were like massive towers of metal that dwarfed the towns Lutcas remembered. But suddenly as he looked at the city. A massive ball resembling the sun appeared and exploded in the heart of the city. In a flash the city was ablaze, and a pillar of smoke raced towards the sky creating the shape of a mushroom. When the shock wave made it to Lutcas he opened his eyes again. He didn't make any progress. He laid there helplessly in pain as the serpent once again used the light of his eyes.

This time Lutcas found himself in a uniform once again. He held up large transparent shield against a wave of people. They all held signs and shouted many things. A chant he heard mostly was, "Give us the power, stop the hate!" "Give us the power, stop the hate!" or something to that degree. As he held his ground one of the people managed to reach over his shield with a weapon and say the chant. He then pulled the trigger causing Lutcas to open his eyes again.

Again, he was sent into another vision that was sheer chaos. He saw man turn against men, mothers to their own children, rulers offering salvation, people claiming their own lives, torture of the innocent, the silence of righteousness, and many more. They all happened in different times and settings that Lutcas couldn't comprehend. But as he gazed at it, he became appalled at the sight of humanity, he lost hope.

He now laid on the ground with his back down. He had no more strength to move. More so than strength he had no will to move either. This made it clear to him now. No matter which one of them got the Strings, they would be no better off than before. This being, the unharmonized one held all captive who were in its reach. There was no point in fighting it, for no amount of good intention and a strong will can defeat the Unharmonized One.

Then the sun came up, finally dawning a new day. Suddenly He was revitalized again, and he could hear the sound. But this sound was much more beautiful than any he heard before. Full of energy again, Lutcas sprang up to investigate. He looked as he saw all his friends get back up disoriented from the power of the Unharmonized One. The attention of the great and terrible beast turned towards the sun that radiantly showed over the sea of clouds below. From its brilliance there was a silhouette of a man walking over the clouds to the platform they were standing on. Lutcas saw the musical aura that emitted from this figure, they were smooth and harmonious like only one he saw before. Once close enough Lutcas heart sprang for joy, for it was Coda. Coda stood there in the same shape he was in when was killed. Except now he wielded a harp with bright and radiant strings on it, even more radiant than the Strings of Harmony once were.

The Unharmonized hissed and said, "No! Impossible! You allowed yourself to die. You fell into death. How are you here?"

Coda gave a warm smile and said, "I did, didn't I? Well, it looks like your favorite weapon just wasn't potent enough, rebel."

Using Lyle's corpse as a puppet, he used the Lyre to send another shockwave of silence at his newly appeared foe. The shockwave hit everyone, but there was no silence.

Coda chuckled and said, "That trick again? Please. Now let me say something to remind you and to show everyone else who I am. I am the one who weaved this world together with music. I am the one who gave the gift of its power so all could participate and rule as I gave life to all. I am the Conductor, creator of all things!"

The Unharmonized One, again, hissed and lunged at Coda with its massive jaw. Coda in response ran his hand across his Harp and a glorious music was produced from it creating a mighty wave of energy. This caused the Strings of Harmony on the Lyre to snap in half and turn to dust. The Unharmonized one writhed and spasmed as his discord could not be in the presence of such harmony. Suddenly he jolted to the far east like a bolt of lightning. Following him were the other Concertmasters who emitted chaos like he did. This was not the only thing this impact did. Suddenly the dark clouds beneath them scattered allowing light to shine below. Beneath everyone's feet the hulking podium tower split into two and crumbled to dust. The tower and the floating city met his fate. Lutcas was ready to fall, but he found himself floating above and slowly going down.

Lutcas overjoyed to see Coda shouted, "It's you! But how did this happen? You were dead, weren't you?"

Coda once again smiled and embraced Lutcas in the air, "Lutcas did you not hear what I said? I told you this wouldn't go the way you thought. I have now defeated the one who wielded a great mighty weapon, death. But as you can see it was not enough to take me down."

Lutcas looked at the ground below him and saw the gaping hole in the earth as well as the vast crumbled and darkened sea that was the land below him, "Coda I must ask. What will happen now?"

"Lutcas I will go to the other students and tell them this. I will go back to Podiem and bring it back to where it once was before. In the meantime, I want you and my students to share the music I have taught you with the survivors below. Let them contribute to this restoration. Then when the time comes, I will be back."

Lutcas was excited and he said, "I think I got it. Will you see me again when you return?"

"Oh, trust me Lutcas. You will know when I'm back. Plus, I will bring others that want to see you too."

Soon everyone that was in the middles and upper districts of the city landed gently on the ground. Coda in a flash of radiance vanished leaving Lutcas and his companions on what was left of Orchestrasus.

People in groups ran toward them seeing what happened and they all asked questions like, "Who was that?" "What just happened?" "What is going on?"

Lutcas and the others looked at each other and explained all that happened. The survivors heard what happened and were amazed. The students of Coda emerged from the rubble and spread the word of what happened. Shortly after, Lutcas and the others began to show them the music that Coda taught them using their voice. To demonstrate, Lutcas went up to the edge of where the kingdom used to be. The land in front of him seemed to have flaked off and was replaced with a horizon of purple chaos. Lutcas took his Lute and began to hum as he played his music. The music emitted from him turned some of the landscape in front of them back into green lands with blooming flowers and plants. Witnessing this the others join quickly filling the land back with life.

Before Lutcas continued, Pan approached him and said, "Hey Lutcas, I just noticed something."

"What is Pan?"

“I was investigating the rubble. There was so much battle going on and for some reason no bodies were found. Was this the work of Coda?”

Violina approached them interrupting them while also answering their question, “Well if it is I am sure he has got something big planned.”

Now it took a while for everyone to spread across Symphonia and restore what they could. Some even chose not to participate in its restoration, some even trying to hinder its progress. But for Lutcas, he was just happy to see lush green landscapes full of animals and trees again. Lutcas, Violina, and Pan had made their way east, restoring as they went. They were unable to go any further once they reached the ocean, so they headed back to help everyone else. Suddenly as they got closer to the middle of Symphonia, where Orchestrasus use to be, they saw something incredible. In the sky was the holy city of Podium floating towards the crater where it once was before.

Violina, amazed, shouted, “Wow, what a beautiful sight to see!”

Pan folded his arms and smiled when he said, “Ya it sure isn't it. It's a shame that Chornelious wasn’t here to see it with us. We basically saw the whole world together”

“Well, I suppose it is a good thing that I am here, isn’t it?” said Chornelious, acting like it wasn’t a big deal.

Wide eyed, the three turned to their left to see Chornelious standing there with them. He was well kept and almost glowing. He turned back and gave them a smile. Without hesitation the others embraced him at once.

Pan who now shed some tears of joy asked, “How can this be? You were dead!”

Chornelious answered, “Well Coda was the preview to what was yet to happen. Now look at me! Back and better than ever. I’m back because he is back!” he said while pointing to the Kingdom now touching the ground.

But suddenly before it touched a great flash of light occurred. Lutcas opened his eyes and saw that he was back at the eastern shore. Around him were all the people who ever lived in Symphonia. They were all facing the shore that now had a massive bridge of light stretching to the horizon of the ocean. In Front of this gate was Coda who, like Chornelious, shone more brightly than ever before.

Coda spoke to all Symphonia, “My dear subjects. Rejoice for the new kingdom of Podiem is here. But just as I have done in the beginning, I have always let my creation have a choice. Here before you are a bridge that will take you to the far east, the land beyond the sea. There my sovereign doesn’t reach. It is as some of you sought out before, a land without me. So, if you choose to live in such a place go ahead and walk the bridge, but I’m sure many of you have made the choice already.”

Lutcas was surprised to see how many people began to walk the bridge. He didn’t recognize most of them, but he did recognize a select few. One of those was Sonare who began to walk the bridge. Lutcas knew that she had said mean things to him, but his prior feelings for her didn’t allow him to change his mind. But he also knew that this was her choice to make, and with a heavy heart he let her make it. Soon after they walked the bridge everyone began to embrace one another, for many were separated by death which was now defeated.

Sometime after this event, Lutcas found himself under his favorite tree playing his tune of thankfulness. It was time for the harvest festival and many all around the recreated Symphonia joined in. Lutcas looked at the sky and saw that the music lines running through its existence were orderly and harmonized. The same went for the grass and all the people around him.

In the far distance are the tips of newly constructed buildings of the city of Podiem. In such a short time the ability to create has been increased. This is used in new technology, buildings, clothes, games, and many more wondrous things. From the city was the everlasting radiance, which always shone allowing there never to be a night again.

He looked around to see who was enjoying themselves in this time of celebration. Guil, Zamir, and Lyle were at a table playing some sort of complex strategy board game. Pan and Bendzo were running around playing a sport with the other young men who joined the celebration.

Chornelious and his teacher were at a table talking about tinkering and what to make next. Violina was holding her new baby as Tekoa was making silly faces to provoke its laughter. Next to Lutcas was the love of his life as she rested her head on his shoulders. She was more beautiful and kinder than Lutcas would have previously ever hoped for.

She stirred and lifted her head and she asked, "Dear do you hear that?"

Lutcas stopped playing to listen to the sound she heard. He heard an approaching animal. He looked over and running across the field was a familiar little creature. It was Note with his floppy ears running right towards his faithful companion. Lutcas got up and ran to embrace his dog who began to lick him on the face and wag his tail in happiness.

Alas this was the story of the world of Symphonia. One story that its inhabitants would never forget. A story of a world created by music and a world that fell into discord, only to be restored and recreated by the being that loved it so very much. Lutcas and his companion now had an eternal future of an ever-expanding land with infinite possibilities of creation and growth. Alas, all was set right and harmonized.

THE END

www.ingramcontent.com/pod-product-compliance
Lightning Source LLC
LaVergne TN
LVHW010548160826
845677LV00013B/3044

* 9 7 9 8 4 4 5 8 4 4 7 1 6 *